Behind the bookcase w

Elle stepped back. "C
leave it alone. I had a bad feeling about coming here. All
morning my unlucky number kept turning up. Did you know
there are rumors this bungalow is haunted by an Andy Warhol groupie who OD'd in the bedroom?"

The former compound of Andy Warhol sat next to Uncle
Harry's, and by "next to" I mean a couple of acres away.
Back in the day, Harrison Falks handled a good share of
Andy's and other famous local artists' works.

"Why in the world would you have an unlucky number?
Now who's the sissy?"

I bent down and peered through the hole in the doorplate.

A human skull propped on a small table grinned back at
me. Its head bone wasn't connected to its neck bone—or
any bone, for that matter. "Oh my God!"

"I was right! There is treasure!" Elle shoved me aside,
took a screwdriver from her back pocket, stuck it in the hole,
and turned. Then she kicked the door with her boots and
charged in.

The scream that followed could have woken the dead.

Or maybe not.

Perhaps there was something to an *un*lucky number?

Berkley Prime Crime titles by Kathleen Bridge

BETTER HOMES AND CORPSES
HEARSE AND GARDENS

Hearse and Gardens

KATHLEEN BRIDGE

BERKLEY PRIME CRIME, NEW YORK

BERKLEY
PRIME
CRIME

An imprint of Penguin Random House LLC
375 Hudson Street, New York, New York 10014

HEARSE AND GARDENS

A Berkley Prime Crime Book / published by arrangement with the author

ISBN: 978-0-425-27659-4

PUBLISHING HISTORY
Berkley Prime Crime mass-market edition / May 2016

PRINTED IN THE UNITED STATES OF AMERICA

10 9 8 7 6 5 4 3 2 1

Cover illustration by Marjorie Muns.
Cover design by Diana Kolsky.
Interior text design by Kristin del Rosario.
Hamptons map by Lee Goldstein.

Penguin
Random
House

*Marc, this one's for you. May we share many
more Montauk sunrises and sunsets.*

ACKNOWLEDGMENTS

To my friends on social media, my readers, bookstores, and the mystery community, thank you for embracing me with open arms.

Thanks to everyone behind the scenes: Joshua Evan, Lindsey Taylor, Judy and John Drawe, Ellen Broder, Michelle Mason Otremba, Ann Costigan, Lee Goldstein and everyone at Backstreet Antiques.

A special thank you to Victor Caputo, the Director of the Wm. Cullen Bryant Library in Roslyn, Long Island, for supporting authors, especially this one.

And again, thanks to Lon Otremba for sharing more fabulous recipes from his secret vault.

To the best agent ever, Dawn Dowdle at the Blue Ridge Literary Agency for your commitment, encouragement, and guidance. My editor, Robin Barletta, thank you for believing in me and Meg Barrett. My publicist, Danielle Dill, you do a stellar job of getting the word out and it's much appreciated.

Last but not least, MONTAUK, you are the END and the BEGINNING.

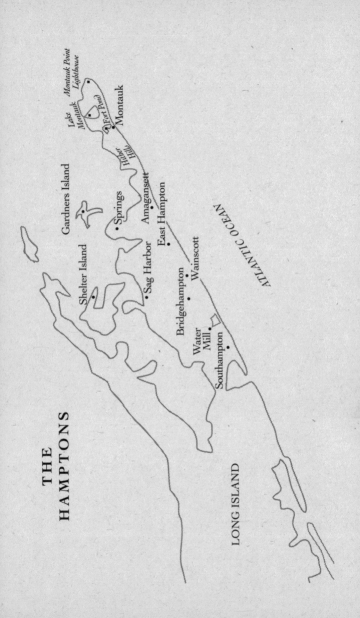

THE
HAMPTONS

Montauk Point
Lighthouse

Lake
Montauk   Fort Pond   Montauk

Hither
Hill

Gardners Island

Springs   Amagansett

East Hampton

Shelter Island   Wainscott

Sag Harbor

Bridgehampton

Water
Mill

Southampton

ATLANTIC OCEAN

LONG ISLAND

"You have been served." Four words you never want to hear.

Last April, I was on the dilapidated porch of 221 Surfside Drive, ready to begin renovations on my cottage in Montauk, when a sweet little old lady in a hand-crocheted beanie and scarf sprinted toward me. She had one hand in her pocket—I swear I saw the outline of a gun—and used the other to shove a subpoena in my gut. Then she flew down the steps to her granny-mobile, like Bambi escaping a forest fire.

An heir of my cottage's former owner had crawled out of the woodwork to lay claim to my precious little parcel of land. Six months later, the will remained in probate and the hearings kept getting postponed, thanks to Justin Marguilles, Hamptons real estate lawyer extraordinaire and a shark with a rep close to the one in *Jaws*.

So, here I was, still in my four-room rental, yellow tape barring the entrance to my dream home in true crime scene fashion. Not that I was complaining. I still got to wake up every morning in a cozy beachfront cottage with the mighty Atlantic only steps away.

A horn honked. I grabbed my handbag from my newest purchase, an antique pie safe with its original milk paint. My old pine breakfront had been scarred with bullet holes. Salvageable, but too chilling a reminder of how short life can be. On my way out, I remembered to set the alarm and lock the top lock—a safety measure I'd added after last spring's nightmare.

An October sun painted the ocean with silvery white brushstrokes. The shadow of a harvest moon hung in the afternoon sky.

"Get a move on Meg Barrett. We have junk to excavate!" A feather from Elle's hat escaped the truck's window and danced on the crisp ocean breeze. "Hurry, or Uncle Harry might reconsider his generosity."

Elle Warner was a friend and former coworker from my days in Manhattan as managing editor of *American Home and Garden* magazine. She owned a thriving antiques shop in nearby Sag Harbor and also did freelance work for insurance companies in the Hamptons area, occasionally calling me in to assist. In turn, I sometimes asked her to help with my fledgling interior design business, Cottages by the Sea.

Elle's great-uncle Harry was none other than Harrison Falks, one of the most revered art brokers of the twentieth century. Ninety-one-year-old Uncle Harry owned a compound in Montauk valued in the multimillions. His main

house sat on a cliff six miles away from the Montauk Point Lighthouse and a few miles up from my oceanfront rental.

The house was named Sandringham after the ancestral home of English royalty. It was a slightly smaller version of Queen Victoria's "informal" holiday retreat, with a red brick facade, gables, and turrets. Today, Elle and I were rescuing, free of charge, furniture and knickknacks from one of the beach bungalows on the compound.

Elle parked the pickup in front of Sandringham and we took the sandy path that led to the beach. I'd anticipated the strong ocean wind forecasted by the weather report and had taken out my hearing aids. I wasn't a fan of the high-pitched whistling sound they made if I wore them in blustery offshore winds. I'd explained to Elle, it was like talking to someone on their cell phone while they walked outdoors on a breezy day. The sound heard by the person on the receiving end could be quite irritating.

The bungalow we were looting sat a mere hundred feet from the ocean. It was the last of six that needed to be moved inland by flatbed truck and tucked safely behind deeply rooted sea grass and a cyclone fence. All six bungalows had been sitting unoccupied since the mid-eighties. Unfortunately for Elle and me, the other five's contents had been dumped into a dozen industrial-sized Dumpsters and carted away to parts unknown. What a waste of perfectly recyclable décor.

I looked at the exterior of the bungalow. It had real potential. In my mind, it was a cottage, but I had to admit it followed bungalow criteria: one and a half stories, low pitched roof with broad eaves, a large front porch, and shingled siding. The brick chimney needed some work,

but all in all, even without seeing the interior, I wished the flatbed truck would drop the bungalow at my place.

Elle beat me to the door and rushed in.

I followed her inside, but not before a twister of sand filled my mouth and eyes with briny grit. Bungalows typically opened directly into a living room, and this one looked frozen in time. "This place reminds me of where the Big Kahuna took Gidget, planning to deflower her."

Elle was already flipping over furniture. "Whoa, baby! Look at this set of chairs. I think we've hit it big!" She used her sleeve to brush away years of grime, uncovering a red paper logo. "It's Eames, the midcentury furniture icon. And by the way, what's a gidget?"

"It's a romantic surfing movie from the *Beach Blanket Bingo* days. A sixties classic. Haven't you ever heard of 'Moondoggie'?" *Gidget* had been one of my mother's favorites, surprising considering she'd spent her whole life in Detroit and never so much as put her pinkie toe in the ocean; a great lake or two, maybe. Perhaps *Gidget* was the reason salt water ran in my veins and I had no problem watching surfers at Ditch Plains Beach for hours on end.

"Way before my time, and you know I only watch classic mysteries—Great-Aunt Mabel's faves like *The Thin Man, Perry Mason*, and anything Hitchcock."

I looked at her '60s "après-ski" boots—her words, not mine. "You'd love the movie and the clothing especially, seeing you're the queen of all things vintage. Come over. We'll have a sleepover and watch *Gidget* on my new laptop."

Elle removed a package of wipes from her bag. "A laptop! Welcome to the new millennium."

She moved on to the built-in corner cabinet on the oppo-

site side of the room. Built-ins were another feature of bungalows, along with an open floor plan without hallways to take up needed space.

I started on a wall shelf filled with midcentury art glass. First, I took a picture of the shelf with my cell phone, then bubble-wrapped each piece and placed them in a carton. I took out a Sharpie and transferred the photo number to the top of the carton and sealed it. Elle had taught me well. "All done. What's next?"

"I have to have that mounted fish," she cooed.

On top of a tall bookcase filled with thick hardcover art books was a huge wooden plaque on an easel. Attached to the plaque was a large fish's head, complete with a dead glassy eye. The body had long disintegrated.

"And why do we want that thing? It's gross."

Elle was already on the ladder. "The plaque's worth money. Vintage teak is hard to come by. It would sell in a second to a wealthy novice who gets lucky fishing off Montauk Harbor, the sportfishing capital of the world." She reached up and removed the plaque and handed it to me.

Fish dust trickled down. "Ewww."

"Sissy. Hey, wait. There's a door behind the bookcase. Come up and see."

Elle stepped down and I climbed up. Sure enough, there was the outline of a door. "Don't get excited. Probably an old broom closet."

"Hurry. There might be vintage treasure."

We stood together on one end of the bookcase and pushed. No good. The bookcase was too heavy. We removed half of the art books, mostly Pop Art, and stacked them on the floor and tried again.

Behind the bookcase was a knobless door.

Elle stepped back. "On second thought, maybe we should leave it alone. I had a bad feeling about coming here. All morning my unlucky number kept turning up. Did you know there are rumors this bungalow is haunted by an Andy Warhol groupie who OD'd in the bedroom?"

The former compound of Andy Warhol sat next to Uncle Harry's, and by "next to," I mean a couple of acres away. Back in the day, Harrison Falks handled a good share of Andy's and other famous local artists' works.

"Why in the world would you have an unlucky number? Now who's the sissy?"

I bent down and peered through the hole in the door-plate.

A human skull propped on a small table grinned at me. Its head bone wasn't connected to its neck bone—or any bone, for that matter. "Oh My God!"

"I was right! There is treasure!" Elle shoved me aside, took a screwdriver from her back pocket, stuck it in the hole, and turned. Then she kicked the door in with her boots and charged in.

The scream that followed could have woken the dead.

Or maybe not.

Perhaps there was something to an *un*lucky number?

We ran out the bungalow door and headed toward Sandringham. I tried not to trip on the uneven beach terrain or get blinded by the sand spraying in my face from Elle's Clydesdale-inspired boots.

When we turned to take a trail that led to the front of the main house, Elle grabbed my elbow so I could read her lips. She knew, even if she shouted, I couldn't hear over the din of the breaking waves and buzzing wind. "This way. It'll be quicker."

As we ran, I dialed 911 and handed off my phone to Elle. I knew there wasn't a reason to hurry, because the body we'd just seen in the bungalow was long dead. It just seemed like the right thing to do.

Elle rapped on the mammoth sliding glass doors. A Grace Kelly blonde in her midforties came toward us

looking like she'd just stepped off the red carpet in Monte Carlo. She slid open the door.

"Oh my, I know you, don't I?" She directed her stare at Elle.

"Hello, Celia, it's Elle, Uncle Harry's great-niece."

"Oh, yes, of course. You're the one who wears the old-lady pins and thrift store clothing. If I remember correctly, your great-aunt was a Warner. Her people were potato farmers."

"Yes, until my great-grandpa sold the farm for millions."

I knew Elle's story was true. Back in the early part of the twentieth century, potato farms were a big thing in the Hamptons. Now, few farms remained. They'd been sold to celebs and tycoons as prime spots to build their mega estates. The Hamptons weren't nicknamed the American Riviera for nothing.

Elle said, "Is it okay if we come in? We have an emergency."

"Quickly. This room is temperature and humidity controlled."

We stepped in, and I caught a whiff of Celia's strong perfume and sneezed. A pet peeve of mine: women who wore so much perfume, it arrived in the room before they did.

Elle said, "Bless you."

Celia looked at me like I had the plague. I didn't like her snooty 'tude, so I dropped our bombshell. "We just found a body in one of the bungalows."

Celia put her hand to her mouth and made a pouty O with her lips.

"The police should be here any minute," Elle added.

Celia stood to the side as we entered a large space with white marble floors.

This addition of Sandringham was nothing like the rest of the mansion. The walls were made completely of glass. Above us was a transparent section of the ceiling. I looked up into the underbelly of a glossy white Steinway. If I was ever invited upstairs for a recital, I'd be sure not to wear a skirt.

White leather sofas and sleek chrome and leather chaises melded perfectly with the modern art: Warhols, de Koonings, Lichtensteins, and Pollocks, just to name a few, were set either on clear acrylic easels or trapezoid sections of wall open at the top, making the artwork seem to float. There were a few zany, but powerful, sculptures spaced around a room the size of a MoMA exhibit hall. Every side or coffee table was made out of Plexiglas, allowing the art to take center stage. A clear spiral staircase was in the center of the room, leading to the second floor. Outside, nature's aquarium, the Atlantic, was only steps away. Inside, we were the ones in a huge fish tank.

"Come this way." Celia led us toward a back wall. With the toe of her designer shoes, she tapped a piece of marble. *Open sesame*, wood panels parted and exposed the original nineteenth-century part of Sandringham.

Celia walked ahead and turned the corner at the end of a long hallway, perfume trailing in her wake.

We followed the long Persian-carpeted hallway into a grand foyer with coffered ceilings. Classical art in ornate antique frames with brass nameplates hung from the rich mahogany paneling. Inset into the paneling were cubes

displaying busts of seventeenth-century wigged aristo-crats.

Someone banged on the front door. Celia advanced to open it but was cut off by a man with longish brown hair that looked strategically messy. His not-quite-faded summer tan was a perfect backdrop for his blue eyes. He was dressed casually in jeans, a pink polo shirt, and loafers, but they were nice jeans, a nice polo, and even nicer Gucci loafers. "I'll get it, Mrs. Falks."

"Thanks, Richard," Celia said.

He gave her a roguish smirk and bowed, as if playacting, then went to a keypad hidden behind a hinged portrait of a scowling gentleman. After Richard performed a complicated routine on the keypad, a green light turned red, and the huge front door opened inward.

Detective Shoner stood at the doorway. He looked at us and rubbed his eyes.

"We're not a mirage, Arthur." Elle went to him and leaned her five-four frame into his five-five frame. Elle and I met Detective Shoner last March. I suspected the detective and Elle had a thing going on. Elle's behavior just confirmed it.

Detective Shoner stepped in and closed the door. "What's this about a dead body?" He was dressed impeccably, a perfect match to this formal side of the mansion.

Richard said, "Dead body?"

"And you are?" the detective asked in his usual non-bedside manner.

Celia came forward and introduced herself as Celia Jameson Falks, saying she hoped the detective didn't

think this messy business had anything to do with San-dringham. *As if!*

"Body? Where?" Detective Shoner repeated, non-plussed.

Elle remained mute, so I said, "We were working in one of the bungalows on the estate and we found a skeleton."

Even without my hearing aids, I heard a clattering com-ing from the back hallway: a thump, scuttle, thump, thump. A wizened form, reminiscent of the skeleton we'd just found, moved toward us. Harrison Falks piloted his wheeled walker like a B-52 on a mission. Elle stuck her hand out and pressed it against his chest to stop his momentum.

"Who forgot to invite me to the party?" A rivulet of drool pooled onto Uncle Harry's huge lower lip.

"Good morning, Unc. It's Elle, your great-niece. Remember?"

Harrison Falks's milky eyes looked her over from head to toe. Then he smiled. "Little Elf. Did you hear the one about the basset hound and the bullfighter?"

Elle looked dumbfounded.

He glanced around the foyer. "Anyone?"

Celia said, "For God's sake, Harrison. Your stupid jokes will be the death of me."

Uncle Harry took one of his hands off the walker and waved it in the air. He started to teeter, so I grabbed the walker to keep it from rolling out from under him.

Richard, who I assumed was some kind of butler, major domo, and nothing like the regal Carson from *Downton Abbey*, shoved me aside. "I've got him."

"Come on, you bunch of nincompoops, what's your

answer?" Uncle Harry lifted the walker and cracked it hard against the marble tile.

Richard jumped and went to stand behind Celia. I was able to read his lips when he whispered, "Who's the nincompoop?"

"Hey, sir," I said.

"Call me Uncle Harry, young lady."

"Uncle Harry, it's Meg. I met you last week when Elle brought me here for tea. I'm stumped. Please tell me, what's the difference between a basset hound and a bull-fighter?"

Uncle Harry stood perfectly still. He opened his large mouth and started to wail. His upper dentures separated from his gums and fell to his lowers. He mumbled with tear-filled eyes, "I don't know, I just don't know. What's the answer? Tell me."

I couldn't stand to see him so distressed, so I fudged it. "A basset hound is a dog and a bullfighter is full of bull."

He readjusted his teeth. "Yes, that's it. By Jove, you've got it." He closed his mouth and scooted toward the rear hallway. To my astonishment, he touched a section of mahogany paneling, and the wall slid open. After a few clanks with the walker, he disappeared inside an elevator, and the panel slid back in place.

Celia said, "Where the hell is that nurse of his? Why do we pay her such an exorbitant salary? She can't even keep track of him."

A curvaceous woman, looking the opposite of any nurse I'd ever seen, sauntered down the ornate winding staircase with a tray in her hand.

"Nurse. There you are." Celia walked to the bottom

step. "Are you going to keep tabs on my husband or just let him roam about willy-nilly?"

Nurse's hair was long and wavy, in a striking shade of russet. Despite the fact she looked to be around forty, her huge breasts looked perky beneath her sweater. "He took the elevator while I was fixing his bath. And Celia, the name is Brandy, not Nurse. As you know, I'm also Harrison's personal assistant, who just happened to have taken nursing classes after he fell ill." She looked at Detective Shoner but didn't say anything.

I could picture Celia and Brandy in a catfight. *Meow!*

"Harrison's probably back upstairs by now," Richard said.

Detective Shoner opened the front door. "Enough of this. Elle and Meg, please show me what you found."

We led Detective Shoner to the bungalow. He put on a pair of gloves, opened the door, and walked inside. We tried to follow but he shooed us away.

"Aren't you cold?" Elle buttoned up her coat and pulled up her hood, the feather on her hat long gone. In this buffeting wind, I was surprised her hat hadn't followed suit.

"I'm good." I was shaking, but not from the cold. My insomniac middle-of-the-night trips to the beach, dressed only in pj's and a robe, made me immune to foul weather. "So, whose body do you think we found?"

"Forget that. Look, someone's coming this way. Maybe he's the killer?"

"We don't know anyone was murdered. Maybe the door got stuck."

"Right. And the bookcase magically moved on its own to block the door."

"Shush."

As the man got closer, I saw he was in his forties and ruggedly handsome. He reminded me of Gregory Peck in *To Kill a Mockingbird*—my favorite movie and book. He held a walking stick in one hand and in the other a clear plastic bag filled with sea grass, roots and all.

"Hello, ladies, is there something I can help you with?" I was pretty sure I'd read his lips correctly. Elle said nothing, no doubt thinking this man with a heavy five-o'clock shadow was a serial killer.

"No, we're okay. Just waiting for someone who had to step inside." I didn't disclose the fact a homicide detective and a skeleton were in the bungalow.

Elle said, "And who are you?"

"I'm the Falkses' neighbor. And you would be?"

"Elle Warner, Harrison Falks's great-niece."

"We have to be careful with who comes and goes around here. We get a lot of lookie-loos because of the Andy Warhol connection." He nodded his head to the west, where I knew Warhol's former compound stood.

I stuck my hand out and said, "Meg Barrett, nice to meet you," just as Detective Shoner exited the bungalow.

Not a man of subtleties, Detective Shoner walked over to us. "Who's this guy?"

The man said, "Nathan. What's wrong? Has there been a break-in?" He zeroed in on the badge hanging from the detective's neck.

"Not sure of anything until we process the scene. Do you have a last name, Nathan?"

"Morrison."

The detective handed Nathan his card and told him to

come down to the station for a statement. Nathan seemed hesitant about leaving but finally walked east, clutching his walking stick and grass specimens.

We left Detective Shoner and a crew from the East Hampton Town Police on the beach after I convinced Elle we wouldn't be able to remove any goodies from the bungalow. Not even Detective Shoner was allowed to touch anything until the CSIs from Hauppauge, a town seventy miles away, arrived.

We grabbed lunch at Candy Kitchen in Bridgehampton. Naturally, we sat at the old-fashioned soda fountain counter for our grilled cheeses. The rest of the afternoon and evening was spent in Sag Harbor, working on our fixer-uppers in Elle's carriage house/workshop.

Elle had filled me in on what little she knew about her great-aunt Elsie's part of the family and the inner sanctum at Sandringham. Celia was Uncle Harry's third wife. Celia had a daughter from a previous marriage, Kate. Uncle Harry's son had married a local Montauk girl and had a child named Liv, who now lived on the estate, along with Celia's daughter; both girls were in their early twenties. With the exception of a few daily housecleaners and a cook, named Mrs. Anderson, that left Richard and Brandy, valet/chauffeur and nurse/assistant, to round out the list.

But who was the skeleton in the bungalow?

It had been a week since our discovery. Georgia, the proprietor of The Old Man and the Sea Books, was pruning roses on her white picket fence. "Do you believe all these flowers in October?" She clipped a pale peach bloom and waved it under my nose.

"Spicy, yet sweet."

"The way I like my men," she said.

I coughed. "Don't make me blush. I can't think of Doc that way." Septuagenarian Georgia began dating sexagenarian Doc last June. "Doc" Marshall Heckler was a buddy of my father's from when they both worked for the Detroit PD. Doc was a retired coroner and my father a retired homicide detective. Doc was the only family I had on the Eastern Seaboard.

Georgia went into the bookshop, and I followed. With the exception of a dusty old attic at an estate sale, The Old

Man and the Sea Books was my favorite place to hang out. A converted cottage dating from the 1930s, it even had a working fireplace fronted by two cushy wing chairs. A stack of logs and kindling waited for the first cold snap. I half hoped the weather would turn foul—not like the last late-season hurricane—just cold enough to put a chill in my bones so I could reheat them in front of a toasty fire.

The thought of bones reminded me of the body in the bungalow. "Last week, Elle and I found a skeleton at Sandringham," I blurted out. The skeleton hadn't made it into the news. The police promised not to publicize it until they received the autopsy results and notified next of kin.

"Are you kidding? Whose? Harrison Falks's? He's older than the hills." Georgia was an expert on all things Montauk and a patron of the Hamptons art scene.

I went to the counter and poured myself a cup of Earl Grey from the electric teapot. "You can't say anything until the police announce it, but Elle and I were cleaning out one of the bungalows and found a skeleton in a secret room. I'm not sure, but it looked like the room was used as a recording studio. It was windowless and even had padded walls."

"Gracious me. It probably was. Back in the seventies, a lot of artists, musicians, and groupies flocked to Harrison Falks's and Andy Warhol's compounds, even the Rolling Stones." She grinned. "Me included." Georgia opened the small fridge under the counter, took out a slice of lemon, and plunked it in my tea. "Of course, Andy's was much harder to get into, even though he barely came out here."

Everyone in the Hamptons knew the Rolling Stones' song "Memory Motel" was written about the motel that

still stood on Main Street in Montauk. Most were under the impression the Stones stayed at the tiny motel/bar that looked like it hadn't changed in sixty years, but I'd learned from Georgia they didn't. They just used it as a watering hole.

"Wow, can't picture you as a rocker."

Georgia's white hair was cropped short to keep the wind from slowing her down on her daily six-mile bike ride to the Montauk Point Lighthouse and back. She was my same height, five seven, but weighed about fifteen pounds less.

I poured some water from a small carafe, graciously placed there to cool customers' tea to drinkable status. "I don't know how to gauge the time period it takes a body to morph from flesh to skeleton, but I'm assuming this guy or gal must've been there for a while. It's funny, a corpse of bones is so much more palatable than one with flesh."

"Yes, hilarious. I can't think of anyone gone missing around here. Oh, wait. Liv Falks's father, Pierce, disappeared about twenty years ago, along with Helen Morrison. And so did Pierce's father's Warhol painting of a can of Aqua Net hairspray valued in the upper millions. Warhol gifted the Aqua Net to Harrison Falks. Everyone assumed Pierce and his lover Helen ran off together and took the Warhol."

"Aqua Net hairspray? You're kidding, right? Iconic soup I understand, but hairspray?"

"Supposedly, only the family ever saw the Warhol. The reason the public found out the picture was a can of hairspray was because Harrison thought his son and his lover had absconded with it. By broadcasting its theft, it would

make it harder to fence. I don't think Harrison cared as much about the painting being returned as he did his black sheep of a son. Tragically, a few years after Pierce's disappearance, Pierce's wife drowned in a yachting accident off Montauk Point."

"So, who is Helen Morrison?"

"Nathan Morrison's wife. His family estate, Morrison Manor, lies next to Sandringham. When the majority of the family land was sold to pay taxes, Nathan and Helen were forced to take up residence in the Morrison Manor gatehouse."

I thought about the man I'd met the week before on the Falkses' beach outside the bungalow. As my father would attest to, scorned love was the modus operandi in many a homicide. "Hmmm. That's complicated. Pierce was married but having an affair with his next door neighbor?"

"Yes, and Pierce had a child, Liv. The child was the reason for the marriage.

I set my cup on the table between the wing chairs, and my heart hiccupped when I spied a new book by Patrick Seaton.

Georgia followed my eyes as they darted from her to the table. She went to the table and picked up the book, *Tales from a Dead Shore—A Biography of Tortured Poets*, and handed it to me.

Patrick Seaton was my recluse neighbor. He lived on the other side of the nature preserve, next to my rental, and occasionally left melancholy poetry in the sand on his beach. Patrick Seaton had moved to Montauk after his wife and child were killed in an automobile crash. We were kindred spirits. Not that I could compare my ex's cheating,

or even the loss of my mother at a young age, to losing his wife and daughter in a tragic accident. But we shared a love of classic poetry and the ocean. And it made living alone a little less lonely.

"Maybe I should buy *Forensics for Dummies*?" I went to the shelf and pulled it out.

"You're no dummy. Plus, we have Doc and your father for any cutting-edge insight into crime. You have other reading to do, Patrick Seaton's new book."

She rang up the book and slipped in a couple of home and garden magazines, my addiction, free of charge. We had an understanding, if I came across any vintage New York seltzer bottles in turquoise, her addiction, they went straight into her collection.

Georgia walked me to the door. "I can't believe I forgot to tell you. Patrick Seaton was in last week with his publicist, Ashley Drake. She bought a Long Island *Zagat*'s. Patrick just stood in front of the poetry section with his hands in the pockets of his black pea coat, collar turned up, all dark and brooding. He didn't say a word to me and walked out when Ashley grabbed him by the arm. They made a handsome couple. Time for you to step up and introduce yourself, before Ashley snatches him away."

"I'd be happy for him if he found someone, after what he went through. And I've told you and Elle, I like things just the way they are. Now that you-know-who has been out of the picture for the past few months, delivering one of his yachts to Australia, I'm putting all my attention on my new romance—my very own cottage."

My latest crush, Cole Spenser, and I had become

almost-lovers last spring. But his home was in a different state and mine in Montauk. Case closed. At least for now.

Mr. Whiskers came out from the back room. Another reason I loved the bookshop was the back room where Georgia kept vintage and antique books. The cat wound his way in and out of Georgia's legs. He looked at me and hightailed it to the seat of a wing chair. I'd rescued Mr. Whiskers last May from a Dumpster when I'd been diving for vintage treasure. I'd thought his glowing eyes were a piece of Tiffany glass. Originally, Georgia and I planned to share custody. She was supposed to keep Mr. Whiskers in the cold months, and me in the warm. This past summer I was homeless because I'd rented out my cottage for the season to make some extra money, so he stayed with Georgia. And apparently, by his 'tude, he wouldn't be coming back. I stuck my tongue out at the cat. "Fair-weather friend."

Georgia laughed, removed a cat treat from her jean pocket, and tossed it to him. "Thought you couldn't do anything on the property until you settle your court case with phony-baloney Gordon Miles, great-nephew and owner of your cottage—my arse! I used to bring hot meals to Old Lady Eberhardt and I know she didn't have a soul in the world after her husband died."

Mrs. Eberhardt had been the original owner of the cottage. After she passed away, she left the house in her will to the church, who I bought it from. "I can't go into the cottage, per se, so I've decided to hire a landscape architect to draw up plans for the garden."

I hadn't disclosed to anyone, with the exception of Elle, that last summer I'd taken the liberty of setting up shop in

the glass folly I'd discovered on *my* property. The little Queen Anne gem of a structure had been covered with vines and hidden behind eight-foot spikes of bamboo. I'd subleased my rental cottage for the months of June, July, and August at a seasonal rate of thirty thousand dollars, a bargain in this 'hood, and spent the summer fixing up the folly, even camping overnight in good weather. When I wasn't at the folly, I bunked at Elle's carriage house.

After I left The Old Man and the Sea Books, I grabbed a latte from the Montauk Coffeehouse, hopped in my Wrangler, and headed to my future home-sweet-home. A few miles later, I pulled into the narrow dirt drive. Rhododendron branches scratched at the Jeep's windows in welcome.

My appointment with landscape architect Byron Hughes wasn't for another half hour, but I needed time to go through the bursting-at-the-seams file box with garden ideas I'd been saving since the closing last April. Or should I say *supposed* closing. Elle and I decided Byron Hughes warranted his hefty retainer. Byron was almost as famous in the Hamptons area as Frederick Law Olmsted of Central Park fame was in his heyday.

I'd found out Grey Gardens in East Hampton—the former home of Big Edie and Little Edie Beale, Jackie Bouvier Kennedy Onassis's relatives—and my cottage in Montauk were designed by the same architect, Joseph Greenleaf Thorpe, at the turn of the nineteenth century. I'd come to call my cottage Little Grey. And if I wanted an endowment from the Montauk Landmark Committee, I needed to restore Little Grey to its former glory. Seeing I wasn't allowed to touch the house until the court ruled in

my favor, I planned to draw up plans for the garden. I'd take care of the design of the cottage myself based on old pictures and blueprints I'd found in a second-floor closet.

Last spring I'd macheted a path to the front door of the cottage but purposely left the way to the glass folly undisturbed. My secret hideaway. And the perfect place to envision a glorious garden.

Before heading to the folly, a.k.a. deer tick central, I bent down to make sure my jeans pooled over my boots—too many stories of Lyme disease gone undetected. When I stood, I glanced toward Little Grey. The front door was undisturbed, yellow tape barring Gordon Miles's and my entry.

Only, something was askew.

I went closer.

Dangling from the door handle, at the end of a hangman's knot, was a partially decomposed seagull.

Before I could let out a yelp, a car's engine sounded. A black Range Rover pulled next to my Jeep. Byron Hughes stepped out like a knight in dazzling armor. My mouth, still open, opened wider. I'd never met Byron in person, but I had seen numerous society photos of him in *Dave's Hamptons*. His tall frame was lean and fat-free. His hair was a sandy brown with gold streaks. Natural? His skin a burnished bronze, which he most likely maintained on a yearly basis: Aspen and St. Barts in the winter, the Amalfi Coast in the spring, and, of course, the Hamptons in the summer. For an instant, Byron's gorgeousness eclipsed the hideousness of the strangled gull.

I cursed Gordon Miles and any future generations he might propagate. Who else would have done something so

heinous to the poor gull? Not usually the shrinking violet type, I wasn't about to allow this Greek god of a man to see me as a wuss. I bit my bottom lip and pulled it together.

Or so I thought.

When Byron reached the front porch, he handed me a bouquet of Montauk daisies and a bag from The Old Man and the Sea Books. I collapsed into his outstretched arms like a cheap umbrella. He had me at daisies, but a book put it over the top.

After a few minutes, I pried myself from Byron's steel-cage embrace. Embarrassment reared its ugly head. "Sorry about the crushed flowers."

"Don't worry. There are more where they came from."

The timbre of his voice was rich and deep. I pointed to the seagull.

"Why don't you wait by my car? I'll take care of it." He took out the silk pocket square from his suit jacket, walked up the steps and across the covered porch, then reached for the doorknob. The carcass swayed gently in the morning breeze. The poor bird. I turned away so Byron wouldn't see my tears and hurried to his car.

His license plate read BYRON3. I could only imagine what kind of cars BYRON1 and 2 were. I never understood the charm of owning vanity plates—I was too modest, or too cheap, to consider buying them. At least his plates didn't say LORDBYRON, of course, too many letters for a New York plate.

I cringed at my reflection in the Range Rover's dark tinted windows. Black mascara trailed in spikes down my face. I'd make the perfect stand-in for a Kiss band member. I licked my pointer finger and tried to erase the smudges,

only managing to create two little bat wings, which extended from the outside corners of my eyes to my ears. Now I looked like an Edward Gorey gothic cartoon from the opening sequence of a PBS *Masterpiece Mystery!*

As a distraction, I reached into The Old Man and the Sea Books shopping bag and pulled out my gift from Byron, *The Illuminated Language of Flowers*, by Jean Marsh and illustrated by Kate Greenaway. I quickly thumbed through the index and looked up daisies. Daisies meant farewell. Which made the daisies and the book an oxymoronic welcome gift.

I glanced over at Byron, just as he was about to drop the silk-cocooned gull into a rusty trash can.

"Wait!" I ran toward him and wrenched the gull from his hands. "He deserves a proper beach burial."

I thought I saw an eye roll.

"You might catch a disease. Look at all these insects." He peeled away the top section of the pocket square and revealed an entomologist's dream.

I cringed but wasn't swayed. We Michigan gals were tough. The summers of my adolescence were spent at my grandfather's house in Traverse City, or Up North, as my family called it. Up North was a wonderland, another universe from Detroit's urban sprawl. My summers included building a fort next to a stream that emptied into Lake Michigan.

I became a loner at a young age. Having a hearing loss I didn't know about until much later wasn't a conduit to close friendships. I had only two playdates with Patsy, the little girl who lived next to my grandfather. Her mother told my grandfather, who told my mother, that Patsy

thought I was stuck-up. I realized later, Patsy probably tried to talk to me when I wasn't facing her, and I hadn't heard a word she'd said. So I spent long summer days alone, surrounded by Nancy Drew, centipedes, garter snakes, and pollywogs. I wasn't a big fan of the crayfish. Their pasty beige exoskeletons and pinchers creeped me out. However, that didn't stop me from putting one in the basket of Patsy's bike.

"Do you have any idea who would do this to you?" Byron pointed at the gull.

"I have a good idea. I'll take him home and bury him in front of my cottage."

"I thought this was your home?"

"Well. Yes and no. I'm in a dispute with someone over ownership. But, in the meantime, I want to draw up plans for the garden. I guarantee you, it will soon be mine."

"Sure you want to make the investment?"

I tried to see myself the way he must: smeared mascara, holey jeans, a Detroit Tigers hat and T-shirt, clutching an insect-ridden seagull. "Follow me, I want to show you a few things."

CHAPTER

FOUR

It was such a welcoming feeling, walking into my tiny four-room cottage. I'd lucked out renting it because my buddy, Barb Moss, Montauk real estate agent extraordinaire, took pity on me when I burst into Sand and Sun Realty during a snowstorm, looking for an immediate oceanfront rental. Fortunately, the owners had just handed Barb the key. The owners were on a two-year waiting list for a top Hamptons architect who would replace the charming four-room cottage with a mega beach house— the reason for my two-year lease.

The kitchen was small, with room for only one piece of furniture and a small table to go against the cushioned banquette. No dishwasher but a vintage turquoise "icebox" still tickin' after sixty years of service.

I grabbed a Vernors, a made-in-Detroit ginger ale, from the icebox, then sat on the sofa so I could call Elle

on my landline phone. She would be waiting for a report on Byron Hughes.

"So, he was gorgeous and rescued a damsel in distress," Elle said.

"Well, I wouldn't go that far. Although, he did have a certain charm. He even brought me gifts." I remembered my first impression this morning of Byron as a knight in armor, and the ground shifted from all the nineteenth-century suffragettes rolling in their graves.

"He's a catch. Be extra nice to him and maybe he'll do the job for free."

"Before you pimp me out, I don't think I stand a chance with him. Out of my league. And the only reason I got lucky enough to pay in the low thousands for blueprints was because it's October, not March."

"He's not out of your league! You were engaged to Michael. His pedigree wasn't chopped liver."

"Michael was a user. He would've never made it as editor in chief of *American Home and Garden* without his ex-wife's publishing connections." Michael was my former fiancé and boss, whom I'd found in bed with his ex-wife, a.k.a. Paige Whitney, of Whitney Publications fame. Michael was also the reason for my escape from Manhattan to Montauk. Even though I had to leave behind my dream job at the magazine, it was the best decision I'd ever made.

"The whole gull thing is disgusting. I think you should tell the police," Elle said.

"Crime is pretty rare in the Hamptons, but I don't think a dead seagull will make the police blotter in the *Montauk Journal*. Do you?"

"Maybe not, but be careful. Between this and the skeleton at Sandringham, you'd better take things as a warning. I dreamt last night I couldn't fit into my Edith Head dress from *The Birds*. An omen, don't you think?"

"You told me about that dream months ago. And, you also told me the dress was from *Vertigo*."

"Semantics. It's a Hitchcock movie, for God's sake."

Elle's great-aunt Mabel had been an assistant to the famous movie costume designer Edith Head. Aunt Mabel willed Elle many items from classic '40s, '50s, and '60s movies, along with a few hundred pieces of costume jewelry, and an entire store filled with antiques and vintage. Lucky girl.

I said, "Let's talk tomorrow afternoon, when we meet at your place with our finds."

"Sounds good. By the way, I called Sandringham and talked to Uncle Harry for a whole two minutes before Celia grabbed the phone and told me, in no uncertain terms, the discovery in the bungalow was to be kept top secret. As if I'd upset my great-uncle."

"Celia didn't seem like the caring type when we saw her at the estate, chastising your great-uncle like a child. I hope you've got Detective Shoner on call to let you know when they ID the body."

"Why would I?"

"Time to step up that relationship. We need an inside track to the investigation."

"Oh no, you don't! You almost got murdered last spring."

I looked at the base of my landline phone. Elle's words filled the screen at such a fast pace, I could hardly keep up.

Most of my home time was spent hearing-aid-less: no feedback, and as tiny as they were, they still irritated my outer
ear canal. My house phone transposed everything into
words, like the captions on foreign movies. Occasionally,
things got spelled incorrectly, like Elle's last sentence. It
read, "You almost got merlot last spring." I wish. In fact,
I had an open bottle in the fridge. But I always stuck to my
after-five drinking curfew.

"It can't hurt to know what's going on in case it involves
your family. I doubt there's any danger. That skeleton had
been sitting there for a long time."

After I hung up with Elle, I spent the next three hours
working on a proposal for a potential Cottages by the Sea
client. My rates were quite different than Byron Hughes's.
I didn't charge for my time or designs. I just invoiced a
reasonable markup for the items I placed in my clients'
cottages. That made me very popular, but not very rich.

Dinner consisted of Stuffing à la Mac and Cheese: follow
the boxed stuffing microwave directions, dump in a nuked
cup of macaroni and cheese, mix together, and you've got
a meal to satiate your worst hormonal carb crave.

My father, the best home chef I've ever met, would have
a canary if he knew about tonight's meal. However, his
gastronomical genes hadn't missed me completely. I'd
learned using fresh herbs in cooking wasn't for gourmet
chefs only. I grew my own year-round. I had herbs in a
windowsill planter and in two gardens, one on the side of
my rental and one at Little Grey, hidden behind the folly—
my secret garden.

Herbs helped elevate fast-food and microwave dinners
to another level—a palatable one. I pinched off a few leaves

of sage and thyme from the windowsill planter and added them to my Stuffing à la Mac and Cheese. Oooh la la. My father had taught me a tip about storing fresh herbs. He told me to only wash them right before using. And if I needed to store fresh herbs in the fridge, I shouldn't wash them, just wrap them gently in a damp paper towel, then put in a Zip-loc bag with trapped air.

After dinner and a few more hours of work, okay one hour of work, and one on the Internet surfing for design inspiration, I bundled up and stepped onto the deck. The wind off the ocean was merciless. I flipped down the flaps on my fur-lined hat and secured the chin strap. Then I grabbed the vintage Red Rose Coffee tin from the plant stand and went to the beach.

The sky was clear, freckled with crisp white stars. I took out my flashlight and aimed it on the milk-mustache foam left by the huge waves beating the shore. I found a stick wide enough to use as a shovel and dug a hole. I opened the tin, turned it on its side, and slid the seagull corpse into its final resting place.

In my head, I recited the words from my mother's eulogy, written by Samuel Butler. *I fall asleep in the full and certain hope that my slumber shall not be broken. And that though I be all-forgetting, yet shall I not be all-forgotten. But continue that life in the thoughts and deeds of those I loved.* I thought about the skeleton in the bungalow. Was it foul play or accidental?

Foul play was just a nice way to say murder.

It felt like someone was nearby. My rental butted up to a small nature preserve on one side, and on the other, my neighbor was a seasonal occupant. I was isolated. A

fact I usually reveled in, but not tonight. Tumbleweeds of kelp somersaulted across the beach. I turned to go, and the weirdest feeling crawled up my spine, like the hairy legs of a tarantula.

I'm not a soothsayer, but I must admit, between the seagull and the skeleton, I had a bad case of the ooks. And without my hearing aids, a banshee could be clomping toward me with a butcher knife and I wouldn't know it.

I tore up the steps, locked the French doors, and with spastic fingers set the alarm.

I tried to start each day with a simple but powerful five-minute meditation. As I looked out at the ocean, I repeated over and over again, "Thank you. Thank you. Thank you."

Elle had called to confirm our plans for the day and to tell me the skeleton from the bungalow was positively identified as Harrison Falks's son, Pierce. Not a huge surprise. Pierce's death was ruled suspicious and a possible homicide. The CSIs deduced someone locked Pierce in the recording studio and placed the bookcase in front of the door. Another no-brainer. Pierce had no keys or wallet with him. The room was empty, except for the desk and chair. One question on everyone's mind, including the paparazzi, was where the heck was Helen Morrison, not to mention the Warhol painting of Aqua Net hairspray?

Today's fifty-degree weather set the stage for a perfect day of garage and yard saling. I'd programmed each estate

sale into my cell phone's map app. Three sales were in
Bridgehampton, two in East Hampton, and four in Amagan-
sett. Elle was covering Sag Harbor, Wainscott, and Water
Mill.

Before leaving, I separated my singles, fives, and tens
from my large bills. In my shoulder bag I had my trusty
loupe, a keychain tape measure, baby wipes, and a pen-
light for dark corners. In the back of the Jeep were four
huge zippered plastic bags like you could find in dollar
stores. I'd learned the hard way it was important to zipper
the bag shut as you collected your loot so no sticky fingers
could make off with your booty.

The most important thing before you headed to a sale:
a stomach empty of liquids, not even a sip of coffee.
Homeowners weren't too keen on sharing their bathrooms
with strangers, and once you hit the vintage trail, you
didn't want to traipse back to town for a restroom. I'd seen
people waiting in line drop like flies because they needed
the loo. Not me. I was a camel.

I pulled onto Route 27. There was more traffic than
usual. The Hamptons International Film Festival started
on Friday. Soon, every hotel in a twenty-mile radius
would have NO VACANCY signs.

The first sale was disappointing. I came away with
only a Japanese doll with a damaged face, stuck to a wood
base under a glass dome. The doll would go straight into
the trash, but once I removed the glue from the base, I'd
have a vintage cloche to play and display with.

Another disappointment, at the first sale, was seeing
none other than Tara Gayle, my professional and personal
archnemesis. Our history wasn't good. She was my com-

petition at estate and garage sales, and we'd both dated the same guy. I smiled at the memory of this past June when I saw her walking along Montauk Highway with a big stick, stabbing litter, dressed in a reflective orange community service vest, penance for stealing from a nearby estate. The jumpsuit was a step down from her usual designer wardrobe.

The next sale in East Hampton kept me busy for hours. It was the thing dreams are made of. Even the trash on the curb netted a few projects I knew had rosy futures. When I saw what the third-floor attic hid, it set me back a minute, reminding me of my barricaded cottage with its attic of treasures. Treasures I hadn't been able to get my mitts on because of Gordon Miles. But my personal credo was: live in the moment. After seven trips up and down the stairs with goodies, my angst disappeared. The bags I'd brought were full, so I made do with empty laundry baskets I found in the basement.

Weary, but satiated, I drove to Sag Harbor. I passed slowly through historic Main Street, then turned right on Sage Street. I parked in the back of Mabel and Elle's Curiosities. The shop took up the bottom level of an early-nineteenth-century captain's house. It was painted sand beige with white gingerbread trim and black shutters and even had its original fish-scale shingles. At the top of the house was a widow's walk with a full view of the harbor.

The wraparound porch had two high-back rocking chairs, a porch swing, wrought iron tables, and plant stands. The flower shop, Sag Harbor Horticulture, supplied the porch's flora and fauna, in this case: mums, pumpkins, and ornamental cabbage, along with cornstalks and bales

of hay, all for the measly price of Elle displaying their business cards in her shop. That was how small business worked in small towns—even the Hamptons.

Mabel and Elle's Curiosities had been in business for fifty-five years and was a favorite stop for many a Sag Harbor tourist and local alike. Three years ago, after the death of Aunt Mabel, Elle took over ownership, adding her name to the letterhead. Elle kept the front of the shop as it was back in her great-aunt's day—stuffed to the rafters with odds and ends.

In the back of the shop was a room without Aunt Mabel's influence: the White Room. All the smalls, a decorator term for knickknacks, and upholstered furniture were in white, accented with whitewashed wood tables, even the wide plank floor was painted white. Elle's White Room had been photographed in all the top home décor magazines. She liked to change it up every season, but still kept to the white theme.

Elle's living space was on the second floor. Her bedroom was on the third. On the third floor she'd torn down walls without the approval of the Sag Harbor zoning commissioners, our little secret, and created a perfect loft that faced the bay.

After I unloaded my Jeep, I went inside the carriage house. I put the day's "finds" on top of the ten-foot workbench, next to Elle's. We discussed Pierce Falks's murder. There wasn't much to analyze, except for the sadness of the situation. Elle had also informed me that over the past weekend, Tara Gayle had come into Mabel and Elle's and grabbed one of my business cards from the checkout

counter. For the life of me, I couldn't understand why Terrible Tara would want my business card. Elle also mentioned Tara had spent an inordinate amount of time in the White Room. I hoped Elle had checked Tara's handbag when she left—thievery was her modus operandi.

I sat on my stool and said, "Okay. I'll go first." It was magic time—where Elle and I pulled out the day's catch and determined what restoration needed to be done. Sometimes nothing was best. Sometimes pitching items straight in the trash was best. "Amateur midcentury female portrait, paint with wood stain glazes to faux age it. Eight dollars. Sell for thirty-six."

"Okay. Floral, wrought iron chandelier with chippy paint, electrify. Twelve dollars. Sell for two fifty."

"What a steal!"

Elle's grin said it all.

We continued until we decided to call it a draw.

I took pictures of each of my lots, dividing items by the location. Instead of a file name, I put the amount I'd paid at each sale. An easy way for me to keep the books for Uncle Sam.

Elle put her items in the huge cubby against the north wall of the workroom. I had a smaller space on the opposite side. Fair was fair. Plus, my stuff didn't stay long. If I didn't use my items in my current design project, I'd give Elle first dibs for her shop. If she passed, I'd sell to local dealers.

When it was time for me to leave, Elle walked me to my Jeep. "Glad you agreed to go to the funeral with me tomorrow."

I said, "Of course." I'd be lying if I said I wasn't looking forward to Pierce Falks's funeral. It would be an affair to remember and a good place to get a feel for the players at Sandringham, or should I say my suspect list. I sounded a little cocky. Believe me, I wasn't. I just had a bone to pick with myself for not figuring out who murdered the Queen Mother of the Hamptons last spring until it was almost too late.

I waved good-bye, and set out for my three o'clock appointment with a potential Cottages by the Sea client.

I'd spent yesterday finessing my presentation for a mother/daughter property in Montauk's Hither Hills neighborhood. Last week, I'd stopped at the property and was given a tour. There was a good-sized, four-bedroom contemporary beach house, and a half an acre away, a traditional Hamptons shingle-style cottage with three bed-rooms. Both sat on their own separate hills and had amaz-ing views of the ocean.

Sylvie and Rebecca Crandle were a famous mystery writing team—S. R. Crandle. Their last book recently made the *New York Times* bestseller list. They wanted a Montauk retreat to keep the writing juices flowing. I couldn't think of a better place.

I pulled into Sylvie Crandle's drive. When I got out of my Jeep, a golden retriever bounded toward me. I knew there wasn't a need to worry if goldens were friend or foe— they were always friend. And I was right. The dog licked my hand in welcome.

"Hey, girl." I wasn't psychic. She wore a pink bandana around her furry neck.

I'd toyed with the idea of getting a dog for protection and company, especially after meeting the love of my life last spring: Tripod, the three-legged dog. Tripod was traveling the open seas with his master, Cole, the gorgeous blue-eyed devil I'd also met last spring.

Sylvie's golden retriever led me to the stairs in front of her cottage, just as the door opened and someone stepped out.

Tara Gayle!

She had on a shaggy fur vest. Animal killer. In Tara's hand was a large portfolio case, like the one I was holding. Oh no. She was poaching clients, just like she tried to poach my man last spring. Tara was a former antiques shop owner and an Internet seller, but never an interior decorator.

I thought I heard the sound of an asp hissing as Tara passed me on the steps.

I snarled, "Tara."

She snarled back, "Meg."

Sylvie held open the door. "Hi, Meg. Come inside. I made pumpkin bread. It's still warm."

When I showed Sylvie my storyboards, she seemed excited. I'd tailored each cottage's interior design with her and her daughter's individual aesthetics in mind. She had e-mailed me photos of her daughter's loft in Soho and her Upper East Side apartment, giving me a good idea about each woman's preferences.

My appointment went well, but it was too soon to pat myself on the back. Sylvie promised she'd call to let me know if I was hired. There was only one other designer in the running. Guess who?

*   *   *

True to her word, when I returned home, there was a message on my machine. Sylvie called to say I was hired. But only to decorate her daughter Rebecca's shingle-style cottage. The job of decorating her contemporary went to Tara Gayle.

Then I remembered what Elle had told me earlier, that Tara had taken my business card from Mabel and Elle's. She was out for revenge because I'd outed her to the police for stealing. I could only imagine the spiel of lies Tara told Sylvie. Did Sylvie know Tara had a police record? I could tell her, but it might be more amusing to watch Tara crash and burn.

Later that night, I took Patrick Seaton's book, *Tales from a Dead Shore—A Biography of Tortured Poets,* to bed with me. The first poet listed was Lord Byron. Quite a coincidence that the name Byron was popping up all over the place.

Lord Byron's tale of woe started when he was born with a clubfoot. It not only caused him physical pain, but psychological. When he was young, he nicknamed himself *la diable boiteux*, French for "the limping devil." Despite his handicap, Lord Byron enjoyed adventure. And like myself, he was passionate about the sea.

In 1810 he swam from Europe to Asia, across the Hellespont Strait. Today, swimming the strait was an annual event. Lord Byron's even accredited with being the father of long-distance swimming. Unfortunately, his life ended badly at the age of thirty-six, not from disease, but more likely from the unsterilized instruments used in the barbaric,

but popular at the time, medical procedure of bloodletting. Patrick ended his biographical passage with a quote from Lord Byron:

> *Roll on, thou deep and dark blue ocean, roll!*
> *Ten thousand fleets sweep over thee in vain;*
> *Man marks the earth with ruin; his control*
> *Stops with the shore.*

I fell asleep with dreams of Byron Hughes in a sword fight with Patrick Seaton, battling for my honor. In the dream, Patrick had a definite limp.

Sunday morning was dark and cloudy. The scent of fall leaves mixed with the salty brine of the ocean. Fort Hill Cemetery offered a gorgeous view of Montauk: the ocean to the south, Fort Pond to the west, and Montauk Harbor and the Long Island Sound to the north. Georgia, owner of The Old Man and the Sea Books, had lectured me about its history. In the mid-1600s, the land the cemetery stood on was the scene of a bloody battle between the Narragansett Indians and the Montauketts. "Montaukett" translates to "hilly land." The Montauketts were able to live in peace with the white man but were nearly exterminated by warring tribes from New England.

The land at the base of the cemetery was aptly nick-named "Massacre Valley." The Narragansetts not only killed a slew of Montauketts, but as a final blow, went on to kidnap the Montaukett chief's daughter right in the

middle of her wedding ceremony. With all that said, it would be a beautiful spot for a wedding—and it wasn't bad for a funeral—as far as that goes.

I thought about my mother's gravesite in Detroit. Before she died, my mother made my father promise we wouldn't spend time weeping on her tombstone because she didn't plan on being anywhere near it.

Crows dotted the cemetery grass, and Halloween's spooky vibes settled over the black mourners like a proverbial shroud. The pallbearers removed the casket from the hearse.

I never understood why hearses had windows, windows with white satin curtains. No one was looking out, and with the curtains, no one could see in. For cozy appeal? To soften the fact a loved one was dead but afforded the best luxury money could buy? When I died, I wanted to be put in a pine box, no open casket, and to be planted under a tree with a view of the ocean.

The minister droned on with the traditional "dust to dust" sermon. He looked like Edgar Allan Poe: gaunt, high forehead, bushy eyebrows, and sunken eyes. Uncle Harry sat in a wheelchair with Brandy behind him. Her bosoms sat like a shelf over his drooping head.

Uncle Harry seemed to have aged ten years since the news of his son's demise, putting him in his early hundreds. The reverend aimed his booming voice at Uncle Harry, causing him to shake with each syllable hurled in his direction. Uncle Harry's hearing aids looked old-fashioned and clunky. I made a mental note to send my audiologist to Sandringham with a host of newer technological wonders. What people didn't realize was every

person's hearing loss was individual, like DNA, depending on what range they were missing.

I scanned the crowd and was able to figure out who was who from Elle's descriptions and their position around the casket. Liv, the deceased's daughter, stood next to her grandfather. She was a natural beauty and would never need a stitch of makeup. She had rich mahogany doe eyes and blue-black hair. Her eyes were clear and innocent and filled with pain. I resented her makeupless face. The bare minimum I needed to step out the door was blush for my fair skin and black mascara for my pale eyelashes. Liv wore black riding attire and had the perfect posture and frame for an equestrian. I'd bet dollars to Gleeson's doughnuts, she owned her own horse and spent most of her time at Montauk's Deep Hollow Ranch, just a hop, skip, and jump from Sandringham. Deep Hollow's claim to fame was that Teddy Roosevelt used to hang out there.

Kate, Celia's daughter and Uncle Harry's stepdaughter, had ginger freckles and hair, green eyes, and her mother's perfect nose. You could tell Kate's black dress wasn't her choice, probably borrowed from Celia. The dress must've been made of wool because Kate scratched at the long sleeves like a dog with fleas. Celia kept elbowing her to stop.

Elle saw me looking at the only other person I didn't know. I read her lips when she mouthed, "Mrs. Anderson. The cook."

There weren't any strangers at the gravesite, only immediate family and staff. Even though Elle stood next to me, I felt like an outsider. Nathan Morrison was noticeably

missing. He probably wasn't a big fan of Pierce for having an affair with his wife, or he felt guilty because logic suggested Helen murdered Pierce and had taken off with the Warhol.

Elle nudged me. "Did you feel that?"

I did. A sudden gust of wind entered the soles of my shoes and whistled up the marrow of my bones.

"There's something unsettled about this place."

"It's a cemetery. You can't be more settled than that."

"I have the heebie-jeebies. Let's beat the family to the parking lot. I want to stop at Psychic Sue's for an amulet. Generic crystal, I think. I'll put it on my lighted chakra color wheel so I can take full advantage of its healing powers. I'll get you one too."

"I'm good. I still have the amethyst you gave me last spring. Not that it did much good."

"You're alive, aren't you?"

She had a point.

Elle turned the pickup onto South Essex and took a right on South Emerson Avenue, the road that housed Montauk's prime oceanfront hotels. She parked on the grass of Psychic Sue's Surf and Tarot.

Neon surfboards stood against a large sea green cottage. Surfing season was still on in Montauk. Smoke curled from the stone chimney—smoke or burned sage— you could never tell with Sue.

Elle tooted the horn and waved. "Look, it's Doc."

At first, I thought she was mistaken, but it *was* Doc.

Doc minus his trim white beard. My father always laughed at him because he spent hours wiping it after one of Father's scrumptious gastronomic creations.

I lowered the pickup's window. "What did you do with your beard? Where's my Doc?" I stuck out my lower lip in a pout. I'd known Doc since I was three, and I'd known his beard for just as long.

Doc held a clear cup filled with green liquid in his long-fingered surgeon's hand. The cup was the size they used to dispense medication in movies like *One Flew Over the Cuckoo's Nest*.

One of Doc's white eyebrows formed a perfect peak. "Where have you two been?"

He'd never seen me in anything but jeans. Certainly not somber church attire. "We just came from Pierce Falks's funeral."

He asked, "Will I see you at Paddy's tomorrow?"

"Yes." Paddy's Pancake House was the site of our designated Monday morning breakfast date.

Elle leaned over. "Hey, Doc. Isn't that Mean Green Harmony juice the best?"

I was floored. Detroit's meat-and-potato man drinking health juice? New age meets old. I had a feeling Georgia from The Old Man and the Sea Books had something to do with his Zenformation.

Sure enough, Georgia emerged from Sue's. She held a piece of paper in her hand. "Marshall. You forgot your surfboard receipt."

Wow. Doc and surfboard in the same sentence. I hadn't tried surfing, and I'd lived in Montauk for almost two years and was thirty years younger.

Elle went into the shop to purchase her crystal. I kissed Doc and Georgia hello and good-bye and walked a short distance to the beach. The rolling, turbulent waves mesmerized me by their consistency. Who needed crystals for peace of mind when the ocean could deliver such a moving tribute to life? Not always soothing and serene, but always there. I thought about Pierce Falks being locked in a room so close to the ocean without being able to see it. He couldn't even hear the waves in his soundproof tomb. What had he done to make everyone assume he'd taken off with Nathan's wife and stolen the Warhol? If he'd been murdered because of the Warhol, then why hadn't it shown up? Unless it was in someone's private collection, for their eyes only? But how long could you stare at it for enjoyment? A Pissarro I could see. But a can of Aqua Net?

I thought of my friend and Montauk Realtor, Barb, who was on a second honeymoon cruise with her husband of thirty years. I'd kept her in the loop about Pierce and Helen and the missing Warhol. She'd been very upset with my putting down Aqua Net, seeing it was a staple of her mother's and now hers. I always wondered how she kept her beehive hairdo intact between appointments at Curl by the Sea.

Someone tapped me on the shoulder.

"Thought I'd find you here. It's time to go to Sandringham for the wake," Elle said. "I want to get a good seat to watch the show."

Now that the Hamptons International Film Festival was on the horizon, Elle had informed me that Celia invited a bunch of Film Festival celebs to Sandringham

for Pierce Falks's wake. "Do you think I'm dressed appropriately?" Since my move to Montauk, I hadn't kept up on the latest fashion trends, just decorating trends—a far cry from my Manhattan schmoozing and entertaining days at *American Home and Garden*. Elle didn't have a problem keeping up with trends because she only wore vintage.

"You can't go wrong with a little black dress. Here, let me add something." Elle took off one of her gigantic rhinestone pins and stabbed it onto my chest.

"Hmmm. Maybe a bit much." I was happy the sun wasn't out because I could blind someone with the sparkle of the rhinestones.

After Elle removed the brooch, a good-sized hole remained. "Oopsy. Come to the car. I might have something in my train case."

"Train case?"

"Picture a sixties Pan Am stewardess's carryon luggage."

There was nothing in the "train case" to cover the damage made by the brooch, so I had Elle drop me at home so I could change. I told her to go on to Sandringham and I'd meet her. This way, if I felt out of place or the wake turned into a snooze fest, I'd have my own wheels and could skedaddle home in time for my favorite home and garden fixer-upper TV show.

As soon as I entered the cottage, I ran upstairs and changed into another simple black sheath dress. I was officially bottomed out of funeral attire. If something happened to this dress, I was doomed.

The cottage was freezing. I went onto the deck and

grabbed some kindling from under a tarp. When I stood, I noticed something hanging from the gate at the top of stairs, which led down to the beach. Then I heard a wolf howl.

There weren't wolves in Montauk.

The Montauk Monster? The disgusting thing washed ashore years ago on Ditch Plains Beach. Someone took a picture of it and then, before it could be autopsied, the carcass mysteriously disappeared. Once you saw the photos on the Internet, they haunted you for weeks. There was a debate on what the thing actually was, ranging from a raccoon, to a shell-less sea turtle, to an alien.

Why did I have to think of the monster now?

Where was Tripod, my three-legged canine friend and protector? Probably stealing sausages off the barbie, Down Under with Cole, his master.

I dropped the wood and crept toward the gate, or at least tried to in my three-inch heels. You'd never catch me in six-inch heels. As I got closer, an orange bucket hung from the latch on the gate. Harmless enough. Maybe my neighbor Patrick Seaton brought me a present? The reclusive author had left extra kindling near my kitchen door once before.

Then I thought of the dead seagull at Little Grey.

When I was a few feet away from the gate, the toes of my shoes squished something slimy. Before I could turn and run, my feet gave way and I went sliding into the gate. Bam! My head hit the bucket, and its contents spilled onto my head and shoulders.

I screamed.

I tried to stand but slipped again, my knees and hands

swimming in gook. The smell was so bad I refused to inhale. I crawled back to the deck, through the open French doors, and collapsed on the rug. I took a deep gulp of air but the odor remained.

Some miscreant had poured fish guts on the area in front of the gate. The bucket contents were the icing on the cake. And I was the cake. I was covered with fish heads, scales, and entrails!

I stripped down and threw my clothing and shoes onto the deck. I wiped my feet on the rug, then threw it outside. I ran to the cupboard, got out a large paper bag, and, naked as a jaybird, went back onto the deck, where I put the clothing and shoes into the bag. Then I tossed everything over the railing, including the rug, not caring where it landed.

Okay, be brave, Meg Barrett. Your father didn't raise you to be a wimp.

I locked the door with my elbow and very slowly went up the stairs to the bathroom. I removed my hearing aids and got into the shower. It took five washings to get my hair to rinse clean. Words couldn't describe what pooled on top of the drain. I was one step away from adding my stomach contents to the mix.

CHAPTER

❧❧❧

SEVEN

I hid the Jeep outside the gates to Sandringham, hoping when I returned it would have turned from a rotted pumpkin to a golden carriage. The sky was filled with sooty mauve-tinged clouds, ready to let loose the downpour it threatened all day. I had a good five-minute walk on six-inch red-soled shoes I'd only worn once in the past two years. They pinched my toes and found every pothole on the dirt lane. I hobbled toward the sweeping front portico, using my vintage ivory-handled umbrella as a cane.

Richard stood in the open doorway, a dumbfounded look on his face.

He took my umbrella. "We do offer valet service. Everyone's in the gallery." He pointed to the hallway on the right side of the staircase. "We haven't been formally introduced. I'm Richard Challis, Mrs. Falks's chauffeur, concierge, and assistant."

"Meg Barrett." I stuck out my hand, but instead of taking it, he did a southern France double-double air-kiss: left-right-left-right. I knew the rules. The receiver offered the right cheek first. No lip to cheek, just cheek to cheek with soft smooching noises. Rules for the traditional double-cheek air-kiss were the same, only halved.

I'd learned about the southern France double-double salutation from my father's instructor at the Culinary Arts Institute in Detroit when I was invited to the class's final exam. My tough, retired homicide detective father had prepared a traditional rustic meal you'd find in a small out-of-the-way cobblestoned bistro in Provence, but raised it to Cordon Bleu level by adding a few decadent cream sauces typical of the cuisine of southern France—where his instructor hailed from. My father took a chance mixing north with south, but it paid off. He aced his exam, and the recipe could be seen framed inside the institute's showcase of honor.

Where did Richard learn his air-kisses? He didn't have a French accent like my father's gourmet guru. In fact, if I wasn't mistaken, he had the familiar midwestern twang I'd grown up with in Michigan.

The soiree/wake was held in the modern addition of the house or, as Richard called it, the gallery.

As I stepped into the gallery, the low buzz of cocktail conversation, like the sound of a fly when trapped under a window shade—only multiplied by a thousand—enveloped me. I fumbled for the keychain in my handbag, which held the remote for my hearing aids, and lowered the volume. I was better off reading lips.

The ocean, through the floor-to-ceiling glass, was the perfect backdrop for the ultramodern décor and art. Whoever designed the room stuck to the rule of floating furniture and defining it with a rug—only, in this case, the white rug was hard to define against the white marble floor. The ocean and the room were quite magnificent.

Elle sat in the corner on a clear Plexi stool. Uncle Harry was next to her in his wheelchair. Elle held a wineglass filled with clear liquid. In the other, she clasped Uncle Harry's hand. After the news of his son's death, I had a feeling he wasn't up for the walker.

Uncle Harry's skin tone matched the color of the churning Atlantic—gray, gray, and more gray. I glanced at the other guests. Like Elle, their glasses were filled with clear liquid. I'd been to a few highbrow society parties in my time and knew it wasn't the guest's choice to choose white wine, vodka, gin, or champagne. It was the host's. Spilling red wine, even fine bourbon on a white rug or chaise was a no-no and an even bigger no-no if someone bumped your elbow and your cabernet splashed onto a de Kooning or Pollock.

I grabbed a glass of wine from a roaming waiter and made my way over to Elle and Uncle Harry.

Elle stood and offered her seat. "I'm so happy to see you. Brandy left me with Uncle Harry forty-five minutes ago, and I need to use the ladies' room. Wow. You clean up nicely. So happy you wore red. There's too much black in the room. Love the stilettos."

Like I had a choice. I was pretty proud of myself for keeping my cool. What I really wanted to do was shout

it from the rooftops that I'd been SLIMED. "Thanks. No problem. Anything I should know?" I looked at Uncle Harry's nodding head.

"Nothing to know. Just look for Brandy. He doesn't look so good."

That was an understatement.

Elle darted in and out of the mourners. I wouldn't consider half of the people invited as mourners; they probably didn't even know Harrison Falks, or his deceased son. Celia took center stage, laughing, giggling, and flirting with any man over eighteen. I didn't see her glance once in her husband's direction. I set my wineglass on a—you guessed it—Plexiglas side table and looked out the window. Two figures stood under the floodlights, in view of anyone who wanted to see. They were in a heated conversation, arms flailing, spit flying. It was Brandy and Richard. I wished I had a better view so I could read their lips. The only words I could make out were from Richard because he faced me—they were "committed" and "testify."

Uncle Harry opened his eyes. He looked around and demanded to be taken to his room. He must have thought I was Brandy. Though you could never confuse the two of us, especially in the chest area. "Let me get Celia to take you up."

"I doubt you'd be able to tear her away. You take me." He put his hands on the wheels of the wheelchair and pushed forward.

"Sure, Uncle Harry. No problem." I looked out the window. Brandy and Richard had disappeared.

On my way through the gallery, I almost bumped into two people I never thought I'd see at Sandringham. Byron

Hughes, star landscape architect, and Justin Marguilles, star attorney, whom Gordon Miles hired to kick me off my property. And they were both chatting like old Harvard buddies. If they were friends and I cozied up to Byron, maybe he could sway Marguilles to drop the silly lawsuit.

I kept my head down as we left the gallery. I wasn't sure where Uncle Harry's bedroom was, but I remembered the last time I was here, he'd taken an elevator hidden in the foyer. I found it and wheeled Uncle Harry inside. The doors opened on the second floor and Uncle Harry pointed the way. When we stopped in front of a double door carved with ornate flourishes, I pushed the button to the right of the doors and they opened inward.

The original Sandringham in England had been built for Queen Victoria. The mammoth suite we walked into was built for a king.

Uncle Harry said, "Please help me onto the bed."

"Of course." I maneuvered the wheelchair next to a bed the size of a small yacht and was totally surprised at how little Uncle Harry weighed as I helped him up. He lay back among the white linen monogrammed *F* pillow shams, and I tucked a cashmere throw around his frail body.

"Do you want me to take out your hearing aids?"

His eyes were teary. "First, please hand me that glass of water. I want to tell you a little about my son, Pierce. He wasn't always a scoundrel."

I handed him the glass. He drank like no one had given him liquids in weeks. His hand shook as he placed the glass back on the nightstand. Water splashed on the glossy veneered top and, without thinking, I took the corner of the pillow sham and sopped up the liquid.

Uncle Harry smiled. "You must love old things. What
do you think of my collection?" I followed his gaze to the
twelve-foot-high wall opposite the bed. Every square inch
was crammed with oil paintings in ornate gold frames with
brass plaques. All the paintings were clearly from the Hudson River School: grazing sheep and cows and hilly pas-
tures with winding rivers.

"Lovely. What made you want to represent modern art?"

"I was a businessman. Back in the early seventies I knew
the writing was on the wall. My second wife Tansy, Pierce's
mother, was one of the 'it' girls at the time and also a print
model. She was the muse for many an artist who hung out
in Springs. Tansy was the inspiration behind the Aqua Net
painting by Warhol."

"I assume she used lots of Aqua Net?"

"There was an advertisement for Aqua Net showing
Tansy driving in a convertible without a hair out of place.
It got Andy Warhol's attention. Warhol started in advertis-
ing, you know."

I pulled over a chair that belonged in a museum, hoping
my hundred and thirty pounds wouldn't collapse the deli-
cate Regency legs. I reached into my bag and turned up the
volume to my hearing aids. Reading Uncle Harry's lips
wasn't easy. The muscles on his right side seemed slack. It
was possible he'd had a stroke sometime in the past. "Tansy
must have been beautiful."

"Oh. She was." He closed his eyes but kept talking.
"Blonde, blue eyes, fair skinned, perfectly proportioned
facial features and a wide mouth. The perfect artist's muse.
Scandinavian. Mrs. Anderson, our chef, is Tansy's distant

cousin." He opened his eyes. "Mrs. Anderson could be your mother. You have the same coloring. Tansy was the biggest flirt I've ever met, but we all forgave her. She was ethereal, from another time-space continuum. That's why I left that particular bungalow for last. It was where Pierce always hung out to be closer to his mother. It was his refuge of sorts . . . I never thought it would be his final resting place." He reached again for the glass of water and brought it to his lips.

After he returned the glass to the table, he looked at me. A fog had descended.

"I'm Scandinavian. Swedish on my mother's side."

He gave a series of rapid blinks. "Who are you? Where's Brandy? We have to find Helen. She has to pay. She has to pay! And what about the baby? The wee baby?"

Still fully clothed, Uncle Harry laid back and pulled the throw up to his chin. He licked his lips. "Did you hear the one about . . ."

A soft voice called out, "Granddad. I've been looking everywhere for you." I turned my head toward the doorway, where Liv Falks, Pierce's daughter, stood. Liv seemed to be the only one looking for her grandfather. Certainly, his wife Celia didn't seem to care.

I walked toward Liv. "He wanted to leave the party—I mean wake. I'm Meg Barrett, a friend of Elle's."

If she noticed my uneasiness over the "party" faux pas, she didn't show it. She held out her hand. "Liv Falks. I saw you at my father's funeral. Thank you for coming."

Uncle Harry twisted toward her. "Livvy, my Livvy. Come sit next to me and tell me the story."

"In a minute, Granddad. Let me walk Ms. Barrett to the stairs."

Liv led me down the hallway, then turned left. She touched something on the wall in front of us and the wood panels opened, exposing the second floor of the glass gallery with the Steinway piano and the clear section of flooring. There wasn't a third floor to match the roof line of the old part of the house; instead there was a forty-foot-high tinted glass ceiling with copper rafters, giving the gallery a greenhouse effect.

On the first floor of the gallery, the wake was in full swing. The mellow stringed ensemble from earlier had added percussion. Was this the raucous way everyone in the Hamptons celebrated death?

Liv stopped at the dividing line between the original part of the mansion and the modern addition. "Thanks again for bringing Granddad to his room." She waved her arm toward the scene below. "This is a little much for him. For all of us."

"How are you taking it? I'm so sorry about the loss of your father."

"I'm just happy he was found and all the rumors weren't true. I knew he'd never steal a painting and leave me alone without a word. I may have been only three when he disappeared, but I knew he loved me. He was an artist. He published picture books he made just for me. One for each birthday. My mother gave me the last book on my fourth birthday, right before her accident." She took her right hand and ran it through her silky hair. "I can't wrap my

head around the fact that my father was murdered, with no water or food. How could anyone be so heartless? And to think he was so close to Sandringham the whole time. My mother thought he left with *her*. Everyone did."

I assumed she meant Helen Morrison.

"My father did some sketchy things. Things I read about in the paper after he died. But did he deserve this?" She looked at me, as if I had an answer.

I wanted to help her. I knew what it was like to lose a parent at a young age. But to lose both your parents, around the same time, seemed inconceivable. "If you want, I can look into things for you. My father is a retired homicide detective. And I know Detective Shoner from the East Hampton Town Police. Call if you need anything. Even a cup of coffee. I live right down the road." I handed her my business card. My father had taught me motive was a pie-in-the-sky thing. No rhyme or reason on what might set someone off. The person who murdered wasn't always a stereotypical adolescent who tortured small animals or set fires, sometimes it was the kind little old man who held the door for you at the post office.

"Have you always lived at Sandringham?"

She had dark circles under her eyes. "Yes, between boarding school and Brown. I just graduated last May."

I looked down and saw Celia's daughter, Kate, sitting stiffly next to a Plexiglas beverage cart topped with discarded cocktail and wineglasses.

"It must be nice having someone your own age living here."

Kate must have felt us watching because she glanced up and gave a weak wave, then took both hands and put

them around her neck like she was hanging from a noose. She mouthed, "Save me."

Liv smiled.

The noose gesture reminded me of the strangled gull.

Liv said, "Kate can be a little intense, but look who's her role model."

Celia stood next to the actor twins from one of the popular crime scene investigator TV shows—Maui, Seattle, or Poughkeepsie. Who could keep track? Both actors were gorgeous but way too young to be interested in Celia.

Then she led the twins over to meet Kate. If looks could kill, Celia would have been a doornail.

When Celia walked away, one twin on each arm, Kate reached for a partially empty wineglass and chugged. She continued to drain every drop of liquid from each glass on top of the cart, not caring that a group of guests had gathered to watch. It was a good thing Celia was on the other side of the room, chatting with a famous director, and didn't see her.

Score one for Celia. Subtract two for Kate.

Liv looked at me. "Kate's father isn't the greatest either. He has lots of money, nothing compared to Granddad. But when he divorced Celia, he cut her and Kate off without a dime. I understand cutting off Celia. But Kate? His own flesh and blood? Kate's father can't even be bothered to see her. He spends his summers on Shelter Island, only a few miles and a short ferry boat away."

"Well, living at Sandringham can't be too shabby an arrangement for Kate or anyone else."

"True. I love this house—the old and even the new addition. Celia built the modern addition right after she

married Granddad. Prior to that, all the modern art was stored on the third floor."

I glanced down. Elle was talking to Nathan Morrison. Nathan hadn't been at Pierce's funeral. I was surprised he'd showed up for the wake. Elle didn't seem to view him as a serial killer any longer. Then I realized she was holding on to his arm and keeling left to right, trying to get her sea legs. Elle was tipsy.

Then the worst thing happened. I heard a distinctive laugh. More like a cackling. Even if I hadn't been wearing my hearings aids, I would've recognized the nails-on-a-chalkboard sound. At the bottom of the circular stairs, Tara Gayle was flirting with Byron Hughes.

Oh no, you don't.

I turned to Liv. "I better get back to Elle."

"You have a choice," Liv said. "You can either take the secret stairs in the old wing or the circular stairs to the heart of the action."

"I'll take the circular stairs." Of course, if I hadn't seen Tara, I would have taken the secret stairs. What Nancy Drew wannabe wouldn't? But Tara wasn't moving in on my landscape architect if I had anything to say about it.

Unfortunately, Tara saw my descent and quickly took Byron's elbow, steering him out to the side terrace. I had to make a decision: rescue Elle or follow them outside. Sisterly love trumped hate.

A few minutes later Elle and I waited at the front of Sandringham for the valet to bring Elle's truck. Richard was nowhere in sight. Of course, I wouldn't let Elle drive

inebriated. I helped her onto the passenger seat, buckled her in, then handed her a full bottle of water I'd taken from an eight-pack in the bed of the pickup. "Drink."

I went around the front of the truck, opened the door, jumped onto the running board, and got in.

Elle chugged the water, then put the empty bottle in the drink console. "Did you see Tara Gayle tonight? What a poser. Walks around like she has a stick up her . . ." Elle hiccupped. "I'll have to tell Uncle Harry to take her off any future guest lists. Pull up the moat when she comes to call!"

"Too bad her shop, Champagne and Caviar Antiques, had to shut down last spring."

"Because of you. And Bridgehampton is all the more better for it."

"Thanks, friend. Why don't you bunk down at my place and you can drive me back for my Jeep in the morning?"

Her only response was a few short snorts. Elle was in la-la land.

I put the truck in gear and pulled away, happy I didn't have to walk to my Jeep in my killer shoes. When I reached Egret Lane, my Wrangler was where I'd left it. Still a pumpkin.

Elle's pickup was easier to drive than you would have thought—actually, a lot smoother than my tub of rust. I thought of all the wonderful damage I could do with a pickup truck and the right estate sale. Then I remembered the hefty sum I'd given Byron Hughes and realized I'd have to make do with what I owned free and clear.

*   *   *

All was quiet when we reached my rental. I helped Elle
inside, propping her against the pie safe cupboard as I
punched in my alarm code. I followed behind her up the
stairs and into the cottage's only bathroom. It was small
but had a claw-foot tub and the largest daisy showerhead
on the market. I left her inside, and waited on my bed
under the sloped ceiling. The bed's headboard consisted
of four vintage shutters with crescent moon cutouts,
painted in a sun-washed blue with undertones of turquoise.
The white matelassé jacquard duvet and lofty goose down
comforter came from a high-end French bedding
website—costing me almost a month's rent—but well
worth it. I kicked off my shoes. They were going straight
in the donation pile. Pink Ribbon thrift shop would probably clear three hundred dollars when they sold them.

Elle came out of the bathroom. I offered her the bed, but
she insisted on sleeping on the sofa. I grabbed the duvet,
brought it downstairs, and lit a fire in the flagstone fireplace.
After I was sure Elle was safely snuggled under the duvet,
just the tip of her nose sticking out, I went outside.

I was an idiot to go to the beach after the fish-gut
episode, but I wouldn't let anything keep me from my
nightly visit. I grabbed a heavy claw hammer from my
toolbox and took it with me for security. When I got close
to the gate at the top of the steps leading down to the beach,
the wood planks were wiped clean. The bucket was placed
in front of the beach grass. Patrick Seaton must have
cleaned it up—which meant he had my back.

I planned to call Detective Shoner in the morning to report the incident, but I wouldn't tell Doc the worrier. I took the steps down to the beach. On the sand in front of Patrick's cottage, I found:

> *We are all in the gutter,*
> *But some of us are looking at the stars.*

Oscar Wilde. This was the first semi-uplifting quote he'd written since the first time I'd found poetry on his beach, almost two years ago. Perhaps Georgia was right. Patrick Seaton was moving on.

CHAPTER

EIGHT

Early Monday morning, Elle drove me back to Sandringham to pick up my Jeep. We'd found Nathan Morrison standing next to my car, writing down my license plate number. Apparently, I'd parked on his property. He seemed genial enough when he saw us, especially when he saw Elle: a sober, but hungover Elle.

After picking up the Jeep, I had dragged Elle along to Paddy's Pancake House to meet Doc for our Monday morning standing date. Doc had been happy to see us, but I could tell he was upset we couldn't talk turkey about Pierce Falks's murder. Every time Doc asked Elle a detail about the state of Pierce's skeleton, including the sights and smells in the room, she closed her eyes and stuck her fingers in her ears. I'd told her about the fish-gut prank, so that might've had something to do with her squeamishness.

After Paddy's, Elle and I sat in the gazebo on Montauk's

village green, comparing notes about last night's wake. We each had an apple fritter and a cup of joe in our hands. I tore off a chunk of fritter and stuffed it in my mouth. "I saw you talking to Nathan at the wake. Anything I should know?"

"I'm a little hazy about last night. My wineglass never seemed empty."

"The sign of a good host."

"You mean hostess. Celia surely was in her element."

"Back to Nathan. What did you learn—besides that he looks like Gregory Peck?"

"Wow. You're right. Those eyebrows." Then Elle shook her finger at me. "Oh no, you don't. This isn't something you can figure out. Pierce was killed twenty years ago. Maybe I shouldn't even tell you, but Uncle Harry said we could go back in the bungalow and continue with the clean-out."

"Yay."

"I don't like that look in your eyes."

"Nathan?"

"Nathan was best friends with Pierce and practically grew up at Sandringham. He remained close to Uncle Harry and Liv, even after he'd thought his best friend had taken off with his wife. He lives in a gatehouse on the property adjoining Sandringham. It's been in his family for four generations. The oceanfront mansion that went with the gatehouse burned down in the Prohibition days, and the land was sold to the town when he couldn't keep up with the taxes. Nathan's great-grandfather used the ocean as a way to bring in bootlegged liquor. Barrels of booze were stored in the mansion's wine cellar turned

speakeasy. One night his great-grandfather fell asleep in the cellar with a cigar in his mouth. He and all those barrels went up in flames, along with the ancestral homestead."

I drained the last drop of coffee from my cup. "I went to a Montauk Library lecture with Doc last month about pirates on the East End."

"Anything to do with searching for treasure interests our kind."

"Our kind?" I grinned. "We are a special breed, aren't we? All I know is people have been using the shores of Montauk for their nefarious undertakings since Long Island was under British rule. Back then, Long Island was part of Connecticut. Pirates loved Montauk because of the open ocean on one side and the bays and inlets on the other. Captain Kidd not only buried treasure on nearby Gardiners Island, but there are rumors that the two small ponds at the base of the Montauk Point Lighthouse hide more of Kidd's loot. That's how they got the name 'The Money Ponds.' Folklore says one of the ponds is bottomless."

"I'll have to remember that when I scour your beach for sea glass. I might find a gold doubloon or two."

"Doubtful. We're talking three-hundred-plus years ago. The Gardiners Island treasure was dug up by authorities as evidence for Kidd's trial. He was sentenced to death and died on the gallows."

A troop of seagulls waited at the bottom of the gazebo steps for stray apple fritter scraps. Fat chance. People didn't line up outside Paddy's Pancake House just for their coffee. "Did you ask if Nathan had any idea who'd want to kill Pierce?"

"Of course not. Especially with his wife as the number one suspect. And no, I didn't ask him about the missing Warhol either."

I soaked in my surroundings. The weather was glorious for mid-October. It was hard to believe a nor'easter was scheduled to hit on Wednesday. The grass was still verdant under a mosaic of crimson and burnt orange leaves. Something strange and wonderful hit me. I felt at home. Montauk had become my touchstone. Life was simple, but never boring. The people were real and if I needed a shock of culture, I only had to travel 16 miles due west to East Hampton or 116 miles to Manhattan.

Friday, when the Hamptons International Film Festival opened, the minions would descend on the East End like a cloud of five-hundred-dollar-an-ounce perfume. And guess what? I'd be right next to them, ticket in hand for my chosen indie movie premiere. I could stand shoulder to shoulder with celebs if I wanted. Well, if not next to them, then near them. Life didn't get much better.

The only glitch I saw in my future was if Gordon Miles won the lawsuit and I lost Little Grey. Sure, I'd get my down payment back, but where could you find a cottage on the ocean for that price?

Answer: nowhere.

We walked back to my rental, passing quaint, unpretentious shops: a fudge store, a florist, a toy store, a bakery, a jewelry and clothing boutique, and a coffee shop. We turned off Montauk Highway and strolled by St. Paul's. St. Paul's was the church who sold me my cottage. It had been left to them by Mrs. Eberhardt.

Elle complained the whole way. She wasn't an exercise

fiend, nor was I, but I loved the fact that town was less than a mile away. As we walked, I filled Elle in on the shouting match I witnessed at the wake between Brandy and Richard, and my time with Uncle Harry and Liv. She seemed happy Liv was such a devoted granddaughter.

When we got to the rental, I showed Elle my storyboard for Rebecca Crandle's cottage. After it received her stamp of approval, she headed back to Sag Harbor to relieve her part-time shop worker, Maurice.

Off-season, Mabel and Elle's Curiosities was closed on weekdays. For the next couple of weeks, because of the Hamptons International Film Festival, Elle adopted an open-seven-days-a-week policy. Elle had regular showbiz clients who came to her when they were in town, to feed their collecting addictions. Elle didn't need the money, just the satisfaction of someone finding that special one-of-a-kind item that would make their day. Elle's great-aunt had left her very wealthy, and it was thanks to her loan that I was able to pull off the down payment on Little Grey.

I sat on the sofa to make a phone call to my father. He was already on the case to find some kind of proof Gordon Miles wasn't who he said he was.

Jeff Barrett picked up on the first ring. "Hey, kitten."

"Hi, Dad. What's for dinner tonight?"

"Well, let me see. Sheila's got me on this new farm-to-table kick. We're leaving in a few minutes to go foraging for wild herbs and greens. I plan to make homemade sausage with gnocchi in a sage broth. We'll see. It depends what the forest yields."

Sheila was my father's new bride. They were married less than a year. In the beginning, I had a hard time with

Sheila's intrusion into my father and my table-for-two life, but he was in Detroit and I was in Montauk. It was time we both moved on in the romance department. And Sheila wasn't that bad.

I looked at the screen on the phone to double-check I'd read what he said correctly. I had. "Foraging for greens in Detroit, the Motor City? Where?"

"Actually, on one of the old automobile moguls' estates in Grosse Pointe. It's been turned into an organic farm and natural animal habitat. There's a vast forest on the estate and it's only two miles away. It's run by the university."

"Well, make sure they point out the poison herbs from the safe. Did you have a chance to do any digging? And I don't mean for wild turnips."

"Yes, but I don't think you'll be too happy. Sergeant Gordon Miles is a war hero. He came back from the Middle East after a four-year tour. He was held in the mountains, missing in action, for half that time by some rebels. Sorry to bring you the bad news."

Darn you, Gordon Miles. Now you're a nice guy? Maybe the seagull was just a prank by a local teen. But what about the fish guts?

"How about any genealogical ties to the former owner?"

"More bad news. The former owner, Mrs. Eberhardt, did have a nephew who recently died and his name was Joseph Miles. Gordon's father, I assume."

"Ugh. I need time to absorb this. I better run. Give my love to Sheila."

My father said, "Will do. Don't give up yet on your property. The other side still has to prove their case. Love you."

"Love you back."

"Oh. One more thing. Tell Doc to stop texting me and make an actual phone call."

"Will do." Doc texting? Must be Georgia's influence, the seventy-year-old who acted like she was thirty.

After I hung up the phone, I thought about my attorney. He wasn't anything like smooth Justin Marguilles. He was a kind, elderly Montaukian nearing retirement age. I trusted him. He had kind eyes.

I got up and grabbed a Vernors from the fridge, then sat on the sofa thinking about Gordon Miles. Even if Gordon was related to the former owner, why couldn't Old Lady Eberhardt have left her estate to the church if she wanted? I'd bought it from the church. Now that I thought about it, what did the church think about Gordon Miles's claim? What if they already gave the money from the sale to some missionaries, or helped the homeless, or invested in some other altruistic project?

I hadn't told my father that my preliminary hearing about Little Grey was scheduled for today, at four thirty. I'd finally be able to set my sights on Gordon Miles, and let my gut tell me if he was a good guy or bad.

I left the cottage an hour before my scheduled court appearance, wanting to stop off at Little Grey to make sure someone hadn't left me another present, like the pitiful seagull. I took the path to the back of the folly, wanting to do a little foraging of my own. I had some annual herbs on their last legs. Elle called me the Herb Whisperer because I talked to my plants. Didn't every gardener?

I carried an antique flower basket on my arm, amazed something so old could still be useful. My rosemary bush was out of control. I couldn't even find the marjoram I'd seen on the day of the strangled gull. And, of course, the mint had taken over, per usual. Sometimes I thought early botanists made a mistake classifying mint as an herb—it was more like a weed. However, nothing was better than a few leaves of chocolate mint in your peppermint tea.

When my basket was overflowing, I lifted the wrought

iron Chinese cricket by the door, retrieved the key, and went inside. When I'd first found the folly, I had to use a machete to clear the way. The key had winked at me as soon as the first ray of sun hit metal. Divine providence. At least to my way of thinking.

Officially, a folly is a structure with no purpose, decorative and frivolous in appearance. Mine was built in the Queen Anne style. It was once painted white, and had large-paned glass windows with all the early bubbles and streaks of late-nineteenth-century glass. Over the doorway was a fan window in a starburst pattern. Once I held the deed to the land, I'd turn the folly into either a potting shed or a design studio—sometimes I lay awake at night fighting with myself over which to choose.

I turned the key in the door and entered. It was just as I left it. A cot folded in the corner, a kerosene lantern, which gave off an amazing amount of light, enough to finish the entire collection of Victoria Holt books I reread this past summer in homage to mine and my mother's love of Gothic suspense novels. Where my land stood was sometimes called the Montauk Moors because of the thirty-foot-high cliffs—just like in my Gothics. It was still a dream of mine to visit Cornwall, England—until then, Montauk would do nicely.

The folly décor was kept simple. I used mostly found items. I'd brought in an aqua carriage house door, worn and faded by years of salt air and sun, that doubled as a tabletop. I'd placed it over two large electrical spools I'd liberated from the side of the road. The iron garden love seat, which was piled with cushions and pillows made from vintage fabric, had been sitting next to the fire pit at the

edge of the property. Outside the folly was Elle's small gas grill I'd borrowed, not a big deal, seeing she hadn't taken it out of the box. I even had an outdoor potty, The Water-closet, which I'd purchased from a swanky local party supplier. I was the first person to buy one outright—not rent it for an outdoor Hamptons gala.

When I left the folly, I swept pine branches across the path to hide my trail, like the Montauketts of yore, not wanting anyone to suspect it was my hideout.

On my way to the Jeep, I went up the front steps of Little Grey, tiptoed across the wide plank porch floor, and peered inside. Everything looked copacetic, except for the salty-wound notice barring entry to the cottage by order of the East Hampton Town Police Department.

When I arrived at the courthouse and walked up the steps, I couldn't get the *duunnn dunnn . . . duuuunnn duun . . . duunnn duun . . . duuunnnnn dun dun dun dun . . . Jaws* theme out of my head. I felt like walking bait, and I wasn't too much off the mark because Justin Marguilles, Gordon's lawyer, stood at the top of the steps. The word "dapper" came to mind. Marguilles would be a perfect mouthpiece for Bugsy Siegel or a modern-day wiseguy.

He held the door open for me. "You're Meg Barrett, right?"

"No comment." It took everything I had to not thank him for holding the door. I needed to remain strong.

"Byron Hughes pointed you out to me at Pierce Falks's wake. I think it would be in all our best interests to settle this out of court. My client has recently been through a

harrowing experience and doesn't want to cheat anyone of anything."

Right. Then why the lawsuit? "No comment."

I went ahead of him through the metal detectors and snatched my handbag from the surprised guard and scurried down the hallway.

The guard called out, "Excuse me, ma'am. Please come back."

Of course, when I turned around, Justin Marguilles was standing next to the metal detector. He took something from the guard and walked toward me.

"In a rush, are we?" He handed me an item that must have fallen out of my handbag.

A personal feminine item.

I grabbed it and stormed away. Could things get any more embarrassing? I might as well go into the ladies' room, stick some toilet paper to the bottom of my shoe, and let it trail behind me like a flag of surrender.

I stepped into the courtroom, and the doors slammed behind me, announcing my arrival. A bailiff stood at the front of the room near a raised wooden platform. The courtroom was tastefully decorated, living up to East Hampton standards.

My attorney, Neil Ruskin, sat on the left side of the courtroom, next to the monsignor. I went and joined them.

Where was Gordon Miles? Waiting in the wings to make his entrance?

Justin Marguilles walked into the room and sat at the table to our right. He looked in our direction. "Good afternoon, Monsignor. Don't forget about our handball game tomorrow. I reserved your favorite court."

The monsignor leaned across me. "As if I could. I plan to whip your butt in retaliation for last week's match."

The *Jaws* theme reprised itself.

We all stood when the judge walked in. Still no Gordon Miles.

Judge Ferry was attractive and her smiley eyes connected with Marguilles every time she glanced his way. She opened the folder in front of her and flipped through the pages. "I've reviewed the case and I have to say I'm leaning in favor of Sergeant Gordon Miles because of the following reasons: in Ms. Eberhardt's last will she states, 'In lieu of any living descendants, I leave my entire estate to St. Paul's Church.' Sergeant Miles was missing in action and thought to be deceased when the will was drawn up. I am, however, willing to hear the attorney for St. Paul's Church and Ms. Megan Barrett so they can provide their side before I make a formal decision."

Two things blew me away. One, my attorney was representing me *and* St. Paul's. If we each had our own lawyer, it might make us look more stalwart. And the other thing—where was Gordon Miles?

I poked Neil and whispered into his ear.

Neil stood and addressed the court. "We'd like to ask the court's permission for a postponement until all the interested parties are present."

Marguilles stood. "As you know, Judge Ferry, Sergeant Gordon Miles is stationed out of the country at an undisclosed location. I have no problem postponing, but there's no guarantee my client will be able to be present when you set a final court date."

Judge Ferry said, "Understood. That is very solicitous

of you, Mr. Marguilles. Mr. Ruskin, can I ask why you feel it's important for Sergeant Miles to be present?"

"Well, Your Honor, we need to establish a connection between Sergeant Miles and Mrs. Eberhardt. We don't understand why Sergeant Miles and Mrs. Eberhardt weren't in communication before her death. Or if they were in communication, then we may be able to prove Mrs. Eberhardt left the estate to St. Paul's with the full knowledge Gordon Miles, her great-nephew, was alive."

Judge Ferry said, "Then we will reconvene at Sergeant Miles's convenience."

After the depressing court scene, I stopped in Amagansett for some retail therapy. When I finally arrived back at my rental, it was cold and dark. I had half a mind to buy a pet for company. I missed the canine companionship Tripod had provided, even if only for a short time.

I went onto the deck for some kindling. There were no buckets of guts in sight.

When I went inside, I started a fire, then microwaved a can of creamy mushroom soup. I poured the soup into a large coffee mug and topped it with sprigs of fresh rosemary and thyme. Then I toasted two slices of Wonder Bread sprinkled with garlic salt. Not too fancy, but the butter I spread on top was fresh from a farm in Southampton. I brought my dinner to my desk, which tonight faced the east end of the beach, and sat. I flipped up the screen to my laptop and searched "Harrison Falks." I found him mentioned in a short piece, talking about Pop Art and Andy Warhol.

If Andy Warhol had been a poet, he could have been an entry in Patrick Seaton's book, *Tales from a Dead Shore— A Biography of Tortured Poets*. When Warhol was an

adolescent, he contracted a nervous system disease that caused involuntary movements of his arms and legs and a loss of skin pigmentation. Defying the odds, he went on to revolutionize the art of the everyday. Warhol started his career as an advertising illustrator. Later, he and his crew from The Factory turned out large-sized photo silk-screened works like his 1963 silk-screen painting, *Eight Elvises,* which sold for a hundred million dollars in 2008.

Warhol also made movies, one called *Eat,* showing a man eating a mushroom for forty-five minutes. Another, *Sleep*, showed a man sleeping for six hours. Hmm . . . did he make these movies before or after a long night at Studio 54 in Manhattan, his favorite celeb hangout?

In 1967, before Warhol bought his property in Montauk, he was shot by an acquaintance and barely survived. He was in chronic pain for the rest of his life. In 1971, Warhol and his manager bought the former Arm & Hammer twenty-acre compound in Montauk for $225,000. The compound sat on top of a thirty-foot cliff and included a house and five cottages built in the '30s. Five and a half acres of the compound, including the house and cottages, were sold in 2007 for just under thirty million dollars, then again in 2015 for fifty million dollars to an art collector. The remaining acreage had been set aside in Andy Warhol's will and was now called the Andy Warhol Preserve.

I found a quote of Warhol's in my research that struck a chord with me, "I think having land and not ruining it is the most beautiful art that anyone could ever want to own."

CHAPTER

TEN

When Elle and I arrived at Sandringham on Tuesday morning, we found the beach bungalow in shambles.

I said, "If a pride of African lions ransacked it, I wouldn't be surprised." A few years ago, a wealthy mogul brought in a planeload of lions from Africa and let them loose on the Hamptons to naturally lower the rampant deer population. The deer had been wreaking havoc on the East End, ticks withstanding. They ate farm crops and caused serious car accidents. The original plan was to bring in a troop of sharpshooters with a daily dead-deer quota. Since African lions weren't outlawed in town bylaws, only mountain lions, natural selection was voted to be the more humane route versus the deer being gunned down. I guess you would have to ask the deer which one they preferred. The lions were released one at a time in

certain areas, then after picnicking were shipped off to their home country and released back into the wild.

"You're right." Elle got on her hands and knees to pick up shards of broken pottery. "On TV, crime investigators tiptoe around taking pictures and bagging evidence. I bet this wasn't the way the cops left it. Look what they did to that box you bubble-wrapped."

"I think you better call your homicide detective boyfriend and tell him about this mess." Something wasn't on the up-and-up.

"He's not my boyfriend. But I am seeing him Wednesday at the East Hampton High Adopt-a-Pet. I'll ask him then."

I picked up a Rolling Stones album from underneath a hi-fi console record player. "Hi-fi" was another one of Elle's vintage words. I could picture a young Uncle Harry and his contemporaries lying back on the midcentury sofa with teak legs, chillin' and smoking some wacky tobaccy. Well, maybe not Uncle Harry.

"The more I think about it, the more I think someone else has been in this bungalow. Maybe looking for the Warhol?"

"Could be," Elle said. "Oh, go ahead."

"Go ahead with what?"

"You know you're dying to—bad choice of words."

Elle was right. Time to check out the recording studio. Curiosity was killin' this cat.

The bookcase was back in front of the door, minus the art books. I easily pushed it aside. At the top of the door, I saw nail holes where at one time there must have been a slide lock. Whoever locked Pierce inside made double-

sure he couldn't get out. What other reason would there be for a lock on the outside? I walked in first. The walls and ceiling were padded with what looked like mattress stuffing now turned rust brown. The room wasn't airtight, as I was sure it started out to be. There was a hole near an electrical plate at the base of the wall where sand trickled in, sugarcoating the purple shag carpet. As for furniture, there were just the desk and chair where Pierce's skull and bones sat. Nothing else. The desk had a drawer, but it was empty, and there was black fingerprint powder on the desk, chair, and doorplate—the only smooth surfaces in the room.

I closed the door to the outer room and tried to imagine what Pierce's last thoughts were before he succumbed to his fate.

"When you first saw Pierce's skeleton, do you remember anything else in the room besides the desk and chair? Clothing? Tattered or otherwise?"

"Ugh. You're just like Doc. I don't remember. One look at the skull and I ran back out. I'm leaving. It's smelly, morbid, and claustrophobic in here. I feel a fainting spell coming on. Stop, already."

I knew from my father that when you found a skeleton, it looked nothing like the ones in old Vincent Price movies. The cartilage that kept the bones attached disintegrated by the time the body turned into bone.

I said, "I'll grab my smelling salts."

Elle walked past me. "Hardy-har-har."

I followed her out. Wordlessly, we slid the bookcase in front of the door. I might have sounded tough, but that room would haunt me for a long while.

On our first trip to the bungalow, we never made it into the tiny kitchen, bathroom, two small bedrooms, and attic room. All the main-floor rooms held the same carnage we'd seen in the living room. Elle wasn't swayed. She pushed all the furniture in the living room against the north wall, then swept the floor with a broom she found in a small closet that was filled with empty rare wine bottles. Thanks to my father, my wine knowledge wasn't too shabby.

After Elle cleared the center of the living room, she took masking tape and divided the floor into four sections. We went from room to room and put all salvageable items inside their corresponding squares: living room, kitchen, bedroom one, and bedroom two. There was nothing of interest in the bathroom except a rusty double-edge razor and an empty bottle of Chanel No. 5. I grabbed the Chanel because if it was vintage, it was worth something. If nothing else, it would make a good bud vase.

"I can't believe I missed this Eames rippled-ash folding screen the first time we were here." Elle looked at the screen like it was a lover. "This baby is worth about four grand."

"And I can't believe I missed all these books on the Hamptons and local gardening. This book from 1975, *Bridge Hampton Works and Days*, is a monthly country almanac and includes tips on local history, agriculture, gardening, birds, and even has community recipes."

Elle grabbed the book from my hands. "I've been looking all over for my copy of this book. My mother's family, the potato farmers, are mentioned."

She handed it back to me.

"Don't you want it?"

"Na. I'll find mine. It'll be perfect research for planning your Little Grey garden."

We boxed everything. Then we piled three boxes at a time into the large red wagon Elle had brought to cart our treasures across the sand, then up the steep incline to her truck. I would have preferred she just pull the pickup directly onto the beach. Even my Wrangler was up for that chore. Of course, the large pieces of furniture stayed where they were. Uncle Harry promised to have the furniture loaded into a panel truck he kept in a garage that had once been a horse stable and send it to Sag Harbor. Uncle Harry used the truck for carting paintings he loaned to major art exhibitions and museums in Manhattan.

Elle told me the small upstairs attic room would have to wait for another day. I tried to protest, but I could see she was exhausted.

While we loaded the boxes, I filled Elle in on what I'd learned about Pierce on the Internet and the major art scandal he was involved in. Pierce used his father's name to broker a Jackson Pollock painting between a mystery client and a museum in Czechoslovakia—the Pollock turned out to be a fake. The mystery client was never discovered. Pierce was charged with fraud. However, because he was only seventeen at the time, his father, Harrison, returned all the money to the museum, and Pierce remained a free man, or boy, but was persona non grata in the art world from that day on.

"Wow. How come I never heard about this?"

"Because you were too young."

I'd called Georgia at the bookstore after my research

on Pierce, and she'd given me a brief history on Jackson Pollock and the area in the Hamptons where he had lived.

Pollock and his artist wife, Lee Krasner, bought a farmhouse in 1945 on Fireplace Road in the hamlet of Springs. Springs was an area of land north of East Hampton and south of Three Mile Harbor. The area had always been famous for its light and unspoiled beauty. Pollock used the shed on the property to create his splatter and drip masterpieces. He would have made another good specimen for Patrick Seaton's book, having died in an alcohol-related automobile accident in 1959, less than a mile from his home.

Artists started coming to Springs as early as 1890, when William Merritt Chase opened an art school. The school closed in the early 1930s. In the '40s, a hotbed of Abstract Impressionists moved to Springs. The locals in Springs were called "Bonackers," derived from the nearby Accabonac Harbor. The artist infiltration continued into the early '80s. It became a place where many bohemian artists hung out when they weren't in Manhattan, at Sandringham, or at the Warhol estate.

Initially, Springs was considered the Hamptons' main blue-collar area: an affordable place to live for local artists and restaurant and shop workers. Not so much anymore. Just like the potato farmers of yore, Bonackers had been selling off their land because of offers they couldn't refuse, forced to move farther inland.

Georgia had also told me that after the Pollock scandal, Pierce was only given a slap on the hand.

When Elle and I loaded the last box on the wagon, I said, "There's another interesting tidbit I picked up from

the Internet. In 2003, in Wainscott, there were twenty-four Pollock-like pieces of art found in a locker. To this day, there's no proof the pieces were Pollocks, mainly because researchers found a synthetic pigment in a few of the works that wasn't available in Pollock's lifetime."

Elle asked if Pierce could have been involved.

I told her anything was possible.

After three hours of backbreaking work, we headed to Sandringham for respite.

We were only allowed entry via the service entrance of the kitchen, per Celia's directive. She didn't want us tracking any filth into the front or back of the house. Elle felt snubbed, like she was a poor relation. I felt more comfortable going in the kitchen door than the stuffy front entrance or the equally intimidating antiseptic gallery.

There were two things I noticed when we walked into the kitchen. One was the heavenly scent of New England clam chowder and fresh-baked bread, the other was the kitchen itself. The room was a perfect mix of old and new, with a huge center island topped in marble. The window over two double farm sinks looked to the west and had ocean views. Over the center island were two mammoth chandeliers suspended from white rafters with traditional crystal

prisms. Two nontraditional white gauzy opaque shades circled the top of each chandelier, adding an unexpected modern twist. The walls were made of exposed bricks showing patina and age, and the blue slate floor looked original to the house. The pièce de résistance was a bowed window with triple shelves filled with culinary herbs.

Mrs. Anderson stood at an eight-burner Viking stove. Above the stove was an open brick oven—the kind you saw in the best NYC pizzerias. "Welcome, girls. You're just in time."

I hoped she meant for the bubbling chowder in the industrial-sized pot and the crusty loaves, plural, of bread with crisscross incisions from which butter oozed.

My father taught me "chowder" came from the French word for cauldron. Chowder originated as a community fish stew to which each neighbor contributed an item that would be cooked in the cauldron—a French potluck pot.

"In time for what, Mrs. Anderson?" Elle grinned.

"Chowder, of course. And please call me Ingrid." She turned to me, smiling. "Hi, Elle's friend. Welcome to my kitchen."

I was caught slightly off-guard. When I saw Ingrid at the funeral, she hadn't been smiling. None of us were. She looked so much like my mother I had to take a seat at the humongous wooden farm table to get my bearings. Of course, Ingrid was probably five to ten years older than my mother when she passed away. And I was only about ten years younger than Ingrid now. But that smile threw me for a loop—I never thought I'd see it again.

Elle took a seat next to me, and Ingrid carried over a tray with four large ironstone soup bowls, four bread

plates, four silver soup spoons, and four blue and white French dishtowels meant to be used as napkins.

I was slightly confused about the four place settings until Kate, followed by Liv, entered the kitchen.

"Oh, Mrs. A., you've done it again." Kate plopped down in a seat across from us.

"Hi, Kate," Elle said. "We haven't been introduced. I'm Elle Warner, your stepfather's great-niece on his first wife's side, and this is my friend, Meg Barrett."

Kate picked up one of the towels and waved it in welcome, then stuffed it into the neck of her Grateful Dead T-shirt. "Hmmm. Wife number one. Can't say I know her."

Elle smiled. "That would be pretty hard, seeing she died about sixty years ago."

Liv interrupted, "Elsie Warner Falks, if I'm not mistaken. She died in childbirth and so did the baby. Sad story."

Ingrid placed an ironstone tureen in the middle of the table and ladled chowder into a bowl. She handed the bowl to Kate because Kate's arms were outstretched and her hands were doing the *gimme-gimme* gesture of a toddler, hard to believe she was in her early twenties.

"Thanks, Mrs. A. Just toss me half a loaf of bread for dunkin' and I'm all set." Kate dipped the uncut end of her bread in the chowder, then bit off a big chunk. Her incisors dripped chowder that trickled down her chin and onto her dishtowel.

Before going in for another dunk, Kate said, "Lots of sad shit in this family."

Liv took a long inhale and shakily took a bowl from Ingrid's hands.

Not insensitive to Liv's feelings, Kate grabbed Liv's hand and whispered, "Sorry."

Elle looked at Liv. "How do you know so much about Aunty Elsie, my namesake?"

"I love history, genealogy, and architecture. Always have. Especially growing up in a house like Sandringham, with all its secret rooms and passages. I almost became a historical architect but didn't want to leave Granddad to go on to grad school."

Elle asked, "What exactly is a historical architect?"

Liv put down her spoon. "Historic architects deal with the preservation of historic structures by using similar resources from the same period in the reconstruction."

I knew there was something I liked about Liv.

Kate said, "I think the old part of the house is creepy. Give me modern any day."

Ingrid passed Elle and me our chowder and half a loaf of bread.

I took my first spoonful. "Holy cow, do I detect chunks of sweet lobster in my white clam chowder?"

"You most surely do," Ingrid said. "Caught this morning. Enjoy while you can. It's nearing the end of the season."

I asked, "How long have you lived here, Kate?"

"I was at boarding school and came here at eighteen. Montauk bored me to death, so I went to live with a friend in the city and took a couple classes at the Fashion Institute. But it was too structured. Couldn't understand their thinking, offering classes like Chinese Trade and the History of Fibers, to name a couple. Give me scissors, a sewing machine, and a glue gun, and I can make something

that would blow those pretentious designers at Fashion Week off the runway. You either have it or you don't."

I liked her confidence but thought getting a broader education couldn't hurt.

Kate pushed away her bowl, laid the soggy towel on the table, and stood. "I've gotta run. I'm roped into helping Mother with Stepdad—a new shrink is coming to give him some kind of test. Hope he passes."

"What doctor?" Liv asked.

"You'd have to ask Stepgranny that one," Kate said on her way out the arched brick doorway.

Liv ran after Kate.

I scraped the bottom of my bowl, sad to see it go. Elle and I brought our dishes to the sink. I rinsed the dishes and Elle put them in the closest of three dishwashers.

"Thank you, girls." Ingrid gave us another one of my mother's smiles and I almost broke down in tears.

"No. Thank you!" we said at the same time.

Ingrid took a seat at the table, pulled out a chair, and propped up her feet. "This is my favorite time of day, between lunch and dinner, when I can thumb through cooking magazines and get inspiration for future meals." She nodded toward a tiered pie holder with three pies. "Let's break into one. What do you think?"

Hell yes! The pies looked like either pumpkin or sweet potato. When I first saw the pies, I assumed they were fake—like the ones we'd used in the pages of *American Home and Garden*.

Ingrid went to get up, and Elle said, "Stay. Just tell us where everything is."

She smiled. "Thank you." Then she went on to instruct

us on where to find things, an easy chore thanks to the
clear glass panes on the cupboards.

We brought the white plates, cotton napkins, bone-
handled stainless forks, sterling pie server, and, of course,
pie number one to the table.

"Pumpkin?" Elle asked Ingrid.

"Pumpkin–butternut squash. My own recipe. I like
making each dish my very own. I'm hoping to publish my
own cookbook."

There was a five-minute silence as we all dug in.
Heaven in a slice of pie.

Ingrid stood and went to a shiny silver coffee urn. She
took out three stoneware mugs. "Coffee, girls?"

She brought it to the table, I added cream, and took a sip.
The coffee was just the way I liked it, a dark roast without
any bitterness.

Elle wiped her mouth with the napkin and put it across
her plate. "That was the best pie I've had in a long time.
Do I have to wait for your book to get the recipe?"

"Of course not. I'll get it for you and a blank index card
to copy it down on." Ingrid went to a rustic built-in desk
with numerous cubbyholes and grabbed some cards and
a pen. Then she came back to the table and handed them
to Elle.

Elle said, "Thank you. Why is Uncle Harry seeing a
psychiatrist and what kind of test does he need to pass?"

Ingrid said, "I'm not sure. This will be doctor number
three. I want to think it's out of concern on Celia's part, but
I don't understand why he's only seeing psychiatrists, not
MDs."

I stood, grabbed my handbag from the back of the chair,

and rifled through it. "That reminds me. I have a business card for my audiologist I want to pass on to Uncle Harry." I'd pulled my hair back in a ponytail and saw Ingrid looking at my ears.

She said, "I've been after him for years to get new hearing aids. The last time Harrison saw someone was before he and Celia married."

As I passed through the brick archway into the hallway, I heard Elle ask Ingrid, "How long have you been at Sandringham?"

I had to make a decision on which way to go. Left or right? I chose left and took the hallway to the formal front foyer of the mansion. Instead of taking the secret elevator, I climbed the curving staircase that spiraled up three floors. I really did want to give Uncle Harry my audiologist's card, but I was also curious about his latest psychiatric test.

When I finally found the door to Uncle Harry's suite, Brandy, his nurse/assistant, was standing outside. She had her ear to the door. As I approached, she put her finger to her lips in the universal "shush" gesture.

Brandy must've heard footsteps coming toward her from the other side of the door because she backed away and stood next to me. The door opened and out filed Celia, Kate, and I assumed the psychiatrist, a white-haired man with a goatee and wire glasses, trying to appear Freud-like but failing because he was so tall and overweight. He was talking to Celia but stopped abruptly when he saw us.

Celia said to Brandy, totally ignoring me, "He's not in good shape. You better let him rest."

Then Kate added, "I think he's somewhere in 1972. Don't know if he's ever coming back. Poor Stepdaddy."

Celia was prettier than Brandy, but Brandy's other assets, two to be exact, might have trumped good looks for any guy with a pulse. Celia, Kate, and the doctor followed the hallway that ended at the modern end of the mansion.

Before Brandy could protest, I stepped inside Uncle Harry's room. He was seated in a tufted high-back chair, fine enough to be placed on a king's dais—very Louis XV. He looked out the mullioned window at the Atlantic. Each diamond-shaped pane of glass filtered through a different hue—some mauve, some amber, some clear. I could only imagine the view from the window on a clear day.

I said, "Hi, Uncle Harry."

He didn't move. He bit at his lower lip and rubbed the pointer finger and thumb on his left hand like he was trying to make them click to the beat of a song playing in his head. He wore his clunky hearing aids.

Brandy pushed past me and touched Uncle Harry on the shoulder. "Harrison, dear. You didn't eat your chowder."

He looked at her. "Brandy. Where's the baby? Why didn't she come home?" Then he turned to me. "Meg. Where is Little Elf?"

"Elle is in the kitchen with Mrs. Anderson. We just had the chowder. It was so good."

Brandy interrupted, "I think Harrison needs to rest and finish his lunch. Was there something you needed?"

"Let her be. It's not often I get pretty visitors."

Brandy didn't respond. She took the bowl of chowder off the side table, went into an alcove, and opened a cabinet. Inside sat a small microwave oven. She put the bowl inside and pushed a button.

I moved closer to Uncle Harry. "What an awesome view."

Brandy brought over the warmed bowl of chowder. "Do you want to eat in the chair or in bed?"

He didn't answer. Just looked out the window.

"Oh, Harry . . ." She tucked a linen napkin under his chin, and pulled a chair from the other side of the room and sat next to him. Then she fed him like an invalid.

I placed the business card on the small Rococo table between Uncle Harry and Brandy. "I wanted to give you the name of my audiologist. I noticed, like me, you wear hearing aids. He's fantastic. Changed my life."

Uncle Harry shook his head at the spoon's advance, pushed Brandy's arm away, and grabbed my hand. "Brandy, call this person immediately."

Brandy gave me a look I couldn't decipher, and I remembered the shouting match with Richard on the evening of Pierce's wake.

I left the room after promising Uncle Harry I'd go with him to the audiologist. As I walked into the sitting room, I heard Uncle Harry asking Brandy about the baby. Maybe Uncle Harry was in 1972 as Kate said, or somewhere in the past. Baby? Whose baby? Harrison's stillborn baby from his first wife, Elle's great-aunt Elsie?

I decided to take the crystal staircase leading down into the gallery so I could marvel at the ocean and the artwork, but when I stepped over the threshold from old to modern, low voices rumbled. Through the clear patch in the floor, I saw Celia and Richard standing with their backs to the window. I couldn't hear their words, but I was close enough to read their lips.

Richard said, "I hope this guy's a winner. I've

researched him and he's been used to testify in many a competency hearing."

Celia leaned in to Richard.

Darn. I couldn't see her mouth.

He laughed, then stuck out his lip in a disgusting imitation of Uncle Harry. Even Celia looked appalled and she walked away.

Did Liv know about their plan to take away Uncle Harry's power of attorney? I turned around to head back the other way before they saw me. As if on cue, an entire corner alcove, with a marble bust on a carved column, moved and Liv stepped into the hallway.

She giggled when she saw my look. "The secret staircase I told you about the night of Father's wake. Wanna see?"

Does a bear . . .

She pushed at the back of a revolving alcove, leaving me enough room to squeeze through, then grabbed the molding and pulled it shut. Oh, if only Elle could see this!

There were Persian-carpeted stairs leading up one level and another set leading down. Dimly lit sconces created the perfect shadows for ambiance. Like the rest of the old part of Sandringham, the walls were lined with mahogany panels, minus the art. I wanted to explore the third floor, thinking perhaps Uncle Harry kept one of his wives locked in a room like Mr. Rochester in *Jane Eyre*, but Liv was already waiting for me at the bottom of the staircase.

When I reached her, she pulled a round brass knob next to the stair rail, and the wall in front of us parted. Through the brick archway to the kitchen, Elle came into view, stuffing her face with another piece of pie.

I touched Liv's arm before we stepped into the hallway.

"What an imaginative house, with all its passageways and staircases." I remembered what Elle had told me about Nathan and his family in regards to the tunnels leading from the shore to the cellar that were used for transporting illegal booze. Sandringham was built in the early 1890s and probably had tunnels of its own.

Liv turned. "Yes. I've always admired the planning that must have gone into all of Sandringham's nooks and crannies. Before the funeral, Grandfather just gave me a sketching journal that was one of my father's. I've looked through it, briefly. Many of the drawings are of the interior of Sandringham. All the stories in the picture books my father made for me take place at Sandringham too."

"I'd love to see the journal. I'm a bit of an interior design addict myself." I reached into my pocket and handed her another Cottages by the Sea business card, in case she misplaced the first one.

"Sure. Maybe you can help me organize them. I want to make a book about Sandringham and its history, along with my father's drawings. I think he would've liked that."

"I'm sure he would."

Detective Shoner might also want to take a look at the journal for possible clues to her father's murder.

When we stepped into the hallway, Kate was standing off to the side, out of Ingrid and Elle's view.

Had she been eavesdropping on Liv's and my conversation?

CHAPTER

❧

TWELVE

In Sag Harbor, we unloaded the pickup and piled the boxes from the bungalow in Elle's thankfully empty woodshed.

Over a cup of Darjeeling tea, Elle shared what she'd learned about Ingrid. She came to live at Sandringham about ten years ago and was a distant relative of Pierce's mother and Uncle Harry's second wife, Tansy. Ingrid grew up and lived in Springs for most of her life. She originally worked in a few art galleries in Bridgehampton but found her real passion was food. She started her culinary career in the kitchen of the acclaimed Vic and Tina's Restaurant in East Hampton. Apparently, Uncle Harry came into the restaurant and saw her as the spitting image of his second wife, and made her an offer she couldn't refuse.

Elle and I said our good-byes and I took off for Montauk, wanting to take the long way home, past the harbor.

The sky was dark, lightning zigzagged the horizon, and the wind caused choppy waves on the bay. The swells weren't as high as the ocean waves in front of my cottage, a reason Sag Harbor had been one of America's top ports when whaling was at its peak in the early- to mid-1800s. On a day like this, it wasn't a stretch to picture worried spouses pacing their widow's walks, wringing their lace handkerchiefs in anticipation of their husbands' safe return.

When I turned onto Route 114, the drizzle turned to a steady rain. I flipped on my wipers and thought about Pierce Falks's murder. Just from meeting everyone at Sandringham, I was able to come up with a suspect list. Liv and Kate were ruled out because of their ages. Of course, at the top of the list was Helen Morrison. But what if she didn't kill Pierce and take the Warhol? Maybe she was dead too? Richard, Celia, Brandy, Ingrid, and Nathan were all around the same age. Brandy might have been a little younger, but they were all close to the age Pierce would be if he were alive. Even Uncle Harry had to be thought of as a suspect. And one last person, who'd never be able to defend herself, was Pierce's wife and Liv's mother, Sonya, because she died in a boating accident after Pierce and Helen had disappeared. I wanted to get a look at Pierce's journal and if Liv didn't call me, then I was going to call her. I needed more intel on Brandy and Richard. Elle said she was meeting Detective Shoner on Wednesday at the East Hampton Adopt-a-Pet. Maybe I'd drop in and see if I couldn't schmooze something out of him.

I entered East Hampton. The town was packed with film-festival goers. There was a fender bender at the

crossroads of Route 27 and Main Street, so I decided to park and check out Grimes House Antiques. I rarely bought anything because of the shop's high prices, but that didn't mean I couldn't get inspiration or ideas on what was trending.

Before getting out of the Jeep, I pulled up the hood of my raincoat, then stepped into the pounding rain. The wind and rain lashed at the stately elms as they tried gallantly, but unsuccessfully, to hold on to their foliage. I left my umbrella in the car. It would be useless.

Grimes House Antiques sold mostly Americana, specializing in Hamptons historical items. The exterior of the shop was in the traditional New England style, with white painted wood shingles and two large display windows on either side of a red door.

I walked in and wiped my boots on the front mat, already spying a trinket I knew would set me back a thousand dollars or two. It was a sailor's valentine, almost impossible to find, although there were plenty of reproductions. Even the reproductions sold in the two-hundred-dollar range. Sailor's valentines were thought to be made in the mid-1800s by homesick men who were away at sea for long periods of time. The sailors had access to thousands of small seashells in different pearly hues that were typically glued to the bottom of an octagonal hinged box with a glass top. The designs of the tiny glued shells were usually made in the compass rose or heart pattern, some even spelling out words. Recent research had found that perhaps the sailors weren't the original artists of the shell valentines—more than likely a group of native women

artisans from Barbados, an important stop of sailing ships in the nineteenth century. Did the sailors make them or buy them from souvenir shops? It was up for debate. Believe which story you would—but from what I'd seen, men were always last-minute shoppers.

Grimes House Antiques had once been a nineteenth-century drugstore. On my left stood the original floor-to-ceiling carved mahogany apothecary cabinet with four mirror-backed shelves and a wood counter. Below the counter were wood drawers with original brass pulls and slots to put labels. One section of the cabinet held glass apothecary jars, some with their Latin-named contents still intact. The rest of the shelves held antique oddities, all in early pharmacy décor. Amazingly enough, the ginormous cabinet was for sale—only $100,000. Contents not included.

The rare paper section at the back of the shop was my favorite place to browse. There were maps, posters, Audubon prints, naturalists' handwritten journals with sketches, and matted pages from hand-tinted books going all the way back to the days of early American exploration. If I had tons of disposable income, I'd spend it here, not on a vintage Hermès bag or Louis Vuitton luggage. Elle might beg to differ.

"Can I help you?" Tara Gayle walked toward me. *Ugh*.

Tara had beauty-queen looks, perfect lips, and white teeth. Although her eyeteeth looked a little longer than the average human's—dare we say Vampirella?

I said, "This is your shop? Thought Rita was the owner."

She looked over my head and waved at someone in the

back; it was Byron Hughes in the antique paper section. He must've been bent over looking through labeled port-folios when I walked in. If he'd been standing, his phero-mones would have drawn me like a metal spaceship to Magneto.

Tara said, "I run things now."

Byron motioned to me.

"Excuse me, I see a friend."

She wrinkled her brow and gave me an unbelieving look and said, "Whatever."

Tara went to the front of the shop and sat on a stenciled wooden chest. She took out a file from her skirt pocket and went to work on her nails. Crimson dust fell onto the bleached oak floor. I walked to the back, stopping at a huge poster displaying American beetles in various stages of development.

"Fancy meeting you here," Byron said.

I was glad I'd dressed in my skinny jeans, butterscotch leather knee-high boots, and a long hand-knit sweater, not knit by me, but by Karen Oats, the owner of Karen's Kreative Knitting in Montauk. However, I did pick out the yarn—soft alpaca wool in variegated shades of teal. Knit-ting was on my bucket list, along with surfing. But if it took me two hours to decide on the yarn because there were so many colors and textures to choose from, and another hour poring over patterns while drinking cappuccino from Karen's espresso machine, I could only imagine how long it would take me to learn to knit.

I pointed to the beetle poster. "A little serendipitous, don't you think?"

Byron laughed, a sound I could listen to till the next millennium. And he smelled good. I leaned into him, just to give my olfactory glands a treat.

He pointed at the poster. "Why is it everywhere you go, bugs are involved? Although, I didn't see any at Pierce Falks's wake."

Warmth filled my face. Was I excited that he noticed me at the wake or embarrassed because I passed him by without saying hello? I tried a little misdirection. "I wonder which is worth more, an eighteenth-century naturalist's beetle chart or a twentieth-century Beatle poster—as in John, Paul, George, and Ringo?"

"Probably the latter."

Fanned out on a low table was an assortment of unrolled antique hand-tinted landscape designs.

He followed my gaze. "I'm getting some ideas for a historical project I'm starting in April with the Town of East Hampton. We're working on building a park on the land next to Sandringham."

"Darn. Thought those plans were for Little Grey."

"Little Grey?"

I put my hands on my hips and stuck out my bottom lip.

"Ahh. Your garden by the sea. I thought you didn't want to copy Grey Gardens in East Hampton—wanted to make it your own."

"I do, but we talked about using as many heirloom and local plants from the same time period. I plan on getting landmark status from the town for the cottage because it was designed by Greenleaf Thorpe."

I was happy he was working with the Town of East

Hampton. Maybe he could use his clout to help sway the board once I had the title in my mitts. The Town of East Hampton was all encompassing and included the hamlets of Montauk, Amagansett, Wainscott, and Springs, along with the villages of Sag Harbor and East Hampton.

He picked up one of the renderings and spread it out on the table. "Don't you think this layout might be a little too grand for your property? I remembered an early owner of Grey Gardens had a hard time with her plantings. It took many seasons of trial and error until she got it right."

"Delphiniums!" We said at the same time. We laughed loud enough to make Tara, who was now flipping through a fashion magazine, look up.

I said, "I see we both read the same book."

Byron said, "*Forty Years of Gardening*. Anna Gilman Hill. I have a signed first edition."

Of course you do. Anna Gilman Hill moved from Grey Gardens mainly because of the nor'easters and the fact her favorite flower, the delphinium, couldn't survive, no matter how hard she babied it. Anna Gilman Hill was the second occupant of East Hampton's Grey Gardens, and Jackie Kennedy's cousins, the Beales, were the third owners.

Anna Gilman Hill and her landscape architect, Ruth Dean, planted the garden behind concrete walls imported from Spain as a barrier to the strong winds off the Atlantic. I didn't plan to have Byron Hughes import anything, but I wanted him to give me a landscape similar to Anna Gilman Hill's garden. She used pale-colored flowers to mesh with the sand and sea mist. Little Grey sat on a cliff in Montauk, whereas Grey Gardens was tucked behind

dunes, almost level with the ocean, so naturally, my horticultural requirements would be different.

I said, "I read her book online and printed out all the pages having to do with Grey Gardens. The photos were in black and white—gray gardens, indeed."

"I have to say, I took it for granted you were a 'keeping up with the Joneses' type of girl, like a lot of Hamptons housewives—not really caring what goes into their landscaping, only that it's pretty and has more flowers than the neighbors."

His comment put him just this side of the sexist line, but I gave him a pass. "I'm not a housewife. Not even a wife. And I don't give two figs about the Joneses. Who are they again?"

He laughed that laugh again, and I reached over and stroked his cashmere-sleeved arm. My alpaca yarn made me do it.

"You're a woman of many hats."

Yes. The first time he saw me, I was wearing a backward Tigers baseball cap.

A booming voice called out, "Ms. Gayle! What do you think you're doing?"

Rita must have walked past us while we were chatting. She stood next to Tara. "I hope you're comfortable on my eighteenth-century Pennsylvania marriage chest rumored to be from the Franklin household—as in Ben. One warped board and the price goes down significantly."

Tara shot up like her rear end was on fire.

"If you have time for magazine reading, at least read one on American antiques, not fashion."

Uh-oh. Tara was in the doghouse. She belonged there, trying to pass herself off as the shop's owner.

Tara brushed off the nail file dust from her skirt and put on her stuck-up face. "There happens to be a spread on Bill Blass's former penthouse. *Fashion Times* magazine isn't all about fashion."

Rita Grimes wasn't someone you talked back to. "Well, maybe you can save your reading and nail filing for your break. I just got a shipment of antique lace you need to measure and put on old wood factory bobbins. I'll take care of the store."

Tara stuck her chin out as she passed us. She gave Byron a wink and an air-kiss.

Byron said to me, "Let's make our escape. The last time I talked to Rita, I ended up with a bill even my accountant couldn't make disappear." He put his hand on my back and guided me toward the front door.

We almost made it.

"Mr. Hughes. Mr. Hughes." Rita came scuffling after us. She was a tiny woman, with round tortoiseshell glasses, and dark hair sprinkled with gray that she wore in a tight bun.

Byron stopped for a second, but only to pull out his cell phone. He put it to his ear and said, "Of course, Muriel. Tell Ralph I'll be at his compound in five minutes."

I tried to think of all the famous Ralphs he could be talking about, then realized no one was on the other end. It was a ruse to get away from Rita.

"Sorry, Rita," he said. "Important client. Gotta run."

Rita Grimes wasn't nice to anyone. How come Byron

warranted special treatment? One look in his eyes and I figured it out.

He took my elbow and we went out into the pre-nor'easter squall. His Range Rover was parked behind my Jeep. Beauty and the Beast. He opened the passenger door to the Range Rover, reached inside, and took out an umbrella. He chivalrously held it over me. Before I could swoon, he said, "How would you like to go to the Barkers' party Friday?"

Everyone who was anyone, plus me, who was no one, knew about the Barkers' Hamptons International Film Festival party. It was the invite of the season—right in line with Oscars after-parties.

I almost said, *Shit, yeah!* Instead, in a very demure voice, I said, "Friday? Let's see." I took out my cell phone and touched the calendar screen. Good thing he was busy with the umbrella and couldn't view the barren month of October.

"It looks clear. I have an afternoon thing." *Thing?* "Maybe I could meet you there?"

"Of course." He gave me the regular French double-cheek air-kiss, a little hard to do while holding an umbrella in the horizontal rain. But, of course, he performed it perfectly.

Later, when I walked into my rental, I kicked off my boots and placed a small box of books I'd rescued from the bungalow on the kitchen table. I was going to add them to my barrister bookcase—most were dated from the 1920s to 1940s. Not as old as my large nineteenth-century

collection of gilt-illustrated cloth books, but there was an interesting array of titles, including one thin leather volume on Montauk.

After I left East Hampton, I'd gone to Ditch Plains Beach, where I'd picked up my dinner from Montauk Melissa's food truck. Melissa was famous for the gourmet food she offered daily to the surfers at Ditch Plains Beach. It didn't take long to decide what to order, because there was only one thing you could order, "Melissa's Special Plate." I wasn't surprised that even with the nor'easter on its way the truck had been parked at the beach. Where surfers went, so did Melissa. While I was there, I saw three surfers taking advantage of the huge waves. They were crazy, but I still admired them.

It was too early for dinner, but I opened the box for a preview and saw grilled salmon with mango relish and couscous with asparagus tips. I took a little forkful of the relish. I wouldn't have to add a single herb.

After I paid a few bills I'd been putting off for weeks, I went to the small screened porch that fronted the cottage and looked at the last light of the day. I couldn't believe I was going to the Hamptons International Film Festival. I also couldn't believe I was going with Byron Hughes. I wasn't usually a girly girl who got all excited about what to wear and how to fix my hair, but this was a really big event. If I called Elle, she'd want me to wear one of her vintage dresses. There was a red carpet at the festival, but it wasn't like a Hollywood red carpet. The dress code was more casual. However, the money spent on the casual clothing probably came close to the cost of a red carpet gown.

I went inside and searched on my laptop for photos from last year's film festival—lots of denim, leather jackets, black and white—no full-length gowns and plenty of gorgeous Tinseltown faces. I closed my laptop and looked out the window at the beach. A tall, solitary figure walked the shoreline in the rain. He wore a hooded sweatshirt, the hood pulled over a baseball cap. Patrick Seaton. Getting his last walk in before the big storm. I shot up, grabbed a jacket from the peg in the kitchen, ran out through the French doors, and flew down the steps two at a time.

When I reached the bottom of the steps, he was nowhere in view.

❦

THIRTEEN

Wednesday, Elle and I headed out early for Sandringham. We wanted to beat the nor'easter. Last night I fell asleep dreaming about the little attic in the bungalow.

On the outskirts of town, the Montauk Farm Stand had a line of cars waiting to buy fall's earthy smorgasbord— pumpkins, gourds, and a myriad of squashes, to name a few. Due to the foul weather, each customer stayed in their car and gave their order to one of the Murphy girls, who handed them their bag like a carhop in a *Happy Days* rerun. The most popular farm stand item in the health-conscious Hamptons was spaghetti squash, low carb and gluten-free. The only problem was when I was done pre-paring my spaghetti squash, it would be swimming in butter, hidden under a mountain of Parmesan cheese, with fresh oregano. I did the same with acorn squash, only instead of Parmesan cheese and oregano, I added a cup

of brown sugar and some pumpkin pie spice—the amount of butter stayed the same.

Elle said, "Remind me to pick up a loaf of Lighthouse Bread when I drop you back home."

Lighthouse Bread was made by Lillian Stills, a local who owned a small gourmet shop in Montauk and also sold her wares at the farm stand. Years ago, when Lillian's friends trekked out east for a vacation, she provided them with a basket filled with homemade bread, cheese, chutney, and a bottle of local wine for picnicking at Montauk Point State Park. Demand was so high, especially for her secret recipe bread, crusty on the outside, soft as air on the inside, Lillian was inspired to open a retail shop and Elle and I couldn't have been happier.

I said, "In this wind, the farm 'stand' might be sitting by the time we head back."

"Funny."

Elle drove the truck through the gates at Sandringham.

I turned toward her. "I have something to tell you, and I don't want you to get too excited."

Elle's eyes opened wide as she gripped the steering wheel with both hands. The wind rocked the truck from side to side. "Okay, promise."

"Byron Hughes invited me to the Hamptons International Film Festival's opening night party at the Barkers'."

"Holy bazookas!" she squealed.

My hearing aids sent shockwaves up the side of my skull, reminding me to take them out and put them safely in their case in anticipation of the sixty-mile-per-hour winds coming off the ocean. "You promised."

"Well, whaddya expect? The hottest off-season invite

in the Hamptons with the hottest guy in the Hamptons. I
have the perfect dress."

"Oh no. I'm not wearing a dress. These are serious
Hollywood filmmakers who want to shine for their work,
not their clothing."

"Okay. Okay. I'll just loan you a few pieces of jewelry."

"Do you own anything on the small, understated side?"

"Why the heck would I? That's no fun."

Ingrid had sent word to Elle that as soon as we were
finished in the bungalow, we were to stop at the house for
a special breakfast. I could only imagine what gourmet
delights awaited us. I could already smell the bacon, real
maple syrup, and homemade waffles as we passed the
mansion.

When we reached the bungalow, the ocean was so turbulent, I was afraid a tsunami-sized wave would come along
and sweep it away, taking Elle and me with it. Hurricanes
and nor'easters weren't uncommon in the Hamptons. The
great hurricane of 1938, nicknamed the "Long Island
Express," almost completely destroyed the area. Fifty people on Long Island died, and the winds reached 130 miles
per hour. Then, there were a couple of bad girls, Hurricanes
Irene and Sandy. I wasn't a big fan of hurricanes, but I loved
thunderstorms, especially the light show over the ocean at
night. They were so Gothic—so Victoria Holt.

We walked into the bungalow. I was surprised the furniture hadn't been taken out yet. Probably the last thing
on Uncle Harry's mind.

I beat Elle to the narrow staircase and ran up to the attic.

The attic room was two times larger than the bedroom
at my rental. The first thing I noticed was the dormer

window that looked out at the virulent Atlantic. The view was different than the one from my bedroom because my rental was on a cliff. Here, it felt like the ocean was going to swallow the bungalow whole.

Elle went over to a bamboo easel supporting a large pastel portrait of a woman who resembled Ingrid. "It's not bad. Someone has really captured a restless look in her eyes."

I stood next to her. "I bet I know who the artist is."

"Really? Who?"

"Uncle Harry told me Tansy, his second wife and Pierce's mother, looked like Ingrid. Remember you told me Ingrid was a distant relative of Tansy."

"I bet you're right, but what does that have to do with you knowing the artist?" Elle said.

"Liv and Uncle Harry told me Pierce was a great sketch artist. I bet this is his."

Elle crouched next to an old flattop trunk. She looked at me over her shoulder. "Darn. It's locked."

"I have a ton of skeleton keys back at my place. I'd love to take it. I have the perfect location on my screened porch."

Elle tried to drag the trunk to the doorway. "It's yours, but it's too big and heavy. We'll have to have Uncle Harry pick it up when he sends the truck with the rest of the furniture to Sag Harbor."

We filled three boxes with smalls, some items dating back a hundred years, the usual case in attics. Buy new— put the old in the attic or cellar, or in this case, one of six bungalows on your property.

Elle and I each had our own wagon to pull. Thankfully the wind was at our backs, lending us a helping hand. The heavy rains had started while we worked inside. Elle had

thought ahead and brought heavyweight blue construction tarps and bungee cords. My wagon was lighter than Elle's because it contained only the bamboo easel, the portrait, and a wood box filled with drawing pencils, charcoals, and pastels.

Elle took her wagon to the pickup, while I went directly to the kitchen door at Sandringham. Elle had been smart about the tarps, but like a fool, I'd grabbed my Detroit Red Wings hoodie instead of my raincoat.

Ingrid laughed when she opened the door. "You look like a refugee who just landed on Ellis Island." She had me pull the wagon into the mudroom, not concerned with the wet sand falling in clumps from the tires. I guessed that was why they called it a "mud" room.

She said, "Living on the ocean, you have to make a pact with the sand and the caustic sea spray. If you don't, you'll drive yourself crazy trying to keep them out. Like Celia in the gallery end of the house—one grain of sand puts her into a frenzy. She's not an avid beachgoer either. I've never seen her in the water, not even in the pool."

I took off the tarp.

"Well, I'll be. Cousin Tansy. Pierce did a slew of portraits of his mother after she died—probably wanted to remember what she looked like. From what Harrison has told me, Tansy had little to do with her only son except to buy him extravagant gifts and send postcards from exotic locales."

"When did Tansy die?"

"I think when Pierce was ten or eleven, but Tansy didn't die here. She left Montauk, Harrison, and Pierce when Pierce was a toddler. By all accounts, she was a colorful

character. The reason the bungalow was the last to be moved was because Harrison knew Pierce used to hang out there to feel closer to his mother. It's where she hung out with her artist friends, back in the day. If walls could talk."

I bent down to pick up the portrait. "We thought Liv might want a portrait of her grandmother."

"I'm sure she would love it. She has a gallery set up on the third floor where she displays her father's drawings." Ingrid reached for the doorknob and held open the door that led into the kitchen. I walked through with the easel, portrait, and paint box.

Even her hands were like my mother's: long and narrow, with short, unpolished but buffed nails.

Elle and I were seated at the long rustic farm table. Ingrid sat across from us with a cup of tea—naturally she grew her own leaves.

I wasn't too far off with my prognosticated breakfast fare: breaded and fried center-cut slab bacon, French toast stuffed with a sweet orange cream cheese topped with warm orange/brown-sugar syrup, and the pièce de résistance— scrambled eggs with truffles and small chunks of Brie cheese. The combination of herbs used in the scrambled eggs was beyond anything I could ever come up with. Ingrid needed to get that cookbook on the printing press. Pronto!

I asked, "What does your husband do for a living, Ingrid?"

"I've never been married. I added the 'Mrs.' when I decided to become a personal chef. I was young and wanted to be taken seriously."

After we cleared the table, Elle and I went to see Uncle Harry and to show Liv the portrait from the bungalow.

Liv was by Uncle Harry's bedside, reading out loud from a book. She looked up when we walked in, and put her fingers to her lips, then nodded her head toward Uncle Harry, who was fast asleep. Bringing the book with her, she closed the door to the bedchamber.

Elle and I met her in the small sitting room.

Liv said, "He had a rough night. Brandy went to Green's Department Store to fill a few prescriptions."

Elle said, "We brought you something we found in the attic of the bungalow."

I opened the easel and placed the portrait on it.

"Grandma Tansy. I doubt she would have been a normal grandmother, just like she wasn't a normal mother, from what Granddad tells me. Colorful, yes. Nurturing, no. Why don't you both come with me and I'll show you my father's gallery." She handed me the book she was holding. "This is the picture book my father made for me on my third birthday, right before he disappeared, *The Room Beneath the Stairs*. I read it to Granddad almost every night. It seems to soothe him."

The dust jacket on the cover of the book was white, but the drawing of the room beneath the stairs was in black. The drawing reminded me of the cupboard Harry Potter stayed in when he lived with his aunt and uncle. Then I remembered Pierce was accused of the Pollock art sale forgery. Did that make him a Harry Potter plagiarist too? I hoped not, because Liv seemed to hold her father in high esteem, despite his past transgressions.

Liv reached into her pants pocket and took out an

inhaler. After a few deep inhales, she returned it to her pocket. "Right this way, ladies."

She went ahead of us, carrying the easel and portrait. I held the book, and Elle carried the box with Pierce's art supplies.

When we caught up, Elle said, "Please tell me you're going to take us via the secret staircase Meg told me about."

"Of course. Is there any other way?"

When we were halfway down the hallway, Kate stepped out of a doorway. She looked surprised to see us. "Oh, Liv, there you are. I was looking for you. I borrowed a book from your room. Hope you don't mind."

I couldn't read the title because Kate had it clasped close to her chest, but it was old.

"Sure, no problem."

Kate turned and went into a room next to Liv's, and we continued down the hallway.

Liv stopped at the alcove. She put both hands around the back of a marble head bust, and pulled it toward her. The passageway to the stairs opened. After the revolving alcove shut behind us, we walked up the staircase single file, Elle oohing and aahing from the caboose.

The room Liv took us to on the third floor was huge. My entire rental cottage would fit inside. There was a massive fireplace between two windows. The windows faced east, with a view of the Montauk Point Lighthouse. The room had thick hand-loomed Tabriz carpeting over intricate wood-inlay floors. My favorite part of the room was a wall full of bookcases filled with eighteenth- and nineteenth-century volumes. On a long wall on the west side of the room hung gilt-framed pictures, three or four

stacked on top of each other. The space reminded me of
the Frick Collection in Manhattan. The only difference
between the Frick and this room was almost every picture
was a black-ink line drawing of an interior room.

Liv said, "Most of the pictures are an embellishment of
a room at Sandringham. He inscribed in one of the books
he created for me that he wanted me to use my imagination
regarding what might lie underneath the surface of
Sandringham—another world."

There were four upholstered leather benches equally
spaced in front of Pierce's drawings. Elle and Liv sat down
on a bench and started chatting, while I walked around the
room to take in Pierce's work. He had talent, but there was
something cold and stark about each picture.

I took a seat on a worn leather club chair and thumbed
through the picture book Liv had handed me. It was the
same as the drawings on the wall. Each page was in black
and white. If Pierce had tinted them with watercolor, it
would be more relatable as a children's book. There wasn't
a living soul, not even an animal, in any picture. There
were a few lines of text on each page. The main idea of the
story was it took place somewhere in a spooky mansion
where a treasure could only be found by a clever little
girl—a girl never pictured on the page. Before I turned to
the last page, I saw Elle put her arms around Liv.

Liv was crying.

I put the book down and went over to them. "What's
wrong?" I reached into my pocket and took out the case
that held my hearing aids, and put them in. If I'd been
wearing them, I might have heard the buildup to Liv's
breakdown.

Liv looked beautiful, even with puffy eyes and a red nose. I handed her a tissue from a Louis the Some-teenth desk.

She sobbed, "I'm worried she's going to have Grand-dad deemed incompetent and take away all his rights."

"Who is?" Elle asked.

"Celia. She and Granddad have a prenup. This is the only way she can get control of his money."

I said, "Do you think your grandfather is in his right mind?"

"Only recently has he become confused and forgetful. I mean, I know he's ninety-one, but his decline happened so fast."

Elle took her hand. "How do you know about Celia's plans?"

"I overheard Brandy and Celia arguing about Grand-dad's will. Brandy found Celia sneaking through the papers in his study."

I recalled the conversation I overheard between Rich-ard and Celia and the argument between Richard and Brandy. Maybe Richard was trying to convince Brandy to testify that Uncle Harry had lost his marbles and she refused.

I handed Liv *The Room Beneath the Stairs*. She stroked the book with her fingertips like it was a talisman. "I should get back to Granddad. I don't want Celia any-where near him."

"How about Kate? Is she close to her stepfather?"

"She wasn't close to Granddad before my dad's body was found. Since then, she's been spending more time

with him. I think she's only doing it for my sake, but whatever the reason, I'm happy. She comes across tough, but I know inside she's a marshmallow. Her mother is another story. What you see is what you get."

We took the secret staircase down to the second floor, then we walked Liv back to Uncle Harry's room. When I glanced inside, Kate was sitting next to Uncle Harry's bed.

Elle and I took the central staircase in the front of the house to the first floor. At the bottom, loud voices were coming from a room down a hallway I'd never taken. I grabbed Elle's arm and dragged her toward the voices.

Richard said, in his midwestern accent, "I don't think it's any of your business why I'm in the library. I work here. What's your excuse for hanging around all the time?"

Nathan said, "I'm a friend of the family, Harrison is like a father to me, and I don't have to explain myself to the staff."

Richard said, "That old geezer isn't in his right mind. Just because once upon a time your family had some clout in Montauk, doesn't mean you can lord it over me. How are you handling the fact that your wife murdered Pierce and ran off with the Warhol?"

I stuck my head in the room. "Oops. We thought this was the way to the kitchen. Must've taken a wrong turn."

Elle added an unconvincing chuckle. Her face was the color of watermelon, her freckles the seeds.

I'd been wondering what the library would be like at Sandringham. I wasn't disappointed. It had two marble fireplaces, one on either end of the long room. Shelves of books covered all four walls. There was a brass rail near the ceiling

where you could roll a ladder to your desired location. That was if you picked a volume in the nosebleed section.

Richard was seated at an ornately carved mahogany desk. In front of him, an ancient book was splayed open. His right hand hovered over a notepad with writing on it.

He glanced at us. "Hey."

I said, "Hey."

He put his head back down.

Nathan said, "I'm going to the kitchen. I'll take you." He strode ahead of us. We could barely keep up.

Nathan stopped in front of the archway to the kitchen. He went to step inside but stopped, muttering, "I'm taking care of this now. Not later." He took off in the direction of the front of the house, passing Kate, who was headed in our direction.

Kate held a stack of magazines. "What's up? Planning to raid the kitchen like I am?"

Elle giggled. "How'd you know?"

When we walked into the kitchen, Celia stood behind Ingrid, holding a legal-sized piece of paper. The steam coming off the top of a boiling pot made Ingrid's face look young and dewy, a sharp contrast to Celia's stern face.

Kate walked over to her mother and Ingrid. She snatched the paper out of Celia's hand. "Celia. Give Mrs. A. a break. She can't make three different menus for every meal."

I wasn't surprised Kate didn't call her mother, "mom."

Celia said, "You stay out of it. Your stepfather requires soft food. All you eat is your precious Mrs. A.'s carb-heavy cuisine. I require a raw diet. If you're so worried, why don't you switch over to my healthier menu?"

"I will as soon as you get rid of that trough of red licorice in your bottom nightstand drawer."

Kate sat at the farm table, put her feet up on a chair, laid down the menu, then commenced to rip pages out of a fashion magazine.

Without turning to look at Ingrid, Celia said, "Do as I say *Mrs.*, or I'll talk to my husband."

On her way out, Celia nodded at Elle but ignored me completely.

Kate said, "Don't let her talk to you like that, Mrs. A. I don't."

Ingrid said, "Don't worry about me, Katie. I'm just fine. Now, show me what you plan to make to wear to the film festival."

Elle and I were invited for tea, which we both declined, because we were sadly too full from breakfast. We knew Ingrid's tea most likely involved food. After we said farewell, I collected my wagon and we headed back to my rental. The storm was edging closer.

When Elle pulled the pickup into my drive, she said, "Wow. What a dysfunctional family dynamic they've got going at Sandringham."

"You're part of that family," I said.

"No blood relation, but I am very fond of Uncle Harry and Liv. Do you realize Richard, Brandy, Celia, Nathan, and Ingrid are all around the same age as Pierce would be if he'd lived?"

"Duh! Don't you listen to anything I say?"

"It's pretty clear Nathan's wife did the dirty deed. She's probably living on an island somewhere in the Caribbean enjoying the money she made off the Aqua Net picture."

"I'm just sayin', you never know people. Just ask my dad. I remember this one case where he unknowingly invited a murderer over to dinner. On top of it, the guy was a town councilman."

"Guess who's coming to dinner?"

"You wouldn't laugh if you saw the crime scene photos. I used to occasionally go through my dad's files when he brought them home from work. All that stopped after Councilman Johnson was arrested."

"Well, I better get going," Elle said. "Batten the hatches, matey."

I saluted. "Aye, aye, Captain."

I was happy she wouldn't have to drive all the way to Sag Harbor. She was going to East Hampton to meet Detective Shoner for the Adopt-a-Pet. If anyone could protect her from the nor'easter, he could.

The storm wasn't at its worst.

Yet.

CHAPTER

FOURTEEN

I made coffee in my French press and placed the cup and
the pot on the round etched brass tray table that was next
to my cushioned window seat. I'd already lit a fire, and
the cottage was at its utmost coziest. I stretched out and
looked at the beach, happy I wasn't on it. Too bad I had
to go out later to the Adopt-a-Pet. I really needed to talk
to Detective Shoner, especially with the new developments
at Sandringham with Uncle Harry's competency issue. I
wanted to know if the cops had placed Pierce's murder on
the front burner or back. Uncle Harry and Liv deserved
to see their loved one's killer brought to justice.

I didn't tell Elle I was planning to attend the
Adopt-a-Pet. She would have a dog picked out for me
within seconds. I was a softy when it came to dogs. Especially after Tripod—woman's best friend. The Adopt-a-Pet

started at noon and ended at four. I planned to be there at three forty-five.

The parking lot at East Hampton High School had only four cars in it. Two of the vehicles were Elle's pickup truck and Detective Shoner's Lexus. I followed the arrows to the gymnasium door. Not an easy task. For every two steps forward, the wind pushed me back one.

When I walked in, an elderly lady came toward me. She held an open cardboard box filled with forms. "Oh, I'm sorry, sweetie, we wrapped the Adopt-a-Pet up early because of the nor'easter. The gym becomes a shelter when there's any threat of flooding. We do have one pet we weren't able to find a home for. Why don't you go take a look. Ms. Warner can help you." She pointed to Elle, who stood next to a large animal crate.

I was doomed.

Elle saw me and shouted, "What are you doing here? It must be a sign. I have the perfect pet for you!"

I looked at the size of the crate. "Oh no, you don't!"

"Come see. Your heart will melt."

That was what I was afraid of.

Detective Shoner came into the gym from a door behind the crate and grabbed his coat from a nearby chair.

If I didn't hurry over there before he left, I'd never find out anything about the case.

I walked across the basketball court, thinking it had been years since I'd played—a bonding sport my father and I shared back in Detroit.

When I reached Elle and Detective Shoner, I purposely

avoided looking into the wolf-sized crate. "Detective, I need to ask you a few questions about Pierce Falks's murder."

For a short man, Detective Shoner carried himself like an Amazon. He had impeccable taste in clothing and knew how to dress to compensate for his small stature: monochromatic colors for a streamlined look, narrow vertical stripes, close-fitting clothes, and attention-getting details up high on the body, like a pocket square in a bright color. I'd learned these tips from my ex-fiancé, Michael, who was five ten and told everyone he was six one.

Detective Shoner was also one of the best-smelling men I'd encountered. I was sure Elle agreed, judging by her pink cheeks and starry-eyed look when she glanced his way.

Detective Shoner said, "Ms. Barrett, what could you possibly need to know that you can't find out from your retired homicide detective father or coroner friend?"

"I'd like to know your take on things. Four heads are better than one."

Elle walked up and stabbed a finger in my chest. "Meg Barrett. What are you up to?"

"You saw Liv. Don't you want to help find her father's killer?"

"Of course I do, but I also had a bad feeling when we were in that secret stairway."

"Funny you never mentioned anything."

Detective Shoner interjected, "Okay. I have a deal for you, Ms. Barrett. You adopt this last pet, and I'll tell you everything we know about the case, which I have to warn you, isn't much."

Oh jeez. I looked at him, then the cage, then back to him. "I can't adopt a pet. I might not have a home when my lease runs out, especially if I lose Little Grey."

"Little Grey?" He looked at Elle.

"The old Eberhardt property Meg bought last spring."

"Well, my deal stands." He walked toward the crate and reached for the latch.

Detective Shoner opened the crate door. I stood back, ready for the onslaught. He looked inside. "She's not coming out."

Elle said, "Let me."

Brave soul.

She reached in and crooned, "Come here, baby. Don't be shy."

Baby?

Elle stuck the upper half of her body into the crate. Nails scratched at the bottom of the crate and there was a growl. "Got her!"

Out came Elle and in her arms was the biggest, fattest cat I'd ever seen.

Detective Shoner took the cat from Elle. "She's a Maine Coon. Someone left her at our precinct door. Until one of the officers made the discovery Joe was Josephine, we'd named her One-Eyed Joe. She would have been adopted earlier if we'd thought of the gloves."

Gloves?

The huge cat squirmed in his arms, swiping the air with extended claws. He, I mean, she, had a jiggly white Santa Claus belly. The hair coming out of her ears was long enough to braid. And she had one eye. The other eye was sealed in a permanent wink.

Detective Shoner said, "Elle, give Ms. Barrett the gloves."

Elle handed me a pair of leather work gloves. I had to make a decision because once I held the cat, it would be too late. A one-eyed cat . . . come on.

I put on the gloves. What did I have to lose?

Apparently, *my* eye!

Detective Shoner started to lose his grip, and the cat's left paw reached out and swiped at my temple. I screeched, and the cat fell to the floor and took off toward the bleachers.

After a half hour of cajoling, the cat followed a trail of treats that led to her crate. She gobbled as she went, like she hadn't eaten in years. Inside the crate, Elle had placed an open can of cat food. In she went. This cat's Achilles' heel was definitely food.

"So, what's it gonna be, Ms. Barrett?"

Was he kidding? Blood streamed down my right cheek. Elle dabbed at the wound with one of her vintage hand-kerchiefs.

The cat had finished her meal and put her nose against the grate of the door. Her one eye didn't look apologetic in the least.

"She'll take her," Elle said.

"I can't. I don't have any food or a litter box, and the IGA closed early because of the storm."

"Not to worry." Detective Shoner picked up the crate from the handle on top. It was almost as big as him. "All her things are back in the mail room at the precinct. You can pick up Jo tomorrow. I'm sure everyone will want to say good-bye."

The cat gave me the evil eye, then licked her lips.

"But what about our talk?"

"We'll talk tomorrow. In my office." He gave me a weird look, probably thinking I was an unworthy candidate to be an adoptive parent.

As I walked away, I swear the cat smiled. I saw imaginary feathers sticking out of her mouth.

I maneuvered my Jeep safely out of East Hampton and through Amagansett, making a rash decision to check out Little Grey. You never knew what damage could be done during a nor'easter on a property where the trees and branches hadn't been pruned in decades. And what was even sillier, I took Old Montauk Highway: the twisting, turning roller coaster of a road that followed the shoreline, when I could have chosen the new, straight, safe road to reach Montauk.

On a clear day, Old Montauk Highway brought ocean views so spectacular you might feel you were in the South of France. Bad analogy—especially when thinking of Princess Grace's demise on a similar road in her little sports car. I couldn't even see the Atlantic out the passenger window. Everything was a blur. My trusty Wrangler swayed from side to side. Its roof was made of canvas, and I worried that a piece of flying driftwood might come slicing through.

It took me thirty minutes when it should have taken half that time.

Lots of time to think about the cat. *What have I done?*

I parked at Little Grey and reached in the back for my trusty vintage Coleman lantern, then made my way

toward the folly. I didn't even glance at the porch of the cottage for any bad news. The lantern weighed about two tons because it used six D batteries.

I made it to the folly just as a large branch crashed behind me. I turned and held out the lantern. The branch had severed the remaining arm from a moss-covered Aphrodite-type statue.

Once inside the folly, I lit the kerosene lanterns, took off my soaked hoodie, and wrapped a down comforter around my shoulders. Then I sent a text to myself from my cell phone to remind me to buy a generator. It was cold!

I'd left my hearing aids in for security, even knowing the weather didn't call for it. They amplified the pounding rain on the roof and the clash of the wind chimes I'd hung outside.

Lightning illuminated the windows across the room.

A smushed nose was pressed against the glass.

Someone in a yellow-hooded rain slicker.

I screamed.

One second he was there, the next he was gone.

Adrenaline took over. I reached for my nearest weapon, a claw hand-rake, and rushed out into the deluge. I wouldn't stay inside. The glass folly turned me into glow-in-the-dark prey.

Stupidly, I forgot the lantern. I ran around to the side of the folly where I'd seen the figure in the window. Icy rain hit my face, like shards of glass being fired from a blowgun.

I went back inside the folly and extinguished the gas lanterns and flew out the door, not bothering to lock it. On the way to the Jeep, I brandished the claw rake in one

hand, and the arm from the statue, which I'd tripped over, in the other.

Once I arrived home safely, set the alarm, and chugged a glass of pinot noir, I felt better. I'd have a lot more to talk about to Detective Shoner in the morning when I went to pick up Jo.

Oh boy. The cat had a name. There was no going back now.

I sat on the sofa with a cup of chamomile tea, and thought about Gordon Miles. It couldn't have been him playing those tricks on me. He was on some army base somewhere—fighting the good fight. Or was he? I was almost positive the face in the window was male, or else I'd put Tara at the top of my list. The fact that the dead gull and the face in the window of the folly happened at Little Grey and the bucket incident happened at my rental, proved I was someone's target.

After I lit a fire, I stood at the window and looked in the direction of the black ocean. The nor'easter was in full force. I'd taken out my hearing aids and saw only what was illuminated under the lamppost—the gate at the top of the steps, opening and closing to the beat of the storm. The sea grass blew from left to right, in time to the gate.

Then the lights in the cottage went out.

I was a brave soul but a little gun-shy in power outages, for a reason I'd rather think about later. I pulled my Sunday *New York Times* reading chair and an ottoman next to the fireplace. Then I sat, covered myself in a velvet crazy quilt, and opened my e-book reader. I couldn't concentrate on *And Then There Were None*, even though the Agatha Christie tale was usually a welcome distraction.

An isolated Victorian cottage on a secluded island with a list of suspects, complete with alibis—what wasn't there to love? I turned off my reader and closed my eyes.

Even though my hearing aids were out, I could still hear a tribal drumbeat repeating over and over in my head, along with the visual of the gate violently opening and closing.

It took hours before I could fall asleep.

CHAPTER

∽⤳∼

FIFTEEN

When Thursday arrived, so did the sun. Hallelujah.

I'd gone down to the beach right after sunrise, meditated, then cleared away as much ocean debris as I could without killing my back and having to cancel my date for tomorrow's party. Not that I didn't think about canceling a million times. What if instead of inviting me to the Barkers' opening night party for the Hamptons International Film Festival, Byron had said, "Do you want to go to a brokers' party?" As in real estate brokers?

I didn't even know the address for the Barkers' mega estate. I recalled something in *Dave's Hamptons*, the bible for Hamptons goings-on, about the Barkers living somewhere in East Hampton, near Georgica Pond. Even if I found the place, would they let a no-name like me inside the gates?

First things first. I had to buy something to wear, and

the only place I could think of was Chateau Couture in East Hampton.

I hid my Jeep on a side street and walked into the store like I owned it. Well, not really, but I wore my city face with a full application of makeup. I even added bronzer. I planned to meet these elite East Hampton proprietors on their own ground. It wasn't every day I was willing to drop a couple hundred dollars on a top and pants.

Elle had insisted on loaning me a few items: a vintage cashmere cape in camel brown and an authentic Hèrmes Birkin bag in lipstick red. I might end up feeling like an imposter at the party—but an important imposter. When Elle went to the auction for her Birkin bag, she told me someone across the room bought the same color red, only in crocodile with diamond detailing for $200,000. Get real.

Chateau Couture was a small Madison Avenue boutique with an annex in East Hampton. Their CC logo was purposely, I'm sure, similar to Chanel's. The interior of the shop was one long narrow room with polished dark wood floors and a thick-pile ecru rug. Instead of racks of clothing, the walls had ornate silver hooks from which one outfit hung—complete with accessories. Below the ensemble was a raised wooden box with coordinating footwear. Similar to Montauk Melissa's Special Plate— you were meant to take the whole kit and caboodle or move on to another shop. I had to admit it made things easy, but not much fun. No mixing or matching. Had I made a mistake walking in? I trusted Melissa's Special Plate but had my own taste in clothing, even if it was a tad pedestrian. Every woman knew from an early age what

colors looked best on them and how comfort and quality could be more important than trends and a designer label. The rule for decorating, keep it simple, could also be applied to fashion.

In my cottage designs, I liked to stick to neutral colors, then add a sprinkling of whimsy: a turquoise door, throw pillows in contrasting prints, or a piece of modern nestled between vintage or antique.

A tall twentysomething guy walked over. His black horn-rimmed glasses took up half his face. He was so skinny I assumed he'd stayed inside during yesterday's nor'easter, because if he hadn't, he'd have turned up in Rhode Island. "Can I help you, ma'am?"

Since when was I a *ma'am*? "I'm just looking. Thank you."

He gave me a dismissive look. As he walked away, I couldn't help but blurt out, "I need something for the Barkers' party tomorrow."

He stopped dead in his tracks, then twirled around. "Of course, gorgeous lady. I have the perfect thing for your fair coloring."

I almost asked if he knew where the Barkers lived, but that would tarnish my newfound celebrity status.

Surprisingly, he did have the perfect ensemble.

Five hundred dollars later, "What a steal!" I was told. I took off to pick up Jo and have my chat with Detective Shoner at the East Hampton Town Police Station.

I was seated in Detective Shoner's office with the cat crate next to me, waiting for the detective to return from his break. The occasional claw passed through the crate door,

no doubt looking for my other cheek. "Behave yourself, kitty, or I'll have Detective Shoner put you behind bars for assault."

Oops. Detective Shoner stood in the doorway.

He said, "Any problems I should know about?" Then he reached down, stuck his fingers into the crate, and tickled Jo's nose.

"Nope. Everything's cool on my end. Not so sure about hers."

"You'll be fine. Jo's 'tude is meaner than her scratches."

"Then I'm really in trouble." I touched the side of my face where a scab had formed. A lovely look for tomorrow's party.

"Oh, there's one thing I forgot to tell you. The only way Jo eats dinner is sitting on a chair at the table. All other meals can be eaten on the floor, but come five o'clock, you better have her dinner waiting on a plate, and not a paper one either. Another adorable fact: she's afraid of mice."

Adorable. "Got it. Now, let's fulfill your side of the bargain."

Detective Shoner took off his suit coat, draped it on the clothes valet standing in the corner, and sat at his desk. "Shoot."

"Any leads on who killed Pierce Falks?"

"None. Next."

"Who knew Pierce before he disappeared?" Per Elle, I knew Nathan and Pierce had been friends.

"Celia dated Pierce in high school, and Brandy worked at the estate before Pierce disappeared. Nathan Morrison and Ingrid Anderson lived in the area at the time of his disappearance. Richard Challis said he moved to the

Hamptons after Pierce Falks disappeared, but we haven't been able to confirm that yet."

"How did Celia hook up with Pierce's father, Harrison?"

"Never really asked. Don't see how it's relevant."

"When your guys processed the crime scene, did they find any of Pierce's clothing?"

"I'm really not at liberty to tell you, but seeing your father was on the job, I will share this. The only thing in the room was the desk, chair, and Pierce's picked-clean bones."

"Could the forensic anthropologists determine cause of death?"

"No. They couldn't find any trauma." He tidied a pile of papers on his desk. "If that's it, Ms. Barrett, I have a meeting to get to."

"I think at this point in our relationship you can call me Meg. Especially seeing you have the hots for Elle."

He coughed. "Here, let me take the crate to your car. You can grab the box of her stuff."

By the size of the box, I'd have preferred carrying the cat. What had I gotten myself into? There wasn't room in my small rental for all this.

I said, "One last question. Did your guys tear apart the bungalow? When Elle and I got there, it was a mess."

"Of course not. But we got everything we needed. Maybe a family member made the mess."

"Have you put out a BOLO for Helen Morrison and the Warhol?"

"As a matter of fact, we did. We even had a forensic artist do a sketch of what Helen would look like today. So far, not a peep from the art community."

On the way to my car, I told him about the seagull, fish guts, and face at the folly's window. As I'd thought, he didn't seem that concerned.

When we reached the Jeep, I dropped the box and opened the back, shoving aside a few garage sale finds from earlier to make room for Godzilla—Ms. Godzilla. Detective Shoner placed the crate inside. Jo peered out at me. With the look she sent me, it was hard to believe she was afraid of anything, including mice. Maybe I'd misjudged the cat and she'd been scared at the Adopt-a-Pet from all the gawkers. I reached toward the crate to touch her cute little pink nose, just like Detective Shoner had done.

Swish.

"Ouch!"

Detective Shoner laughed. "You'll get used to her. You have to read her moods. Just know they all depend on the timing between her meals."

As he walked away, I had a feeling I'd been punked.

When we returned to the cottage, I dragged the crate into the great room and unlatched Jo's door. "Welcome home. You're free to come out."

I didn't see hide nor whisker.

Well, two could play that game. I put the litter box on the screened porch and followed the handwritten directions for her afternoon meal. Screw it! I wasn't mixing dry food with warm water. There was even an annotation to test the food on my wrist before giving it to her in case it was too hot. Come on, by the look of her, she'd eat it dry. There was no time for coddling. I still had to stop off at Rebecca Crandle's cottage and do some measuring. I wanted to create an interior that would blow Tara's design out of the water.

I'd composed a "look book," similar to a fashion model's, only this one had my sketches, pages from magazines and the Internet, organized by room. I had a drastic plan in mind. I wanted to blow out the main room so it felt more like a loft, but that would entail getting rid of two walls I hoped weren't load bearing. If Rebecca agreed to my plan, I'd have to raise the budget a bit, and if she wouldn't go for it, I'd probably pay for it myself just to beat Tara.

I grabbed my jacket off the peg by the kitchen door and was ready to walk out when what to my wondering eyes appeared? A giant cat. And behind her an empty bowl. She was quite a beautiful feline. But still scary.

The cat went on a tour of the lower level. Not much to see except the great room and kitchen. There wasn't a door separating the two, just a small counter with two stools. She sauntered onto the screened porch, her belly swaying from left to right. She did her business, then came back inside.

I couldn't help but say, "Good girl, Jo."

With winter approaching, where would I put the litter box? I couldn't leave the door open to the porch. With all the shenanigans going on, it wasn't safe to leave any door open. There was only one alternative: the small closet in the bathroom. I hoped chubs could make it up the stairs.

The light over the kitchen door blinked. My father had installed it during his last visit so I wouldn't miss any visitors if my hearing aids weren't in.

I went to the door and opened it. A woman in a FedEx uniform handed me a cardboard tube and a small packet. I invited her inside. While I looked in my handbag for a

tip, Jo ambled over, and rubbed against the woman's legs.
The cat nuzzled her shins like there was no tomorrow.

I handed her a tip.

"Thanks. Your kitty is a sweetie. What happened to
his eye?"

"Her eye. I don't really know. She's newly adopted."

"Well, it looks like you both lucked out," she said as
she walked out the door. "Have a good one."

I shut the door, bent down, and patted the thick collar
of fur around Jo's neck. It was the first time I'd actually
touched the cat. The same couldn't be said of her to me.
Her fur was soft. Had one of the cops at the station doused
her with fabric softener to make her more marketable for
the Adopt-a-Pet?

Jo plunked down on my Sunday *New York Times* reading chair. The chair was leather—not claw friendly.

"Shoo, shoo." That didn't work. I went to the kitchen
counter and dug through her box for a treat.

That was the ticket.

I covered the chair with a beach towel and sat on the
sofa to open the FedEx packet. I knew what was in the
tube: the plans for my garden at Little Grey from Byron
Hughes. I'd open it later when I had time to savor every
square inch. Inside the packet was an ivory envelope. I
pulled out an embossed card inviting me to the Barkers'
opening night party. Whoooee! I was in.

One thing to cross off my worry list.

After I made a few calls and ate lunch, it was time to
go to Rebecca Crandle's cottage to check out the work
that had been done. But first, I wanted to drool over the
clothing I'd bought for the party.

With my Chateau Couture bag in hand, I galloped up the stairs. I laid out the low-cut top and form-fitting pants on my bed, adding Elle's cape then ran my hand over any wrinkles. I'd even splurged on a necklace that ended at my décolletage, as the shop boy called it with his Parisian/Brooklynese accent. Cleavage was what I called it. On the bench at the end of my bed were my new boots and Elle's Hèrmes bag. Everything came together perfectly. Elle's salesperson, and my friend and fashion consultant Maurice, would be very proud.

When I went back downstairs, I filled Jo's water bowl and hid a new catnip toy tiger under the sofa. I'd thought about buying her a catnip mouse—it was important to face your fears. However, I didn't want to jeopardize the inroads I was making in our tenuous relationship.

Hither Hills was a Montauk neighborhood with rolling hills and an ocean view seen from almost every vantage point. South of Old Montauk Highway was a gated beach only the residents of Hither Hills were privy to. There were no structures allowed south of the highway. Like many parcels of land in the area, the local government made preserving Montauk's natural beauty their number one priority.

I followed Old Montauk Highway, glancing to my left at the top of each hill for a peek at the Atlantic. The ocean didn't just sparkle under the afternoon sun, it glowed. The waves were still huge, but I wouldn't chance learning to surf them. However, the sun helped wash away the memory of yesterday's storm. I slowed the Jeep to read the street

signs on my right. In my side-view mirror, I noticed a white
van advancing behind me. The van was going so fast, its
front tires did bunny hops at the bottom of each hill.

I stepped on the gas.

The van did the same.

Before I had time to think, I took a sharp turn into the
closest driveway. The back end of the Jeep fishtailed 180
degrees. After a few gulps of air, I followed the circular
drive until I was facing the highway.

I stopped to look both ways. The van had made a
U-turn and was hurtling back in my direction. It slowed
as it passed. The sun reflected off the windshield, blocking
the man's face. All I could make out was a neon orange
baseball cap and a meaty forearm. I caught a glimpse
of the last three digits of the license plate—123. Easy
enough to remember. The bad news was, I knew by their
color they weren't New York plates.

After I sat for a few minutes, composing myself, I continued on to Rebecca Crandle's cottage. The logical reason
someone was stalking me had to do with Little Grey. I
wasn't about to scare that easily. But I would be on my
guard.

The key to Rebecca Crandle's cottage was stowed
inside a fake rock near the back door. It took me about
six rocks until I found the right one because I was in such
a frenzy to get inside. Hither Hills was desolate in the
off-season. Cottage owners sometimes returned for holiday weekends but that was about it.

I stepped inside and couldn't believe the difference a
little paint could make. As soon as I got the job, I sent over
my go-to guys, a local father-and-son team, Duke and

Duke Junior, to paint the interior. Now I realized if I broke down the walls, they'd have to come back, costing me more money. Tara's smug face flashed in front of me, and I immediately went to the walls I wanted to remove, tapping to make sure there weren't any support beams. At least something went right. A sledgehammer and Duke and Duke Junior and I'd be all set. I laid out my design plans on the floor. The bead-board wainscoting I planned to put halfway up the walls would give the space a warmer vibe, especially painted to look weathered and touchable. My goal was to make Rebecca's cottage airy and cozy at the same time. Easily done when you lived by the ocean. All I had to do was create a few nooks or alcoves with seating, ideal for daydreaming or reading.

I had the perfect vintage dresser at Elle's carriage house to make into a window seat. I'd get Elle to cut off the dresser's legs then I'd make a cushion for the top. Elle owned a buzz saw and jigsaw—which she wouldn't let me touch because she dreamt I cut off my right hand. I was left-handed, so I didn't know what the importance of the specific hand had to do with it, but I was happy to let her do the work and save a few fingers in the process.

When I'd asked Rebecca Crandle if she wanted me to place her writing desk in front of a window with an ocean view, she'd given me an emphatic "NO!" I remembered when I read Stephen King's autobiography, *On Writing*, how he started writing in the laundry room of his double-wide mobile home. The room hadn't any windows and was smaller than a jail cell. I supposed Rebecca didn't want the distraction. I felt differently. When my desk faced the ocean, it inspired me to create the perfect cottage interior.

There was a small closet under the staircase. I wanted to take off the door and make a storage area on one side and open the back of the closet and put a wine rack on the other. Double-duty storage.

The closet reminded me of Pierce Falks's book with the Harry Potter cupboard under the stairs. I wished I'd finished Pierce's storybook. I was curious as to what had been hidden and what the heroine had learned in the process.

CHAPTER

✧

SIXTEEN

I got back into town right before sunset. The local Montauk school kids were given the task of decorating downtown for Halloween. Every park bench had a stuffed pumpkin-head figure dressed in flannel and jeans. In the off-season, the town returned to its salt-of-the-earth roots, or should I say, salt-of-the-sea roots. People waved hello even if they didn't know you, and no one was in a rush when ordering takeout or picking up a prescription. Don't get me wrong, the business proprietors were always friendly to the influx of summer people, but sometimes I saw eyes roll when the limos pulled up.

When I put the key in the kitchen door, it hit me. I had a pet. A large pet. Possibly a lonely pet.

It took me two seconds to find Jo. She was curled up on my Sunday *Times* reading chair, fast asleep. She didn't even stir when I closed the door. I went over and touched

one of her long white whiskers to make sure she was alive. She opened her eye, looked at me, and closed it.

The temperature outside was in the upper forties, but I started a fire. Something about a cottage, a stone hearth, a roaring fire, and a cat seemed to go together. I went to the freezer and pulled out a meat loaf, green beans, and mashed-potato dinner and stuck it in the microwave. It was only four thirty, but I'd forgotten to eat lunch. I had to admit, having someone in the cottage, even a hostile feline, made me feel a little more secure.

I went to the French doors and looked out. No bucket of guts hung on the gate. Orange peeked out from the sea grass. The bucket must have gotten blown into the neighbor's yard from the nor'easter. I unlocked the door and went outside.

The color of the bucket was Halloween orange and made from plastic. Written on one side in thick black marker was a capital *W*. Evidence! Why hadn't I noticed it before? I wouldn't show it to Detective Shoner or Doc, but I would bring it in to the small police outpost in the center of Montauk.

I sat on the top step leading down to the beach and watched the last light of day being sopped up by the ocean. A heron was on the beach searching for food. *W*. What did that stand for? Why would someone write an initial on a plastic bucket? Logic dictated it had something to do with fishing. Was the person who left the bucket a fisherman? Surfcasting or deep sea? Doc always wanted to take me fishing at Montauk Harbor. Maybe it was time I took him up on it and maybe I'd find a clue regarding who left the bucket. If I ended up finding naught at the harbor, at

least Doc and I could score a meal at Mickey's Chowder Shack—my favorite Montauk eatery.

When I felt calm and centered, I grabbed the bucket and climbed up to my deck. I hid it behind the wrought iron stand I used to store kindling and went inside.

Once inside, I headed straight to the kitchen sink to wash my hands. The cat followed. I put another log on the fire. The cat followed. I went to the microwave, pressed the button for another minute, then took out my frozen dinner. The cat followed. After I added some fresh rosemary to the potatoes, I went to the sofa with my plate. The cat followed. I took a bite of potatoes. She stood as still as a sphinx. Her eye unblinking.

What was I missing here?

I got up for a glass of pinot noir. The cat didn't follow. Instead she jumped up on the banquette, put her paws on the table and looked at me.

I glanced at the clock. It was five on the button.

Dinnertime.

"You're one smart cat. But I'm warning you, Miss Josephine, I will not put up with this behavior if I have guests." Not that I had much company except Elle and Doc. And they both wouldn't care about cats at the table—paws and all.

I washed off a saucer from one of my pots of herbs and opened a can of Purrfectly Organic cat food. This pet was going to cost me a bundle. I placed the dish in front of her. Just as Detective Shoner said, she started eating. Even with the loss of her eye, Jo must have led a charmed life.

After I cleaned Jo's plate and reheated my dinner *again*, I sat on the sofa. I ate while I read another section

about a tortured poet in Patrick Seaton's book. I would've preferred to sit on my Sunday *Times* reading chair but the fat cat was already fast asleep.

Percy Bysshe Shelley was born in a cushy enough environment, the son of a country squire, but was kicked out of Oxford for publishing a pamphlet on atheism. When Shelley married his second wife, Mary Godwin, the author of *Frankenstein*, his first wife's wedding gift to him was to commit suicide by drowning. After that, Percy Shelley lost two sons, one from each wife, and in 1822 he died in a shipwreck on the Mediterranean. He was only thirty-six.

Patrick Seaton had chosen a few select verses of Shelley's "Ode to the West Wind." The poem was written in October almost two hundred years ago on another shore, but with yesterday's nor'easter, his poem couldn't have been timelier.

It was interesting Patrick Seaton didn't quote the final verse in the poem. Perhaps because it wasn't tragic enough, but one of my favorite Shelley lines:

The trumpet of a prophecy! O Wind,
If Winter comes, can Spring be far behind?

I woke Jo and had to half push her out the door to the litter box. It was pretty cold. Tomorrow, I'd rearrange the cottage to be more cat friendly.

Jo came back inside and went to her chair. *Her?* And I went up to bed.

I turned on the light by my bed and went to the closet to get hangers to hang my outfit for tomorrow's party. I was

down to the necklace before I realized my two-hundred-dollar top was missing. I searched the bedroom, which took about two seconds, and the bathroom, which took about one second, then I went back downstairs and searched every inch of the cottage. I stood in front of Jo with my arms crossed. She pretended not to notice.

"Where did you put it? Spill."

She opened her eye, yawned, then went back to sleep.

The top wasn't a deal-breaker, but it did fit me in all the right spots. And I didn't think I had anything else that would work. Had someone broken into the cottage and taken my top? It was such a low-profile crime, then again, the fish-gut bucket perpetrator wouldn't be charged with a felony when he or she was caught.

I stomped upstairs and went to bed.

When I woke, Jo was next to me. Her head was on the pillow on the man-side of my bed.

What had I done?

I wasn't lying when I told Byron Hughes I had an afternoon appointment—well, kind of, because my appointment hadn't been scheduled until after he asked me to the Barkers' party. Today I'd finally meet Gordon Miles. He'd been called to Washington, probably to see his buddy the president, and was coming to clarify his relationship with the former owner of my cottage.

Before leaving for the courthouse in East Hampton, I wanted to stop at the Montauk police outpost in the middle of town to show them the bucket and fill out an official report. Maybe they would send one of their bored-because-it-was-off-season officers to keep an eye on my rental and Little Grey.

Morgana Moss, my friend Barb's sister-in-law, was alone in the office. She only recently moved to Montauk. For twenty-two years she'd lived in the Bronx and had

been a 911 dispatcher for the NYPD. Now she was a gal Friday to the small East Hampton Town Police outpost in Montauk.

"Meg. How wonderful to see you. I just got a postcard from Barb from Florence."

"I heard from her too. I miss her. Especially with all the stuff going on with my property."

"She told me about that before she left. What can our little cop shop help you with, darlin'?" She chewed gum and talked at the same time.

Good thing I was wearing my hearing aids; I would never be able to read her lips.

I explained about the four incidents: dead seagull, fish guts, face in the folly, and menacing van. She took notes like she really cared. She suggested I stay with her until Barb came back. I told her I couldn't because I had a pet to take care of.

Morgana wasn't too keen on cats. She was more of a dog person. As a side job, she raised pups, Maltipoos—Maltese/poodle mixes. She showed me a million photos of Mom and Pop and different litters of pups. Mom was the Maltese. Pop the poodle. I had to ooh and aah over each one before she let me escape. It would take six Maltipoos lined up end to end to equal one Tripod. At the thought of Tripod, I thought of his master, Cole. Then I thought of Byron Hughes. Things didn't have to be complicated, unless you made them that way, as my mother used to say.

Before leaving the outpost, I promised Morgana I'd set my security alarm, even during the day. Then I headed to the courthouse in East Hampton.

The field between Amagansett and East Hampton was

covered with a couple hundred pumpkins in anticipation of Sunday's upcoming pick-your-own-pumpkin day. Obviously, the pumpkins had already been picked, but it was still fun to walk the cornfield looking for that perfect pumpkin while sipping your free hot cider.

I arrived at the courthouse half an hour ahead of time. I wanted to beat Gordon Miles into the courtroom so I could have a little chat with my attorney. I parked the Jeep, got out, and when I got to the courthouse steps I heard, "Hey, Meg!"

Liv Falks stood at the entrance of the courthouse, waving at me. Celia, Brandy, Richard, and Uncle Harry were also with her and Uncle Harry wasn't in his wheelchair. He had his walker and stood upright. He wore a suit and tie, and looked quite dapper. I could see what all his wives had seen in him—well, at least his first two. All Celia had seen was dollar signs.

Uncle Harry had a big smile on his face. His complexion was peachy-pink, instead of ashen-gray.

I walked up to the step next to the wheelchair ramp. "Uncle Harry, you look great. Is everything okay?"

"Better than okay. My third wife, soon to be ex-third wife, tried to have me sent to the funny farm, put out to pasture. She lost, thanks to my champions, Brandy and Liv."

Celia's complexion was a mottled purple. "Harrison, don't be silly. We are soul mates. The only reason I'm here is because your doctor thought you were a danger to yourself. You know I care."

"Phooey. That quack is no headshrinker of mine. You hired him."

"We were all worried about you. Weren't we, Brandy?"

Brandy said, "You were? That's a joke." She put her hand on top of Uncle Harry's.

Celia looked around for support, but no one gave any, including Richard. He knew where his bread was buttered.

Liv said, "Come on, Granddad, let's get home. This calls for a celebration. We'll go to the kitchen and see what goodies Mrs. Anderson has for us."

"No more doctors," he said.

Brandy said, "No more doctors, Harrison." Then she followed him down the ramp.

Liv stayed behind as the rest of the crew headed toward the limo. Richard ran ahead and opened the back door—chauffeur-style.

I said to Liv, "You must be really happy about the outcome."

"Oh, Meg, I am. I have to give most of the credit to Brandy. She stopped giving Granddad the medication prescribed by the psychiatrist, and he got back his appetite and his mind."

I saw that everyone was seated in the limo. Richard was in the driver's seat. I guess it wasn't worth him standing near the limo door to wait for Liv.

"How wonderful. I couldn't be happier."

Liv said, "Why don't you come back to Sandringham? Granddad would love it."

"Wish I could. I have a little thingie to take care of inside, but I bet Elle would love to come. In fact, she's nearby in Bridgehampton, volunteering at the Pink Ribbon thrift shop. If you want, I could text her?"

"That would be great."

The limo's horn honked and Liv started down the steps. When she reached the limo, she turned around and mouthed, "Good luck."

From her lips to God's ears.

When I walked into the courtroom, Judge Ferry was in the middle of admonishing a teen for urinating on the flower-beds in front of the library. The kid apparently spent the night in jail for being drunk and disorderly. His parents looked mortified. The judge let him go with a warning and assured his parents they'd done the right thing in not bail-ing him out at four in the morning. I knew what the jail cells were like in East Hampton. They were clean, usually empty, and the cops were compassionate and caring.

As unobtrusively as possible, I slithered onto the bench in the last row, behind an old guy with a gray beard and red nose. His head nodded over his right shoulder . . . TIMBER! He fell onto the bench, giving me a better view of Judge Ferry.

Judge Ferry spoke to the court clerk, then left the courtroom.

The clerk addressed the room. "Court will reconvene in ten minutes."

Was Judge Ferry the same judge who deemed Uncle Harry competent? If she was, she moved up a notch on my likeability scale.

When the boy and his parents left the courtroom, a few spectators remained. Two men in plaid flannel shirts—one blue, one red—sat on opposite sides of the courtroom. I

got up and moved toward the front of the courtroom. My lawyer and the monsignor were talking to Justin Marguilles, Gordon's attorney. I scurried to join them.

"I'm sorry, folks," Marguilles said. "Sergeant Miles has been detained. He honestly planned to be here but got stuck in Washington."

I piped in, "And you just found this out now?"

"Ah. Ms. Barrett. Yes, I'm afraid so. He's a very busy man. But he did make the effort to come all the way out here for the hearing."

"Can't you video his testimony or something, like they do on TV?"

"Well, that's not his style. He's a people person. His top priority is settling this issue so all sides are happy."

"I don't see how that is possible," I said.

"Oh ye of little faith. We're dealing with Sergeant Gordon Miles. An American hero."

Like I'd forgotten.

Judge Ferry came out and took her seat behind the bench.

Justin Marguilles stood. "May I approach the bench?"

"Yes, you may. In fact, why don't all of you come up."

We stood in front of her in order of height: Justin Marguilles, the monsignor, Neil Ruskin, and myself, but Judge Ferry looked only at Marguilles.

"Your Honor, my client has been detained in Washington, and I've only just learned about it or I would have contacted the court immediately." He handed her a piece of paper with some kind of official seal on top.

She looked it over. "May I keep this?"

"Of course, Your Honor."

Judge Ferry tore her eyes away and looked over at my attorney. "Mr. Ruskin, we'll have to reschedule. My clerk will contact your office when it's back on the docket."

We left single file. Neil held the door for me, and one of the flannel shirt guys pushed past.

Neil said, "This might be a good thing. The longer it goes, the better chance we have of some kind of resolution."

I went through the door. "I hope you're right. Maybe we're better off if the war hero doesn't show up."

Neil gave me a weird look like I was an anti-American Commie. The furthest from the truth.

EIGHTEEN

I would have been down in the dumps from not seeing Gordon Miles, but I had the Barker party on the horizon and only a few hours before I had to get ready. I made an impromptu decision to get my nails done. What little nails were left after staining, sanding, and painting. When I worked at *American Home and Garden* magazine, I had a nail technician come to my office every Friday afternoon. A gift from my ex, who was also my boss. He also got his nails buffed on a weekly basis and the space between his eyebrows waxed. Oh, what I could have done with that info on social media.

My father had called and I'd told him about the fish-gut episode. After he stopped laughing, he told me no more late-night walks on the beach. I hadn't informed him about the strangled gull, the face in the window, or the menacing

white van because I knew he'd have Doc sleeping on my sofa—*tout de suite*.

I called a Yellow Fin taxi to take me to the party, in case I had more than my usual single glass of wine. If things went well with Byron, he could bring me home.

At eight o'clock sharp, my taxi pulled behind an early-model silver Jaguar stopped at the gates of the Barker estate in East Hampton. A guard stood in front of the gates and seemed to be in a heated discussion with the occupant of the Jaguar. I was able to read the guard's lips when he told the driver they couldn't come inside unless they had an invitation. I rolled down my window, just as a woman stepped from the car.

She jabbed her finger in the guard's chest. "I forgot my invitation. Just ask Mrs. Barker. She'll let me in.

I recognized the irritating voice.

The guard said, "That would be hard to do seeing she died last spring." He put his hand on his hip where there was a holster, but it held a baton not a gun. "Get a move on, we're getting backed up."

Tara Gayle turned to look at the long line of cars stopped on the lane.

I couldn't help myself. I got out of the taxi. "Is there a problem? We have quite a backup forming. My date is waiting inside."

Tara looked at me. "You! What on earth are *you* doing here?"

"The same thing you're attempting to do, with one

distinction—I have an invitation." I waved it in front of her. For a moment, I thought she was going to swipe it away with her scarlet nails.

People behind us were getting out of their cars to see what the holdup was.

The guard half shoved Tara back in her car. "Back it up, lady."

I couldn't contain my huge grin. "Wish I could bring you as my plus one, but Byron Hughes has taken that slot."

In her gravelly smoker's voice, she said, "You just wait. You interior designer fraud. Let's see what happens when we finish at the Crandles'. When they compare my decorating panache to your schlocky garbage décor, you'll be lucky if people hire you in Harlem. I'll make sure of it."

I didn't respond. Plus, Harlem was an up-and-coming neighborhood with gorgeous prewar buildings. I just patted the hood of her car. "Better get a move on or the photographer from *Dave's Hamptons* will be adding a few candids for their Naughty-Not-Nice column. Then we'll see who the Crandles prefer."

Tara closed her window. The guard had my taxi and the car behind pull off to the side so Tara could back up. She burnt rubber, just missing my toes. In the scheme of things, it was almost worth losing one or two. Good riddance.

I got back in the taxi and Bud Stevens, my taxi driver, pulled through the gates. Bud also worked the Montauk ticket office for the Long Island Railroad. Most year-rounders carried two jobs to keep afloat until tourist season. When he stopped to let me out, I gave him a generous tip.

The ocean was at the back of the mansion, but it was too dark to see anything as I walked along the torch-lit path.

Boxwood topiaries were trimmed to resemble reels of film. Was that Byron's doing? It was a little brisk, but propane heaters were spaced evenly along the way to keep people from feeling the cold. A huge white tent had been set up on the side of the estate. Music filtered out across the expansive lawn. And yes, there was a red carpet under the long awning at the entrance to the tent.

On my way inside, I rubbed elbows with last year's Best Supporting Actor winner—either that or his stunt double.

Byron and I were supposed to meet at the bar. I pushed through the crowd, breathing in the perfumed air, the perfect blend of male/female, rich/famous with a touch of earthiness. It wasn't hard to find Byron. It was almost as if a light engineer had strategically aimed a spotlight on him. He was dressed casually elegant, no doubt a pro about what to wear to a Hamptons event. When I'd gotten back from getting my nails done, I'd spent another hour looking for my missing top to no avail. I'd thought Jo was helping me until I realized it was five minutes to five. Chow time. A basic white crewneck T-shirt had been my only choice. I still felt appropriately dressed, thanks in large part to Elle's cashmere cape and Hèrmes bag. I would never put down her vintage obsession again.

When I finally reached Byron, I was sweating from the cashmere, but not about to take it off.

"Meg, you look stunning." He put his glass on the bar, took my wrist, and directed me to an area with fewer bodies.

"Thank you. You don't look too bad, yourself."

"Are you a film buff?" he asked.

"Yes. I love this time of year. There aren't many indie films around the rest of the year. You?"

"I enjoy all genres of movies. Mysteries and thrillers are my favorites." He reached over and removed a piece of hair stuck to my lip gloss and tucked it behind my ear. When he saw my hearing aid, he only hesitated for a second. "Come, I have a surprise for you." He still held my wrist, and I worried he'd think I was having tachycardia because of the frenetic beating of my pulse.

He took me to the corner of the tent where there was a doorway that opened to a small room. Against the back wall was a floor-to-ceiling banner that read, HAMPTONS INTERNATIONAL FILM FESTIVAL. In front of the banner was my, and the rest of the world's, favorite iconic actress. Her blonde hair and smiley eyes were lustrous. She had the group of photographers and interviewers laughing at her shtick, her arms and legs swinging in some kind of parody. And she was indeed standing on a red carpet. Byron showed the guard at the door the plastic badge hanging from his neck. I was so starstruck, Byron had to push me inside. I wasn't worthy. This was heaven in the Hamptons. My jaw dropped and my favorite actor took his place in front of the banner. I wondered if Elle would mind if I had both stars autograph her Hèrmes bag.

Byron looked at me and smiled. I must have looked like a geek in an Apple computer store. "How about we get something to eat? The food last year was amazing."

And that was the last time we were alone.

I can't exactly say I became a wallflower, but I was definitely an extra in this movie and Byron the lead. He always tried to include me in the conversation, but with the noise level, I had a hard time hearing. And after my second glass of champagne, I was having trouble reading lips.

The party didn't seem to be breaking up anytime soon and there wasn't any available seating, so I continued to stand behind Byron, like one of his fawning entourage.

Another glass of bubbly, and this Cinderella might turn into her Detroit middle-class self. I'd been known to sing Motown or Madonna tunes at the drop of the hat.

Byron had a definite fan club. Of course, most of his fans were women. I'd been trying unsuccessfully to get his attention, when someone tapped me on the shoulder.

At first I didn't recognize her. Her eyes were lined in black liner so thick, each line was the same width as her eyeball. Her outfit was definitely homemade. It fit her well but was too mature a silhouette for such a young thing. Maybe I was jealous because her top was low-cut, similar to my missing one from Chateau Couture.

Kate said, "Hey there. I'm surprised you're here."

I would've never taken Kate as a snob. "Um, yes. I was invited."

"No, I mean because of Elle."

"What? What about Elle?"

"She had an accident at Sandringham."

My heart dropped into my boots. "What kind of accident?"

"She fell down the stairs. But she's okay. Stepdaddy's nurse took care of her. Just a sprained ankle and a chipped tooth."

"I have to go to her. Is she home in Sag Harbor?"

Kate waved hello to one of the TV twins from Pierce's wake. "No, she's staying at Sandringham. Stepdaddy insisted." She took a step away. "Uh-oh, Mommie Dearest is looking for me. Time to scoot."

I drained my glass and stepped outside to call Elle's cell phone.

She sounded fine, just a little loopy, but assured me not to come over to the estate until the morning. Uncle Harry's doctor was going to stop by with a portable X-ray machine. Wow, must be nice to have money. After I hung up, I called a taxi.

When I finally made my way to where I'd left Byron, he was talking to Nathan Morrison, the Falkses' neighbor. Nathan cleaned up nicely. His dark hair was slicked back and he wore a black T-shirt under a leather jacket, tight jeans, and boots.

Byron introduced us and I told him we'd already met. I listened as Byron talked to him about the project the town had given him in connection to the property that used to be in Nathan's family.

Nathan said to Byron, "Stop by the gatehouse, anytime."

"That would be great. I want to do something special above where the foundation for the old house was. Maybe a folly or gazebo."

Quell my beating heart. This guy was a keeper.

Nathan left us and headed for the exit. I felt sorry for the guy. The twenty-year-old scandal of Pierce and Helen's disappearance with the Warhol couldn't compare to today's headlines and the thought he'd been married to a killer.

Richard was standing at the bar. How'd he get an invite? Of course, Celia. I saw Kate approach Richard. She placed her hand on his sleeve and I read his lips as he praised her for the design of her dress. Then he pulled Kate close and whispered in her ear. Kate took out her cell phone and

showed Richard something on the screen then he kissed her on the forehead. What was going on with those two? Did Mommie Dearest know about it?

Another gaggle of female admirers came up to shower compliments on Byron's landscape genius. A waiter offered me a raw oyster swimming in mignonette sauce, red wine vinegar, and shallots. Not that I needed an aphrodisiac, standing next to Byron. My father had imparted his knowledge on the proper way of eating an oyster by saying there wasn't a proper way. Although, he did say if you chewed it twice before swallowing, you'd get the full ocean flavor. I turned to take a croquette of something filled with truffles and cheese, and saw Celia heading in our direction.

I grabbed Byron's arm. "I think I'm going to have to say good night. A friend had an accident and I have to make sure she's okay." A small white lie. Elle had told me to come to Sandringham in the morning, but I was at my drinking limit and my new boots were killing me. When I took them off, my big toes would probably come to perfect points.

Celia stopped a hundred feet ahead of us to chat with a woman wearing a sari. In the corners of Celia's mouth were little black caviar eggs. Her Chanel No. 5 wafted over to where I was standing. Then, to top things off, Michael, my ex-fiancé, and his ex-wife, Paige, stood a few feet behind Celia. It looked like Paige had spotted me. Only I should have known it was Byron she'd zeroed in on.

When they reached us, Paige said, "Byron, dahhrrling, where have you been keeping yourself? I just want to tell you Windy Willows was the picture of perfection this past season. Even Daddy noticed, and he doesn't notice

anything." Paige Whitney's father was the founder and head of Whitney Publications. *American Home and Garden*, where I'd once been an editor, was only one of their magazines. I'd heard from Elle that Whitney's circulation was in a downslide because they were one of the last companies to hop on the Internet bandwagon. Old-fashioned and stuffy—what Michael aspired to. I couldn't help but notice a ring with a diamond the size of an ice cube on Paige's finger. Paige looked at me. "Oh, it's you."

"Yes. It's me."

As usual, Michael remained silent. He kept glancing at Byron's jacket—probably dying to ask where he bought it.

Paige walked next to me and said in a superloud voice, "I told Michael I didn't have a problem inviting you to the wedding. It's going to be in the city, in the exact spot we first met."

A massage parlor?

She walked closer to Byron and cupped her hand around her mouth and whispered something. I knew what that something was.

"He knows I have a hearing loss. No need to broadcast it, Paige. Oh look, isn't that actress your double? You could be sisters." I pointed to a popular character actress who had an interesting, although well-worn face.

"Let's go, Michael. That's one more seat I can give to my side of the family." Paige retracted her claws before turning back to Byron. "Mummy wants you to redo the area around the duck pond. Would love it if you could fit us into your schedule."

He said, "I'll have my assistant check my calendar. Send my regards to the family."

Paige gave him a toothy smile—a horse toothy smile. She didn't acknowledge me, then walked away.

Michael said, "Bye, Meg. You look good." He followed behind Paige like an obedient hound.

I needed a chill pill, or the steam coming out of my ears would cause my hair to frizz. Something about the two of them brought out the best in me—I was so darn happy they weren't in my life anymore.

"How do you know Paige?" Byron asked.

"Michael and I were once engaged. It's a long story and a short story at the same time. I really should scoot."

"I'll walk you out." He took my elbow and steered me through the crowd, nodding his head at a dozen celebs.

We exited the tent and he pulled me aside, bestowing a kiss on me that would please the archangel and the devil at the same time. It sure pleased me.

I didn't want the kiss to end, but it did when I heard, "Byron, my man. Where have you been hiding?"

Byron introduced me to Ollie Hollingsworth, and I was happy it was dark and ole Ollie couldn't see my red-blotched face. I was a little tongue-tied or should I say, Byron's and my tongue *had* been tied. Finally, I managed a squeaky, "Hello."

Ollie continued, "I bought a new polo horse. Next time you're in Sag Harbor, stop by and take her for a spin. She's a beaut."

As he walked away, Byron said, "Pompous ass. You should see how he treats his horses."

"Do you play polo?"

"I dabble."

I could tell he was being modest. He probably had a

room full of trophies. I'd been to a few matches in Bridge-hampton with my ex-fiancé. I had to pretend I was his trophy, smiling and giving him adoring glances, wearing a flowery chiffon dress and a huge hat that made me look like I had a pinhead, while Michael tried to reel in advertising accounts for *American Home and Garden*. Ahh. Those *weren't* the days.

We walked to the circular drive where my taxi was waiting amidst the super-exotic luxury cars or environmentally savvy smart cars.

"There's my ride. Thanks for the invite."

"You're not taking a taxi. I'll have my driver bring you home."

"I'm good. But thanks."

"I insist."

He went over to the waiting taxi and handed the driver a roll of bills, and the taxi pulled away.

A Mercedes sedan, hybrid, no less, pulled up.

"I really don't want your driver to go all the way to Montauk. What if you want to leave?"

"Don't worry about me. I still have a few people I need to talk to."

I'm sure he did—female people. "Well, thank you." I got on my tiptoes to give him a peck, but he swung me over his left arm and dipped me backward. Then he came in for a landing that had me seeing stars. Seriously, there was a big star standing two feet away. I couldn't help but take a peek, then I relaxed into his lips. A great finale to a great evening.

Byron walked me to his car and opened the rear door. I said, "No *Driving Miss Daisy* for me." I got in the

front passenger seat. As we pulled away, I blew him a kiss out the window.

Byron blew one back. I felt like a giddy teen at her high school prom.

When Byron's driver turned around in the circle in front of the mansion, I thought I saw a familiar silhouette. One I'd seen many times on the beach in front of my rental. Patrick Seaton. And he wasn't alone. He and a woman stepped under the lamplight, and before I could see their faces clearly, we pulled away.

Of course, it made sense a famous author would attend the film festival. I never pictured him anywhere but the beach: in his solitary cottage, spending hours reading and writing, with no social contact because of his malaise concerning the death of his wife and child.

But what if I was wrong?

When I walked into the cottage, it looked like a blizzard had rained down from the ceiling. The entire great room floor was covered in shredded paper towels. Jo stood in the center of the room and looked royally ticked off.

What a prima donna. I thought cats were self-sufficient?

I opened the door to the porch so Jo could go potty and went to work cleaning up the mess. Out of the corner of my eye, I spied Jo with something in her mouth. She dragged it with her to the litter box, kneaded it a few times, then took a tinkle next to my TWO-HUNDRED-DOLLAR top!

Jo seemed to be making a statement on not having full VIP access to the litter box.

After I cleaned the litter box and tossed my top in a bag, I grabbed the box and carried it upstairs. Jo followed me. Once again she stretched out on the man-side of my bed.

And I thought she'd want to hide, worried about my wrath.

I placed the litter box at the bottom of the small closet in the bathroom and took out my towels and linens, tossing them on top of the antique upholstered bench with rolled arms at the end of my bed. I was too exhausted to do anything in an organized way. I glanced at my snoring bed partner. Too bad this was a rental. If it weren't, I'd add a cat door to the screened porch.

Alas, in a few months, when my lease ran out, we might have to live on the street. Especially if the court ruled in Gordon Miles's favor. Which seemed likely. Or I'd have to find a rental for myself and a twenty-three-pound feline terror. Not an easy feat in the Hamptons. I knew how much Jo weighed because the day I brought her home, I stepped on the bathroom scale holding the crate with her inside and then reweighed myself and the crate without her inside.

Woe was me.

NINETEEN

Saturday morning, I knocked at the outside kitchen door at Sandringham. Ingrid answered, a mug of coffee in her hand and a pair of slippers on her feet. "Meg. Have you come to see the patient?"

"Yes, but I wanted to talk to you before I went to see her. How did it happen?"

Elle wasn't clumsy. She could hang and wire a chandelier on a twelve-foot ladder without anyone's help.

"It was just some worn carpeting on the central staircase. It really should be replaced. Don't worry. We're taking good care of her."

I looked at the pan of out-of-the-oven Danish cooling on the granite. "I'm sure you are."

Ingrid poured me a cup of coffee, remembering how I liked it, light and unsweetened, then handed it to me. "The doctor just came. No broken bones, but her ankle is sprained

and he gave her a soft cast and some pain pills. She and
Harrison were singing show tunes the last time I saw her."

"Well, that's a relief."

She sat on a stool at the counter, patted the seat next
to her, and I sat.

She said, "I assume you heard the good news about Harrison's competency hearing? It's like he has a new lease on
life. Brandy weaned him off all the meds his charlatan
psychiatrist had him on—just in time for the hearing."

"If Harrison dies, does Celia inherit?"

"I know from Brandy, who's seen Harrison's will, that
Celia only gets a pittance when he dies. They signed a prenup. In fact, Brandy and I each get more than Celia when
he passes. Liv gets the remainder."

"So that's why Celia wanted Uncle Harry deemed
bonkers, so she could have power of attorney and spend
all his money while he was alive."

"Sounds like it. And it's only been recently that Harrison's financial guys put a limit on Celia's spending. The
last de Kooning she bought was way overpriced. They
suspected she was getting a kickback."

"Uncle Harry lets her buy Willem de Koonings?"

"The money comes from the Falks Foundation. All of
the modern art that's been bought in the last twenty years
is part of the foundation. When Harrison dies, the art will
be donated to the Museum of Modern Art. Celia worked
at MoMA and then was hired as a curator and cataloger
of Harrison's modern art collection. The classical art stays
in the family after his death.

I took a sip of coffee. "Speaking of modern art, what
do you know about Tansy, Harrison's second wife and

Pierce's mother? I heard she was a muse for a lot of the artists who lived here."

"Tansy took off when Pierce was two, after Harrison divorced her. Harrison adored her but couldn't put up with her wild lifestyle. My mother told me Tansy followed an artist she met in the South of France to an art farm in Wisconsin. She ended up living in Milwaukee, of all places, for a couple years before she passed away from lung cancer. I think Pierce was ten when she died."

"An art farm?"

"Like a commune for artists—artists who couldn't get it out of their heads the seventies were over. Before Tansy left Montauk she was almost as famous as Andy Warhol. She was the inspiration for Warhol's Aqua Net painting. That's why Warhol gave it to Harrison. Tansy was not only Aqua Net's star model for their magazine ads, but she used the stuff like it was going out of style. She carried a can wherever she went: in her bag, in her car. After Tansy died, Pierce obsessed about the Aqua Net by Warhol. Harrison kept it out of sight in a room on the third floor for the opposite reason; he didn't want to be reminded of Tansy."

I said, "Did Nathan know his wife, Helen, was having an affair with Pierce before they disappeared?"

Ingrid busied herself with her napkin. "You'd have to ask him. But I think Nathan and the rest of Montauk knew about their affair, including Pierce's wife, Sonya. Remember everyone was young at the time and Pierce had a reputation for being a cheat. He only married Sonja because she was pregnant with Liv."

"Did you know Pierce?"

"I knew of him," she said.

Everyone thought Helen Morrison was Pierce's killer. I wasn't sure. How could she disappear without a trace for twenty years? But more importantly, how could the Warhol not surface after all this time?

"Brandy seems pretty loyal to Uncle Harry. How long has she been at Sandringham?"

"After her father, who used to be Harrison's assistant, died, she moved in and became Harrison's assistant. She took night nursing classes after Harrison's first stroke. She also spent a lot of time here as a child while her father worked with Harrison. Nathan said Brandy's mother was a raging alcoholic and her father would bring Brandy here to keep her out of harm's way. Nathan remembers when he was young Brandy's mother would drive over to Sandringham drunk as a skunk, dressed in her night clothes."

Ingrid reached for the pot and topped off my coffee, then she took a pastry off the tray and fed it to me like I was a baby robin.

From behind a mouthful of ecstasy, I mumbled, "What's in that?" The warm and gooey center dripped down my chin.

"Roasted fig with brie and a dash of red pepper. Cayenne is a good antioxidant. It's been used in Native American cooking and medicines for centuries and contains vitamin C, B-6, E, potassium, and manganese."

"I would have never thought of putting it in a sweet pastry."

She smiled.

"Isn't there something Uncle Harry can do about his current wife, Celia?"

"Between you and me, he had his attorney here yesterday. I have a feeling he's filing for divorce."

I had to ask. "Who's his lawyer?"

"Justin Marguilles. He's been the family attorney for years."

Of course he has. "Was Marguilles Uncle Harry's attorney at the competency hearing?"

"Yes. And I heard he did a stellar job of it."

Darn. Not only was Gordon Miles a good guy, it looked like Justin Marguilles was one too.

I dabbed my chin with a napkin. "Did you know Celia and Pierce were in high school together?"

"Really? No, I didn't. I'm surprised Nathan never mentioned it. I always wondered why there was such bad blood between Nathan and Celia. I bet it had something to do with high school. Nathan and Pierce were inseparable until the forged-Pollock scandal. At first Nathan didn't believe Pierce could have sold the forgery, but when Harrison confirmed it, he had no choice. After the forgery, Nathan should have seen the writing on the wall when it came to Pierce and his wife. Once a cheat, always a cheat."

Ingrid was right. I thought about my cheating ex-fiancé.

I stuffed the last bite of pastry in my mouth and said, "I better go check on Elle, before she thinks I've forgotten about her. Thanks for the food and the gossip."

Before I left the kitchen, Ingrid gave me a plate of Danish to bring to Elle. After she tasted one, I had a feeling Elle wasn't ever going to want to leave Sandringham.

I scared Richard in the secret stairway. I'd never seen a man jump in such an effeminate way. "Sorry. Going up to see Elle via the fun staircase."

Richard gave me a snooty look—he'd apparently been learning from Celia.

"Do you know what room they're in?"

He kept walking, not bothering to turn around. "She's two doors down from Master Falks's suite—on the right."

Had I heard him right? Master Falks or Mister Falks? Either way, it was out of character for him to show so much respect for Uncle Harry. Unless now that Celia lost the competency hearing, Richard decided to switch sides.

When I walked in the room, Elle looked like she was in a production of *Once Upon a Mattress*, she had so many fluffy, downy pillows and comforters surrounding her, it took me a minute to locate her face. She was fast asleep. Her right ankle was propped on a pillow. Darn. How would she drive her pickup?

Liv sat next to the bed, flipping through the pages of a brown leather journal.

I said, "How nice of you to keep Elle company."

"Oh, she's great. I feel bad about the stairs."

"Should I wake her?"

Liv said, "You can try. She's on some powerful muscle relaxants and pain pills."

I looked at the journal in Liv's hands. "Is that the journal you told me about?"

"Yes. I'm pretty excited. I've recognized most of my father's drawings of Sandringham and found two revolving cubbies in what used to be the playroom. And guess what was behind them?"

"What?"

"Tin Easter eggs filled with diamond stud earrings and

jelly beans. I bet my father hid them for me." Her eyes sparkled with the possibilities.

I looked at her ears. The tiny earrings shone almost as brilliantly as her eyes.

"I'll show you how I found them." She opened the journal to the center and pointed to a black ink drawing. Gibberish was written at the base of each cabinet.

"Look." She led me to a full-length mirror next to a magnificent painted French armoire. She turned the book upside down and held it to the mirror. "See."

I did. The gibberish turned into the words, "Eat me."

Her face was flushed, adding to her natural beauty. "I bet this was going to go in the book for my fifth birthday. I was born the second week in March—around Eastertime."

Liv might have been right, but I couldn't get over the fact that Pierce had once again plagiarized a work of fiction. This time it was *Alice's Adventures in Wonderland*. Liv flipped to another page. "These next four pages have me totally stumped. I don't know of any of these rooms, secret or otherwise. Take a look at the décor."

She handed me the book and I examined the pages. I thought the room in the first drawing looked subterranean. There were no windows, and the furniture looked Deco or Nouveau—from the '20s or '30s. There was a bar with stools, and a few oak barrels sat against the wall. The second drawing was of a long winding tunnel cut from rock, with torches attached to the walls. I tried to think of what novel Pierce was borrowing from and could only come up with Mary Shelley's *Frankenstein*, but, of course, that could be because I had Patrick Seaton's book

and the passage on Mary's husband, Percy Shelley, on my mind.

The third page showed a wooden arched door with a small iron-grated window, built into a stone wall, possibly something out of *The Count of Monte Cristo* or *Les Misérables*. The fourth page gave me the clue I needed. It was an exterior shot of the shoreline, not typical for Pierce: a sandy beach, tall grass, and a mansion on top of a cliff. But the mansion wasn't Sandringham. Not even Sandringham before the modern addition was added. The mansion wasn't made out of bricks, but clapboard. Whoa. I thought I had it.

Liv must have seen something on my face. "Tell me, tell me!"

"I think these pages represent Nathan's ancestral home before the fire."

"Morrison Manor. How do you know about the manor?"

"Nathan told Elle about it at your father's wake. And then Byron Hughes . . . Do you know him?"

"Of course. Everyone knows him."

"Well, Byron is planning to landscape the area Nathan's family used to own and turn it into a park for the town of Montauk."

"I've heard the story of the fire. And it makes sense my father would draw Morrison Manor, seeing he and Uncle Nathan were best friends since childhood."

"Uncle?"

She laughed. "We aren't related, but that's what I've called him ever since I could talk."

"Hey, what are you two planning?" Elle was up on her elbows.

I said, "Hello, Sleeping Beauty."

"Liv, don't let Meg sweet-talk you. She has a knack for getting into trouble."

Elle looked adorable with the little chip on her front tooth. It went perfectly with her pixie haircut. I stood by the bed. "Looks like you're the one who got into trouble."

"Oh, this little thing? I'm fine." She wiggled her toes at the end of the soft cast and grimaced. "Holy mother of bleep!"

I helped adjust her pillows. "Relax, missy. You aren't going anywhere. Look what I've brought you." I put a Danish on a plate and handed it to her. "This will cure what ails you."

Elle took a bite. "I've died and gone to heaven."

I offered one to Liv.

"Already had two. But thanks."

Before Liv left the room, she said, "If you want, I can come get you in a few minutes and we can go over to the gatehouse and visit Uncle Nathan. You should see the gatehouse. It's the perfect size. And I know how you love cottages."

I gave her a resounding, "Yes!"

Elle and I chatted until she dozed off. She told me she had one of her premonitions before she tripped on the stairs. But she thought I was the one in danger after I'd called her and told her about my missing two-hundred-dollar top.

Wrong again, O Great Swami.

TWENTY

Liv came back to Elle's room, wearing riding gear. "You ready?" she whispered, looking over at a sleeping Elle.

I joined her in the hall. Liv held a pair of tall black boots in her hand. "I thought it'd be fun if we took the horses. I had them brought over from the ranch. You do ride, don't you?"

"Nope. Never have." Not much horse riding in Detroit or Manhattan.

"Don't worry. You can hop on with me. If you're too frightened, the gatehouse is in walking distance."

Me, afraid of a little ole horse?

We started down the hallway. Kate stepped out from a room next to the guest room and said, "Oh, where are you guys headed?"

"My first horseback lesson," I said.

Liv handed me the boots. "Kate, come with us."

"No. I'll pass. Not my idea of a good time."

Liv's boots fit perfectly. We were both a size 8. Twenty minutes later we were on our way to Nathan's gatehouse. Liv sat behind me and held the reins of a beautiful black stallion with a white diamond on his forehead. His name was Sparky, and I hoped he wouldn't spark while I was on him. It had taken about six tries before I could get up on the saddle. It was quite an amazing feeling sitting on top of such a large beast. I might add horseback riding to my bucket list of learning to knit and surfing.

We took a dirt road that headed east toward the lighthouse. It was very secluded. There were signs posted every couple hundred feet. Either CAUTION, HUNTING IN AREA, ARCHERY NOV. 1–DEC. 31 or NO TRESPASSING: VIOLATORS WILL BE PROSECUTED.

When we turned down a rutted grass lane, all I saw were untamed scrubby bushes and gnarly trees bent and twisted from being battered by storms off the ocean. I'd thought Little Grey was secluded. This brought new meaning to the word.

Liv steered the horse left and we stopped in front of the gatehouse. "The way we came is a shortcut, but you can only take it on foot or horseback. There's another more direct way, via Montauk Highway, but I don't like to bring Sparky near cars. It's the only time I've seen him get upset." She patted the horse's sturdy neck. "I didn't tell Uncle Nathan we were coming, in case he feels he has to entertain us, but I know where he hides the key."

She helped me dismount. As soon as my feet hit solid ground, my knees gave way. I fell butt first and succumbed to a fit of giggles. "Guess I don't make a good cowgirl."

"You did great for your first time. Just make sure you soak in the tub tonight with some Epsom salts. You're going to be sore." She grabbed both my hands and pulled me up from the ground.

Sure enough, the muscles in my inner thighs felt stretched to their limits. I understood why cowboys walked bow-legged.

Liv took out an inhaler from her jacket pocket, put it to her mouth, and pumped three times. I hoped it had nothing to do with pulling me up from the ground. She was a lot smaller than me.

She said, "I learned I had asthma at boarding school. I almost died. I snuck out to a party at a neighboring boys' school, and when our group of girls ran back to make curfew, I had an attack. The headmaster thought I'd done drugs or had alcohol poisoning. I lived to breathe another day, thanks to a smart EMT who realized I had asthma. Now I can't go anywhere without my inhaler."

It must have been hard to lead such an active lifestyle and have asthma. I knew you just had to deal with the cards you were given. No pity parties when it came to disabilities. That attitude not only ruined your life but also the lives of those around you.

Liv tethered the horse to an antique hitching post, then disappeared through the stone archway to retrieve the key.

The only thing I could say about the gatehouse was it was amazing. The exterior was made out of flagstones, similar to the hearth at my rental. The roof had slate shingles, which looked original, although I think it would be impossible with all the nor'easters and storms. In the center of the gatehouse was a stone arch where a gate

once stood. Through the arch was a flagstone courtyard and a fountain surrounded by concrete benches. The stone arch divided the gatehouse into two equal parts, and each side had a stone chimney. The second floor spanned the entire width of the gatehouse.

Liv came back a few minutes later holding the key. She led me under the stone arch. On the left side there was a red door with iron hardware. "Uncle Nathan's not here. His van's gone. When he sees Sparky, he'll know I'm here."

We walked into a vaulted, lantern-hung hallway. The floor was slate and covered with a burgundy runner. The corridor ended at a sitting room with a roughhewn wood mantel and a fireplace where embers still glowed. There were two cordovan leather sofas trimmed in brass tacks on either side of the small fireplace. It was almost a mini version of an English country lodge, similar to the old part of Sandringham.

I looked out the window at a forest of trees, hoping for a glimpse of the ocean.

"Hello, ladies."

I turned.

Nathan held a clear plastic bag filled with some kind of seedpods in one hand and a paper bag from the IGA in the other. "I must have ESP. How about some of my special hot chocolate? Meet me in the kitchen in ten minutes. In the meantime, Liv, you can give Ms. Barrett a tour of my humble abode."

"Please call me Meg. I'd love a tour and hot chocolate."

Liv said, "And while we drink our hot chocolate, Uncle Nathan, I can show you my father's journal and a discovery Meg made."

"A discovery. How intriguing." He walked away, almost having to duck under the door frame at the other end of the room.

In the hallway outside the sitting room, we had a choice: left led to the kitchen, and in front of us was a set of steps. We took the steps. At the top of the stairway there was a short hallway and a door on our left. Liv led me inside. It was a naturalist's room. There were vintage charts of plant life and Audubon-style birds on the walls.

"Besides being an environmentalist, Uncle Nathan is a local wildlife expert. He's recently rescued an endangered roseate tern and had it sent to the wildlife foundation in Riverhead for mending. A few years ago he nursed a wounded baby peregrine falcon." Liv pointed to one of the charts on the wall, which showed the various stages of a peregrine falcon from egg to adulthood.

Against the far wall was a tall antique wood cabinet. It had wide drawers with brass drawer pulls. The top drawer was open, filled with a stack of old maps, foxed with age. The room had the same vibe I loved in the document section at Grimes House Antiques. The top of a drafting desk had a map thumbtacked to the wood. I stepped closer. It was a map of Montauk's ocean shoreline. Three little flag pins were stuck on the map. Starting from the west and moving east were Andy Warhol's estate, Sandringham, and what I assumed was Nathan's former ancestral land. The map looked fairly old, maybe early twentieth century. It was on yellowed paper and looked hand tinted. I was hoping to see an *X* where some treasure had been buried.

I checked the leather volumes in the small bookcase by the drafting table and didn't see a copy of the book I'd taken from the bungalow about Montauk. Maybe after I went through it, I'd give it to Nathan for his collection. I felt fulfilled when I found the perfect home for my old stuff.

We left the naturalist room and took the corridor that connected the two sides of the second story. Windows flanked both sides of the overpass, and there were stunning views of the ocean through the line of back windows. The foundation was evident where Nathan's family's mansion once stood. It was an extraordinary piece of property, and I couldn't wait to see it after Byron Hughes transformed it. Was Nathan upset about making the land into a public park? I would have been, letting people on the property, negating all the NO TRESPASSING signs that had kept the riffraff away for decades.

At the end of the overpass was a bedroom and bathroom. There was room enough for a king-sized bed and two nightstands. At the end of the bed was a humpbacked trunk. Maybe Captain Kidd's? In the center of the room was a spiral iron staircase. The back wall had a large multipaned sash window with another incredible view of the Atlantic. Soon, Nathan would have to add some curtains for privacy.

Liv went to the window and I heard her gasp. "Do you believe this scene?" She pointed west.

I went next to her and looked toward Sandringham. Beyond a boxwood hedge maze was a wooden deck with steps leading down to the beach. Celia and Richard stood below, near the shoreline. They were fused in a passionate

kiss. Instead of Richard leading Celia into the beach cabana, it was Celia who took Richard's arm. She yanked him inside like a tiger with a carcass of fresh meat.

Stepping back from the window, I said, "Does your grandfather know about Celia and Richard?"

"I don't think so. I've always suspected them but never saw them in any compromising positions. Richard came to the house the same time Celia did. Before Sandringham, he was a concierge at the yacht club."

"Will you tell your grandfather?"

"At this point, he probably doesn't care. I'll talk to Brandy. She'll tell me when Granddad is in the right frame of mind. She hates Celia, even more than me. Before Celia, Brandy ran all my Granddad's affairs, financially and socially, and she's always been there for me. Just like Uncle Nathan and Mrs. Anderson."

I followed Liv down the spiral staircase, and we entered a room that was a clone of the sitting room, only it looked like it was used as a study. The room had a fireplace, a flat-screen TV, a wing chair and ottoman, and a desk facing the window. "It's so cozy." What was it about me and small spaces?

We entered the gatehouse kitchen, which was slightly larger than my rental's. The room was simple and well organized, with copper pots hanging from the ceiling, and a four-burner gas stove with a small oven, about as old as my "icebox." Two copper saucepots sat on the stove. One was a double boiler. Nathan added chunks of chocolate from a bowl to the pan with one hand and stirred constantly with the other hand. The back burner had simmering milk. He told us to grab a mug and get in line.

That we did.

He emptied the melted chocolate into the milk, then whisked it together. Before pouring it into our cups, he added an unusual ingredient: a pinch of cayenne pepper.

I said, "I bet I know where you learned that trick. Ingrid."

He said, "How'd you know?"

"I just got a lesson on the antioxidant properties of cayenne."

"Did she tell you the word comes from the town Cayenne, in French Guiana, and can actually settle an upset stomach?"

"No. She didn't."

"I add my own special touch to my hot chocolate. Let me know what you think." He scooped out marshmallow fluff from a glass Ball jar and put it on top of each cup, then he smoothed it with the back of a spoon and torched it, like you did to crème brûlée.

We sat at the small round table.

With the first sip, memories of Michigan winters flooded over me: ice-skating on the lake with my mother, school snow days building igloo forts with my father. I took another sip and said, "Wow, this is the best hot chocolate I've ever had."

Liv said, "Ditto, Uncle Nathan."

Nathan gave Liv a warm look. It added to the room's ambiance: the smell of chocolate and the intimate setting. They shared a close bond. Maybe he'd taken the place of her father in her life?

Liv pushed the journal across the table. "Look at the last four pages. Meg thinks they must have something to do with Morrison Manor. What do you think?"

We remained silent while he flipped back and forth between the four pages.

Finally, after five minutes had passed, he said, "The view of the main house from the shore could be of Morrison Manor, but the other three pages look like something from *The Count of Monte Cristo*. I think Pierce was just fooling around with the idea of Morrison Manor, mixing folklore with reality."

Yes. Or stealing ideas for his next children's book.

We returned to Sandringham via horseback. Liv kept Sparky at a snail's pace. I could tell Sparky wanted to let loose and blamed me for holding him back. Every time I patted his mane, he showed his teeth and whinnied. Between Sparky and Jo, I was starting to get a complex.

I went up to see Elle and we chatted about the film festival. I waited for her pain pill to do its magic, then told her I was leaving. She handed me the keys to her pickup, telling me I might as well take advantage of the truck's large capacity. She didn't plan to leave the estate anytime soon, and I could see why, especially when I looked at her lunch tray— Cascade couldn't have gotten the plates any cleaner.

I parked my Jeep next to the garage, a few feet from Elle's pickup. I got out and saw that one of the garage doors was open. Richard was inside, handwashing the limo, and he didn't appear to be enjoying the job.

I stepped in. "Those rooms over the garage look interesting. Is that where you stay?"

"Yes. Crazy, when there are a million open rooms at Sandringham."

"It looks nice enough. My cottage is smaller."

Richard had perfect features and his dark hair set off his blue eyes, but there was something hard about him. I don't think I ever saw him smile, except when he was making fun of Uncle Harry. I gave him the keys to my Jeep and he said he'd hide it behind one of the sheds.

I could have been insulted, but then I looked at the Jeep and thought it was for the best.

TWENTY-ONE

I didn't stop back at my rental because I was already late to meet Doc at Montauk Harbor, but I'd learned my lesson with Jo. Her litter box was clean and accessible in the bathroom closet. I'd left enough dry food to feed a troop of cats and most importantly, I planned to be home at four forty-five so I'd be on time to put a good meal on the table for my ball and chain.

Weather permitting, Doc and I were going on a short cruise of the harbor on his friend's fishing boat. "Short" because I lied and told him I got seasick after long periods on open water. In reality, I had no problem with boats. I just thought fishing seemed the most boring of pastimes.

Another reason I didn't like fishing was the torture factor when it came to fish too small to fry: ripping the hook out of its mouth as it looked at you with those unblinking eyes while doing the death flip-flop, gasping

for water—then throwing it back into the ocean wounded and scarred.

What was the point?

What I really wanted to do was see if I could find any orange buckets with a black *W* written in marker.

I pulled Elle's pickup into the parking lot at the wharf. Doc waited next to the kiosk that sold tickets for charter dinner cruises, fishing excursions, and the ferry that took you in-season to Block Island, Rhode Island. He looked different without his beard.

I got out of the truck and walked toward him. Hope bloomed when I got closer and saw white stubble on his chin. "Am I late?"

"No, I'm early. As usual." He gave me a peck on the cheek and took my duffel bag. "Sully's all set to go, but I don't think there's time to do much fishing. Maybe drop a line or two."

"Darn." *Yes!*

Doc asked why I had Elle's turquoise pickup and I explained about her fall down the stairs.

It was strange to walk the long dock in October. In the summer it was so busy you were in danger of getting tossed into the drink. There were only a few people working today, but each slip held a boat. The largest boats were for commercial fishing, with their raised hydraulic nets and sparse decks. I lagged behind Doc, trying to read the name on each boat. *Windward Shares* looked too pretentious, probably owned by some Wall Streeter without enough dough to moor at the East End Yacht Club. Based on the boat's newness, I doubted I'd find an orange plastic bucket. *Whale Watcher I*, probably one of those in every

port, looked promising, but there weren't any buckets, not even a clamp for a fishing pole.

A man about Doc's age, with noticeably dyed black hair, waved at us from *Fisher Tales*, a small cruiser.

Doc waved back.

When we reached *Fisher Tales*, Sully hoisted me on deck. Doc jumped on board with ease.

Captain Sully took the helm and we were off. Sully was the type of seaman I'd want on my side if I were on the *Titanic* or the *Andrea Gail*, which, thankfully, was impossible. Every move he made was fluid, from untying the ropes to navigating out of the harbor. He exuded poise and confidence in his crew, and he had a fishing pole in my hand before I even realized it. I hadn't even seen what bait was at the end of the line. Not that that was a bad thing.

We'd just left the harbor when there was a tug on my line. A major tug. "Guys. Guys. Help."

With the assistance of three adults and a strong fishing line, we pulled in my fish—a beautiful striped bass. And she was big enough to keep.

I was the only one to catch anything, and I decided to add fishing to my bucket list of knitting, surfing, and horseback riding—as long as it was with Captain Sully.

Thinking about my *bucket* list reminded me of the reason for my trip to the harbor.

When we pulled into port, I'd insisted Sully divide the fish into three portions. Doc took the bag with our cleaned and filleted striped bass and went to his car to put it in the cooler.

I kissed Sully's rough cheek farewell, then walked to the end of the dock, perusing boat names in search of an

elusive orange bucket. I stopped at *Wrestling with the Wind.*
On a messy deck littered with fish scraps, there was an
orange bucket with a black *W.* Bingo! It was just like the
bucket left on my gate filled with fish guts. I snapped a few
pics with my cell phone and scurried to land, my knees
shaking, but not from seasickness.

Doc said, "Are you okay?"

"Yep. Whattya say we go to Mickey's for a late lunch and
celebrate my big catch. I bet Erin will cook them up for us."

"Good idea. Would you even know how to pan braise
a striped bass?"

"No, but I could always get my dad on video chat and
he could lead me through it."

"True. I could get him on my smartphone."

"Marshall Heckler, you do amaze me. Let's go. It's
freezing out here."

Mickey's Chowder Shack was busy no matter what the
season, and it didn't depend on summer tourists to turn
a profit.

The shack was just that. In the summer months, the windows came out. Clear plastic flaps were rolled up in fair
weather or down in rain. There was wood paneling, wood
floors, and open wood rafters from which hung a large
collection of pirate coconut heads. I was proud to say I'd
donated a few from garage sale finds, and I was allowed a
free cup of chowder every time I came in. Takeout included.
After tasting Ingrid's chowder, I felt guilty it was one notch
ahead of Mickey's.

There were shark jaws on the walls and signs like, IN DOG
BEERS I'VE ONLY HAD ONE. A huge swordfish was stuffed
and mounted above the fireplace. Ernest Hemingway would

probably have felt right at home in Mickey's. The bar was full of locals, all in plaid flannel shirts and caps, each with a different hue of beer in their heavy glass mugs.

Doc went over to give the fillets to Erin.

Mickey, Erin's grandfather, had taken ill last summer. Erin stood behind the counter, shouting out orders. She looked like a fish out of water in a sea of men. She was young and tiny with a great body and a stunning face. I knew from our past conversations she wanted to get out of Montauk. I also knew she felt strongly about family responsibility. The same couldn't be said for her sister, Tara Gayle. Erin told me once that Tara never came into Mickey's. She was too good for the place.

We sat at a table at the window. I looked out at the docked boats. Seagulls bobbed and dived for fish parts tossed overboard from a big commercial boat with two tall poles and a net on an hydraulic pulley. Doc was busy chatting with the table of men next to us. Each man telling a fishing yarn more outrageous than the next. I took out my cell phone and looked at the picture of the boat with the orange bucket. On the side of the wheelhouse of *Wrestling with the Wind* was a line of numbers. I'd let Morgana at the police outpost see if she could contact the harbormaster and get me more info on the boat. I felt close to finding the person who left the bucket of fish guts.

When Erin brought our food, I couldn't believe I was about to eat a fish I'd caught. I now had my own yarn to tell. I wished my father was here to witness it. My mother always laughed about the adoring glances her married girlfriends would send my father when they saw him in his red apron whipping up one of his *Top Chef*–worthy dishes.

That's what I needed, a man who could cook. Where did Byron Hughes stand in that department?

Of course, my father would've never let Mickey's cook his fish. He would have done it himself and it would have been delicious, but so was Mickey's simple panfried version: dusted with a little flour and secret spices.

Doc insisted on paying for the check, and I went over to Erin to thank her for cooking the fish. I thought I was hallucinating when I saw a familiar face through the opening to the kitchen.

Tara Gayle was standing at the sink with a pot in her hand. And she wore a hairnet. Could things get any better?

I didn't say a word to Erin about her sister. Even a lying, thieving cheat deserved a little dignity. I almost made it to the door before I burst out laughing.

Doc asked, "What's so funny? People are going to think you had something nasty to eat."

A guy with a red nose beckoned Doc over to the bar. I told him I would meet him at the Buick.

I pushed at the screened door, and a guy in a blue flannel shirt and a neon orange cap slammed into me on his way out.

Neon orange cap! Just like the guy in the van that ran me off the road in Hither Hills.

I ran out the door after him, but he was already in his van backing out of a parking space. I couldn't catch the beginning letters of the license plate because they were covered in mud, but I did find out the state: First in Flight—North Carolina.

I went back inside and tapped Doc on the shoulder.

"Did you see that guy in the bright orange cap?"

"What guy?"

Guess not.

Doc and I left Mickey's with a greasy paper bag of shrimp fritters and a container of spicy paprika and coarse mustard remoulade. All I needed was a salad and I had dinner. He dropped me at Elle's pickup and wanted to follow me home. I insisted I was fine. I needed to stop somewhere. And I didn't want him to know where.

Morgana had her coat on when I walked into the Montauk police post.

"I'm glad I caught you."

"More stalking episodes?"

"No. Thank goodness. But I think I know who's stalking me." I showed her the photo of the boat with the orange bucket. She told me to e-mail it to her. Then I went on to explain about the orange cap guy and the North Carolina license plate.

"Did you get a look at the guy? Old? Young? What did he smell like?"

Smell like? "Young. Maybe early twenties. Ruddy complexion. And all I smelled in Mickey's was fish and beer."

"Okay. I'll get on it in the morning. Momma is about to give birth."

Morgana was in her fifties. Her mother giving birth would be a miracle.

She laughed. "My dog Sweetie Pie. I'll let you have a pick of the litter."

"Thanks, but my plate is pretty full at the moment."

Just what I needed: a chewing puppy that needed to be trained to go with my vindictive, oversized cat.

I arrived home in time to feed Jo on schedule. I even sat down with a glass of wine to join her. She really was a beautiful creature. I got up from the table a few seconds before she finished, grabbed a pen and some index cards, and took possession of her chair. She pretended she didn't mind. She took a seat on the sofa, but I could tell it was a one-time deal.

I went to work listing all the players involved with Pierce Falks's murder. Later, I'd tack them to one of the blank corkboards I used when working on a Cottages by the Sea project.

Pierce Falks–Victim. Disappeared twenty years ago, the same time Helen, Nathan's wife, and the Warhol of Aqua Net hairspray vanished. Would be in his midforties. Sold fake Pollock when he was seventeen. Pen and ink artist. Idolized his mother, Tansy. Made storybooks for his daughter, Liv. Knew Celia and Nathan in high school.

Sonya Falks–Pierce's wife and Liv's mother. Died in a boating accident a few years after Pierce and Helen's disappearance. Was pregnant when she married Pierce. Suicide? Or accident?

Liv Falks–Early twenties. Pierce's daughter and Harrison's granddaughter. Loves old houses. Was three when her father disappeared. Her mother, Sonya, died in a boating accident after Pierce's disappearance. Not old enough to be a suspect in her father's murder, unless she slipped him a cyanide lollipop, but needs to be on the list because she has Pierce's

old journal and hears things. Gets most of Harrison's estate when he dies. Close to Nathan, Brandy, and Ingrid.

Harrison Falks, Uncle Harry–Ninety-one. Pierce's father. Married to third wife, Celia, stepfather to Kate. His second wife, Tansy, now dead, was Pierce's mother. Keeps mentioning a baby. Like him. Good grandfather.

Tansy Falks–Harrison's second wife. Pierce's mother and Liv's grandmother. Died when Pierce was ten. Former model for Aqua Net magazine ads and the muse for the missing Andy Warhol painting of Aqua Net. Harrison divorced her when Pierce was two.

Celia Falks–Midforties. Harrison's third wife. Her daughter, Kate, is from first husband. Chummy with the chauffeur/houseman, Richard. Seems superficial. Expert in modern art. Used to work at MoMA. Oversaw the building of the modern addition at Sandringham. Tried to have Harrison deemed incompetent. Had relationship with Pierce in high school, then years later married Pierce's father. Doesn't get along with Brandy and Ingrid. Or her daughter. Liv doesn't like her.

Kate Jameson–Early twenties. Celia's daughter and Uncle Harry's stepdaughter. Father disowned her and her mother. Into fashion. Calls her mother by her first name. Rough around the edges. Gets along with Liv and Ingrid. Also not old enough to have killed Pierce.

Ingrid Anderson–Midforties. Live-in cook. Distant cousin to Uncle Harry's second wife and Pierce's mother, Tansy. Doesn't like Celia. Fond of Liv and Kate. Great cook. Looks

like my mother, don't let that take away from her being a suspect. Reminds Harrison of second wife, Tansy, the reason he hired her. She gets more in Harrison's current will than Celia.

Richard Challis–Early forties. Hired by Celia. Majordomo/chauffeur. Pals with Celia and makes fun of Harrison. Had argument with Brandy during Pierce's wake. Richard is having affair with Celia.

Brandy–late-thirties. Uncle Harry's personal assistant then took classes to become his nurse. Has been coming to Sandringham since small. Helped get Uncle Harry off drugs so he could pass competency hearing. She gets more in Harrison's current will than Celia. Doesn't like Celia. And had some kind of argument with Richard at Pierce's wake.

Nathan Morrison–Midforties. Neighbor. Helen's husband. Grew up with Pierce. Best friends with Pierce until the Pollock scandal. Lives in gatehouse on next property toward the lighthouse. His family's mansion, Morrison Manor, burned down in the late 1920s. The land, except the gatehouse, was sold to the town of Montauk. Has motive for killing Pierce and possibly his wife, Helen. Close to Harrison, Liv, and Ingrid.

Helen Morrison–Midforties. Nathan's wife, who everyone assumed took off with Pierce and the Warhol. Killed Pierce?

When I was done with my note cards, I rubber banded them together and put them inside the antique coffee crate I'd turned sideways and used as an end table. Jo sneakily slithered over to my vacated chair and went to town,

giving herself a head-to-tail lick down. I didn't want to try to put the towel underneath her for fear she'd claw the leather in retaliation. I'd let sleeping cats lie.

The tube with the plans for Little Grey was still unopened. I took the tube from the end table and sat on the sofa.

Oh, Little Grey, what is to become of you?

I spread Byron's plans on top of my coffee table. The table was actually three vintage suitcases stacked on top of each other. Each suitcase was filled with old issues of my favorite home and garden magazines. Small spaces demanded out-of-the-box storage solutions. I looked at the plans and was thrilled Byron got me. He really got me. I closed my eyes and envisioned my little plot of land. I was there. I could see it. I could smell it. I would bring the plans with me to the folly to go over them in more detail.

After I rolled up the plans and put them back in their tube, I opened Patrick Seaton's book and read about tortured poet number three: John Keats.

I could tell Keats was one of Patrick Seaton's favorites. Keats's story was sad: he was orphaned by fourteen, ripped off by a trustee of his grandmother's estate, and died at twenty-five. These details were eclipsed by the selected verses Patrick had chosen: all upbeat and full of life.

When I finished the chapter on Keats, I put down the book and said "screw it" to bringing a weapon with me, and went down to the beach. There was a huge full moon, and the ocean looked like it had been sprinkled with fairy dust. A *Peter Pan* moon.

Peter Pan was my favorite childhood fairy tale. Of course, in my dreams, I was Wendy. My favorite part of

the Disney cartoon was the scene with the open dormer window, full moon in the background, and Peter flying into the nursery. My obsession with window seats had a lot to do with *Peter Pan*, and it was only reinforced after reading the book.

Who the hell ever wanted to grow up?

Not me.

I was thinking along the same lines as Sir James Barrie, the author of *Peter Pan*, so I found a pointed piece of driftwood, and left a quote by Keats on Patrick Seaton's beach:

My Imagination is a Monastery
And I am its Monk.

CHAPTER

❦

TWENTY-TWO

Even after my beach meditation Sunday morning, I felt slightly blue. I'd called Elle and she sounded good. Still in pain and ordered by the household to stay put. She asked me to check in on Mabel and Elle's Curiosities. I told her I would. Sunday was the best day for hitting the picker's trail. There were a plethora of garage and estate sales but no Elle to share them with. Even the lure of having Elle's pickup couldn't get me motivated. So instead, I headed to Sag Harbor.

Mabel and Elle's Curiosities hadn't yet opened, and I took advantage and backed the pickup to the carriage house doors. I went inside, put Billie Holiday on the Edison gramophone, and looked at what needed to go into Rebecca Crandle's cottage. Without Elle's help, I had to stick to smaller pieces of furniture. We made a good team. I had never realized how big a part of my life Elle had

filled since I moved to Montauk. We were friends when we worked at *American Home and Garden*, but between spending time with Michael and the magazine's twenty-four seven demands, we never had much time to hang out. It was funny how important girlfriends were when you were single and how easily they could fall by the wayside when you were in a relationship. I promised myself I wouldn't let that happen again.

The pickup was packed and I was happy with my pickings. Before leaving for Rebecca Crandle's, I went inside Elle's shop.

"Hello, Ms. Barrett. To what, on this glorious morning, do I owe the pleasure of your company?" Maurice, Elle's star salesclerk, asked. "Is there a wounded mother bird that's afraid her nest will fall apart without you to supervise?"

"Ha. You know better than I. She trusts you completely. Or is it 'you know better than me,' Professor?"

"Actually, both are correct, although I'd go with 'I.' 'You know better than I know' sounds smoother than 'you know better than me know,' when you add the second 'know.'"

Maurice reminded me of Rex Harrison from the movie *My Fair Lady*. He was tall and thin, somewhere in his late forties. He had an English accent and perfect Professor Higgins diction: The rain in Spain . . . which I had him repeat—ad nauseam. I would respond in guttural cockney groans like Audrey Hepburn in the beginning of the movie. Maurice would make one little change to my appearance: cut a lock of hair or wrap a scarf just the right way and I'd be transformed—Eliza Doolittle–style.

He was also an Edith Head groupie and had worked at

the shop when Elle's great-aunt Mabel was at the helm. Great-Aunt Mabel spent her early life as the assistant to the famous Hollywood fashion designer. Maurice's favorite quote of Edith's was, "The cardinal sin is not being badly dressed but wearing the right thing in the wrong place." *Don't you know it.* I thought of Pierce's wake and my red dress and six-inch red-soled heels.

Today, Maurice just took a tissue and wiped the lipstick off my teeth.

Why hadn't I used him as my stylist for the Barkers' party? It was probably his idea for Elle to loan me the cashmere cape and Birkin.

We had no time for chitchat because the shop was filling up fast. I went into the White Room and took out a few choice items to bring to Rebecca Crandle's cottage. I snipped off the price tags and taped them to a ledger Elle kept behind the counter so she'd know what I'd taken.

I helped a customer decide which vintage jewelry piece to buy. Not my expertise, but I thought the emerald green rhinestone and aurora borealis clasp bracelet, signed Schiaparelli, would look awesome with her red hair. Sold. For four hundred dollars.

Oh, what I could buy at an estate sale for the same amount. Elle owned an Elsa Schiaparelli skirt from the '30s which she never wore because it was priceless. The lobster print on the skirt was designed by Schiaparelli's friend, surrealist artist Salvador Dalí.

I said, "Cheerio," to Maurice and left for Hither Hills.

The down-in-the-dumps feeling wouldn't leave my gut. I pulled the truck over in East Hampton, across the street from Grimes House Antiques. I felt an urge to peruse the

antique paper section. I wanted to see the old landscape
plans for Sandringham and Morrison Manor that Byron
had been looking at the last time I was here.

Thank God, there was no Tara when I walked into the
shop. Maybe she'd been fired and that was why I saw her
in the kitchen at Mickey's, wearing her designer hairnet.
Instead, Rita sat behind the counter cleaning silver with a
polish-coated, nubby hand mitt. She nodded in my direction, which was more than she'd ever done in the past.
Seeing me with Byron on my last visit must have raised
me up a peg or two. Okay, one. Maybe.

I looked through a bin with rolled ephemera and finally
found the blueprints. I saw why he didn't buy them. Eight
hundred dollars each.

A couple walked into the shop, and they must have
been good customers because Rita took off her polishing
mitt and went to the front of the store with a rare smile.

I made sure Rita's back was to me and unrolled the first
blueprint of Morrison Manor on the low table meant for
this exact purpose—well, not my purpose, but a potential
buyer's purpose. I grabbed four books from the case next
to me and used them to hold down each corner of the plans.
I hunched over the blueprint and twisted my body, blocking
Rita's view. I shot off a dozen pictures with my cell phone,
then removed the books and put the blueprint back in the
bin. Then I did the same with the Sandringham blueprint.

When I was getting ready to leave, guilt crept in, causing me to purchase an antique brass inkwell with its original glass ink reservoir and quill-tip pen for sixty-five
dollars. I doubted the quill pen was an antique, but it would
be perfect on Rebecca Crandle's desk. I didn't feel too bad

about taking pictures of the blueprints because when Rita rang up the sale, she acted like she was doing me a favor. She probably wondered how I found the least expensive item in her shop.

As I stepped out of the shop, I body-slammed into Byron Hughes.

He laughed.

I was mortified.

The bag with the inkwell slipped from my hand. He caught it midair.

"Fancy meeting you here." He handed me back the bag.

My body shook from our impact—and not in a bad way. "Yes. I found something to put in a client's cottage." I held up the bag.

"I came back for the Morrison Manor plans. The committee agreed to take money from the fund to pay for them. I had to promise to cut corners some other way."

Beads of perspiration bloomed on my upper lip.

"Why don't you put your bag in your car. I'll make my purchase and we can grab lunch."

"Uh. Sure." I was so articulate.

A few minutes later, Byron led me down a back alley. In East Hampton, back alleys were still something to be afraid of. Not because they were dark and seamy but because they held tiny exquisite shops and restaurants with exquisite prices. Get trapped in one, and you were lucky to come out with only one new coat on your back and an empty wallet in your handbag.

Chez Claudette had enough room for only six tables. One had a reserved placard and as soon as we walked in,

it was removed by an older man in jeans, a button-down oxford, and a suit coat.

He said, "Mr. Hughes, what a nice surprise."

We sat and he presented us each with a handwritten menu. We had four choices.

Byron didn't even look at the menu. "We'll both have the fresh fish plate."

Oh no. Was the honeymoon over? I hated it when men ordered for women. What if I had a fish allergy? Or just plain didn't like fish? He hadn't even looked in my direction.

The waiter went to grab my menu. I put my hand on his. "Scratch the fish plate. I'll have the beet salad with goat cheese."

I didn't feel I'd won because Byron immediately said, "Bring us each a beet salad and the fish."

I was going to press it further, but my cell phone rang. It was Elle's melody, the *Perry Mason* theme, so I answered.

"Meg. You have to come quick to Sandringham. Something horrible has happened!"

"Elle, are you okay?"

"I'm fine, but Kate and Liv aren't. They're both missing. And they didn't sleep in their beds last night."

I explained to Byron and he insisted on following me to Sandringham, but I told him I'd call after I found out more.

Detective Shoner's Lexus blocked the entrance to the estate, so I had to leave Elle's pickup on the lane outside the gate.

I looked ahead. Celia stood on the front portico dressed in a silky robe, her arms clasped around her chest, talking to Detective Shoner with tear-filled eyes.

When I reached Detective Shoner, I touched his sleeve. "Can I come in? I want to see Elle. She called me."

He turned to Celia. "Mrs. Falks, come inside and tell me all the places you've searched."

I followed Celia and Detective Shoner into the foyer. We trooped up the central staircase to the second floor. When we reached Uncle Harry's suite, Elle was sitting outside on a chair.

Before I could get to her, Detective Shoner put his fingers under her chin. "You okay?"

She looked at him. "Yes. Thanks for coming."

Detective Shoner went inside Uncle Harry's room with Celia.

When Brandy came out of Uncle Harry's room, her face was as pink as her sweater. "Celia's always ordering me out. Either I'm Harrison's caretaker or I'm not. And I don't want *her* anywhere near him." She stomped down the winding staircase.

I said to Elle, "Isn't she a little hot under the collar?"

I retrieved the pair of crutches from the guest room that the doctor had left for Elle, and brought them to her. I helped her to a standing position, then we both went to her room. I closed the door. "So, what happened?"

"Ingrid came to bring me breakfast and asked if I'd seen Liv and Kate. Which I hadn't. She went to check and neither one of them had slept in their beds."

"Couldn't they have fallen asleep watching a late-night movie in one of the dozens of rooms at Sandringham?"

"Richard searched the entire place. Their cars are here. And their handbags."

"How about the grounds? Maybe they went horseback riding or over to the gatehouse?"

"Checked. And checked."

I helped Elle back into bed and adjusted her pillows, including the one for her ankle. Elle asked if I'd go to Sag Harbor in the morning to pick up Maurice so he could bring her home. She had a bad feeling about staying at Sandringham—ever the dyslexic fortune-teller.

There wasn't much I could do at the estate about the

missing girls, but I had to do something. I got directions from Elle to Liv's and Kate's rooms. I opened the guest room door and peered down the corridor in the direction of Uncle Harry's room. The coast was clear.

I went to Kate's room first. It was exactly as I pictured. Both rooms to the suite were painted bloodred. The walls showcased modern art posters, all with a fashion theme. Correction, as I looked closer, I noticed they were signed and numbered lithographs. It was apparent the outer room was used as a sewing room. Fabric covered every inch of the floor. The light to the sewing machine was on. A gray piece of material was clamped under the machine's silver foot, a needle poised above, as if waiting for Kate to return any second.

In the bedroom, Kate's bed was made, but that was as far as it went. It looked like the Long Island Express, the hurricane from 1938, had dropped by for a visit. I peeked inside the bathroom and pulled open the heavy rippled glass shower door, praying I wouldn't find a *Psycho*-induced crime scene. I didn't. Outside the shower sat a pair of sandy work boots. The boots were still wet with a chalky demarcation where the saltwater line on the leather ended.

My head and shoulders were under Kate's bed, my nose next to what I hoped weren't a pair of her thongs, when Detective Shoner said, "Anything interesting, Ms. Barrett?"

I had found a small pink jewelry box under a stack of magazines. I stuck it under my armpit before I backed out. I stood. "Um. Nope. But it's hard to tell in this mess."

"Did you think you might find Kate hiding under her bed?"

I palmed the box and stuck it in my back pocket, making

a good show of brushing lint and dust bunnies from my shirt. "Not really. Leave no stone unturned, my father always says. Any news?"

"No. And we can't do anything officially until they've been missing for twenty-four hours."

"Well, it was nice of you to come when Elle called."

His cheeks flushed. "By the way, Ms. Barrett, what room is Elle staying in?"

"Second door on the left toward Uncle Harry's, I mean Mr. Falks's, room."

Instead of following him to Elle's guest room, I turned left in the direction of Liv's suite.

Liv's suite was warm and welcoming. The sitting room had a large oak library desk flanked with bookcases. There was a feminine club chair with an ottoman, an antique floor lamp, and an empire side table. Both the sitting room and bedroom had fireplaces. The bedroom fireplace was huge with a marble mantel. By the room's grandeur, I had a feeling the suite had been Liv's father's. There was a masculine/feminine aura to it.

On my way out, I spied Liv's inhaler on the desk in the sitting room.

Liv had told me Celia had taken two second-floor suites and renovated them into her own apartment-like space. I figured, while I was snooping, I might as well check out Celia's suite down the opposite hallway from Liv's, Uncle Harry's, and Kate's. When I got to the double doors, I pulled down on the gold door handles. *Locked.* There was even a keypad on the wall for security. None of the other rooms in the mansion had alarm keypads. Now I was really dying to get inside.

I went to Elle's guest room to say good-bye, but she was asleep. I didn't think she was dreaming cotton-candy dreams because there were worry lines on her forehead.

Brandy walked out of Uncle Harry's room with a tray of dirty dishes. I waited until she took the staircase down to the first floor. When I saw the coast was clear, I crept down the hall and stopped in front of the open door to her suite.

I stepped into Brandy's suite. It had traditional antique furniture, but anything with fabric, including the curtains, was in a pale pink. No flowery prints, just pink. I peeked in her bedroom and saw a crocheted afghan made out of pink granny squares draped on a rocking chair by the window. The bedroom window faced a western view of the ocean and the bungalow in which we'd found Pierce's skeleton. It seemed so eerie that he had been so close to his loved ones all these years.

In the sitting room, an armoire held a key in the lock. Too tempting to resist. I turned the key and opened it. Inside were Brandy's folded sweaters. At the bottom of the cabinet was a small white suitcase. A locked suitcase. It looked like one of Elle's "train" cases, only flatter. I thought I heard someone coming down the hallway. I quickly closed the cabinet door, turned the key, and exited. I decided I might as well explore the third floor. Maybe I'd find a hidden alcove or revolving bookcase that might lead to Liv and Kate?

Just for fun, I took Uncle Harry's secret elevator up to the third floor. The hallway was carpeted in the same shade of burgundy as the second floor. Before the modern addition, the main house followed a simple rectangular floor plan. Each level had the winding *Gone with the Wind*

staircase in the center. There were rooms interspersed between the two long hallways on the east and west. On the shorter northern hallways on the second and third levels were two cozy turret rooms. Celia's modern gallery covered the southern walls on the first and second levels. If you slid the panels on the first and second floors, you got oceanfront views through the gallery's windows.

If Uncle Harry divorced Celia, would he keep the modern addition or bulldoze it? And if they did divorce, what would happen to Kate without Ingrid?

Most of the rooms on the third floor were locked or looked unused. I'd already been to the Pierce gallery, hoping when I walked in I'd find Liv and Kate playing a game of Monopoly, but the huge room was empty—with Pierce's sketches cold looking and unwelcoming.

A door was unlocked and I knew it was Ingrid's for two reasons, it was tastefully decorated and there were pages stacked on her desk next to a printer: the manuscript to her cookbook. I looked at the top page—Short Ribs Braised in Cabernet and Cognac. I really would love to see Ingrid and my father in a cook-off. In the past, I'd wager my every last cent on my father, but since meeting Ingrid, I wasn't so sure.

The third-floor rooms didn't have sitting rooms, but Ingrid's room was huge. I had a feeling it had once been a schoolroom. The colors chosen were sea colors: pale teals, aquamarine, frosty blues, and sand white. And for a pop of color, the occasional coral red.

On the eastern side of the room was a line of floor-to-ceiling windows, showcasing a priceless panorama of the Atlantic Ocean, towering cliffs, and the Montauk Point

Lighthouse. Instead of a window seat, Ingrid had placed a latte-colored cushioned chaise next to the row of windows. There was a luxurious seafoam green throw draped across the back of the chaise and a book splayed open.

Feeling like a voyeur, something I hadn't felt in Kate's and Liv's rooms, I checked out the title. It was Julia Child's *My Life in France*. My father's fave.

Everything in the room seemed just as I thought. Or maybe not?

Peeking out from under Ingrid's bed was a photo album. I picked it up and opened it. On the first page of the album there was an eight-by-ten photo of a classroom in an artist's studio space. Students were behind their easels and in front of them, sitting on a stool on top of a dais, was a young Ingrid—a scantily clad Ingrid, wearing a toga.

When I looked at the faces of the students, I saw two familiar ones—no, make that three: Celia, Richard, and Georgia from The Old Man and the Sea Books. I didn't have any idea that Richard had been around before Pierce's disappearance. Richard had lied to the police. I took out my cell phone and took a picture of the photo, closed the book, and exited the room.

I patted myself on the back when I found the entry to the secret staircase on the third floor. I'd known where it was located, but I didn't know how to open it until I tipped the small Aristotle head bust forward on its hinge and the alcove swung forward. I took the stairs and paused at the second floor. I considered checking in on Uncle Harry, but I didn't have anything new to add to Liv and Kate's whereabouts and didn't want to upset him. I went down to the

first floor. At the bottom of the stairwell, I pulled the brass knob.

Nathan and Ingrid stood in the middle of the kitchen in a hot embrace.

I quickly closed the panel, then made as much noise as possible before I reopened it. Ingrid held a teacup in her hand and Nathan looked like he was fixing a leg to the farm table.

Awkward. Maybe I didn't know Ingrid as well as I thought I did. I had to keep reminding myself just because she looked like my mother, didn't mean she had a pure heart like my mother. I waved good-bye and exited out the front door in case I had a fit of nervous giggles. I hoped Ingrid knew what she was doing. Helen was number one on my list as Pierce's killer. If Helen hadn't killed Pierce, then Nathan would be my next guess. Celia was in third place. Maybe she still had a high school crush on Pierce and caught him with Helen? Sonya Falks, Pierce's wife, would be my fourth guess. She had the same motive as Celia. Brandy and Richard were tied. Leaving Ingrid and Uncle Harry as the least likely. As I knew from past experience, it could be anyone.

Instead of leaving the estate, I wanted to take a walk on the rocky beach beneath the cliffs of Sandringham and head in the direction of Nathan's former ancestral land. Something urged me on to check out the view of Nathan's family's estate from the shore. I knew Liv was obsessed with her father's journal and the drawing of the house on the cliff. Maybe Liv wanted to check it out for herself, and Liv and Kate went to investigate and got trapped by the tide.

I walked toward the Sandringham garage. The grounds were quiet. With all the recent news and our discovery of Pierce's skeleton and the mention of Sandringham and Harrison Falks's wealth, I prayed someone hadn't kidnapped the girls. Richard had hidden my Jeep behind a huge pine tree on the south side of the garage. The door was unlocked. The key was in the ignition. I got inside the Jeep and took off my good boots and put on the hiking boots I used for seal walks at Montauk Point State Park. They were similar to the pair I'd seen next to Kate's shower. I removed my hearing aids and laid them on the console, just in case a big wave hit me and they got water damaged. I took the car key with me and locked the door.

To my left was a side door to the garage. I checked if it was open.

It was.

The garage was long and narrow. Liv had told me before Celia came into the picture, the garage had been a horse stable. Celia sure had her fingers in a lot of renovations. "Out with the old, in with the new." I hoped Uncle Harry and Justin Marguilles planned for out with the new, when it came to her. Although, I did feel sorry for Celia. She really looked distraught about her missing daughter when I'd seen her earlier on the front portico.

There were a total of twelve cars in the garage, all in varying makes and models, along with the white panel truck Uncle Harry used to transport his art.

Closest to me was a vintage Aqua Shelby GT350 convertible with a white leather interior. My uncle Jim, a car nut, had one just like it, only in a different color, Highland

Green. The Shelby had to be worth about a hundred grand.

I walked next to the car and opened the driver's door and got in. I fantasized I was cruising down Old Montauk Highway on a stellar summer day, wearing a pair of Elle's vintage movie star sunglasses and a head scarf, its ends trailing in the wind. I couldn't help myself and opened the glove compartment. Inside was a vintage can of Aqua Net hairspray, a small hairbrush, and a gold tube of lipstick. The lipstick color was Max Factor's blue red—the perfect shade for a Scandinavian blonde. This must have been Tansy's car.

Stepping out of the Shelby, I looked down the line at the other vehicles. My uncle Jim would have a field day in this garage.

I wasn't wearing my hearing aids, so I didn't notice Richard until he was next to me. Maybe I could make a million bucks on one of those inventor television shows by creating a cell phone app for the hearing impaired: a vibrating alert system for when something warm-blooded was three feet behind you.

Richard said, "It was Tansy's, Harrison's second wife. A 1969 Shelby 302 V8 four-speed, with tilt-away steering, a power top with a glass backlight, front and rear bumper guards. The white leather interior was custom made for her."

I'd never seen this side of Richard. He beamed.

"My uncle has a Shelby."

"I didn't lock your Jeep, if that's what you came for. And the keys are in the ignition."

"Guess you weren't worried about someone stealing it."

He gave me a look like, *duh* . . . He said, "Did you just come from the house? Have the girls returned? I've spent all morning looking for them. They probably just went to a party, drank too much, and spent the night. It wouldn't be the first time. At least for Kate. She might have talked Liv into joining her."

"If I were you, I'd talk to Celia and tell her to call Kate's friends."

I remembered how cozy Kate and he looked at the Barkers' party.

"Good idea." He left out the front door of the garage. I, however, didn't leave. I was curious about Richard's living quarters. Part nosy snoop, part curious interior decorator.

The layout over the garage was fabulous, but Richard's midcentury decorating taste didn't fit the traditional mahogany paneled walls and wide plank floors. I had a feeling they were original to the stable and someone had put their foot down about changing them. All of Richard's tchotchkes were from the same era as the bungalow. He might have pilfered them from the other bungalows before their contents were tossed in the trash.

On the long wall, across from the windows that looked out at the main house, were two huge oil paintings. The first one had swirls of reds and purples and a pair of five-foot-tall creepy eyes peering out from the background. The other canvas showed crazy corkscrews of purple, red, and black. Instead of eyes, there was a gallows-type tree hiding behind the violent splashes of color. I looked closely

in the corners of the paintings to see if I recognized the artist. You never knew in this house. They were signed F. C., and I couldn't think of a famous modern artist with those initials. Maybe one of Celia's rejects? I took a photo of each with my cell phone and sent them to Georgia. Maybe the Warhol of Aqua Net was hidden underneath? They were big enough.

An open laptop was on top of a white '70s-style plastic desk. I tapped the screen. A photo flashed across the screensaver. It was an open page from Pierce's sketch journal. I wanted to explore further, rifle through a few nightstands, and check out his underwear drawer, but as I glanced out the window, Richard was walking toward the garage. He held a cell phone to his ear. Thankfully he moved at a turtle's pace, giving me just enough time to skedaddle out the side door.

I hurried to a set of steps leading down to the ocean on the eastern side of the property. On the western side of the estate, where the bungalows stood, steps weren't needed because of the gently sloping sand dunes that led to the shore.

I walked down the first section of steps and had to stop for a breather on the platform that led to the second set. And here I thought the twenty-seven steps to the beach at my rental were exhausting.

When I reached the bottom, the sand was littered with huge boulders and rocks. Now I could see why Kate's boots were wet if she'd been walking the shoreline. It would be impossible to continue east toward the lighthouse barefoot or in sneakers.

The waves were coming in at a furious rate. The sun had

given way to clouds, and the ocean was the color of wet cigarette ashes. I climbed over a few boulders, but mostly large stones, some pearly white, others inky black. After ten minutes of hiking, I realized I was an idiot. How was I supposed to see what the view of the cliffs at the bottom of the old Morrison property looked like from down here? I needed to be on a boat to get a good picture.

I passed another set of steps and calculated that I was at Morrison Manor—or the cliff on which Morrison Manor had once stood. I squeezed through two huge boulders, the space barely large enough for me to fit through. What I found on the other side was astounding.

A sandy, rock-free beach. Someone had taken the time to haul rocks and boulders to the east side of the beach, creating a ten-foot wall. I stood on the sand and looked up.

Sure enough, I remembered from the drawing that at the bottom of the cliff, under the mansion, was a small beach and a wall made of rocks. Leaning against the cliff wall was a pile of logs reaching up about five feet and in the middle of the beach, a fire pit. It didn't look like there'd been any recent bonfires. The pit was filled with crab carcasses and seaweed, even a soda can, or "pop" can as we said in Michigan, which I retrieved and put in my pocket to add to my recycling pile. People could be such asses when it came to leaving nature, as the word implies, natural. Was that why Warhol used everyday man-made items in his art—to him they were part of nature—human nature?

The tide was coming in. I saw no sign that Liv and Kate had been here. I decided to revisit after I checked a tide chart.

I emerged back through the two boulders and saw Nathan and Ingrid headed in my direction.

They stopped and waited until I reached them.

Ingrid said, "I see you had the same idea as us. Find anything?"

"No. Sorry."

"Well, it was a long shot," Nathan said.

We all headed back together, taking the long way to the dune side of the mansion, instead of the steps. The bungalow where we'd found Pierce's skeleton was still in its same position on the beach. I was surprised it survived the nor'easter.

Ingrid said, "I'm praying we'll walk into the kitchen and the two of them will be sitting at the table, safe and sound."

CHAPTER

❦

TWENTY-FOUR

Kate, Liv, Celia, and Detective Shoner sat at the farm table. Liv had her inhaler in her hand and her father's sketch journal in front of her. Liv and Kate looked like they'd been through hell.

Talk about wishes coming true.

Ingrid ran to the girls and took them both in an embrace. "What happened? We've been looking all over for you."

For once Kate seemed at a loss for words.

Before anyone could answer, Detective Shoner's cell phone rang. He said into his phone, "Be right there." He put his phone back into his pocket then stood. "I have to leave but I'm very happy things turned out all right."

Celia didn't say, "Thanks, Detective," so Ingrid said it for her.

I went to Detective Shoner. "Do Elle and Uncle Harry know the girls are okay?"

"Yes. Please tell Elle I had to go."

I winked. "Will do."

I stood at the counter and took in the happy scene.

Nathan pulled up a chair next to Liv and took her hand.

Liv said, "It's all my fault we got locked in the wine cellar. There was a drawing of a cellar in my father's journal, and I thought I'd discover something special he wanted me to see. Then we opened a bottle of wine and fell asleep. When Kate woke up, she realized we'd left the key on the outside of the door and we were locked in. Neither one of us had our cell phones. She finally used the corkscrew to push out the key from the other side and trip the lock."

By the look on Liv's face, I knew Kate had a fan for life.

Kate stood. "Liv is painting a brighter picture of me than she should. It was my idea to drink the wine."

Celia said to Kate, "You scared me half to death. Come. Let's get you to bed. Dr. Jonas is coming."

"Celia, I don't need a doctor. Just a nap."

Richard entered the kitchen and stopped next to Celia. "I'm glad you girls are okay."

Before leaving, Celia said to Liv, "You were being totally irresponsible for leading Kate into danger. All because of a few of Pierce's sophomoric scribbles."

Liv looked like she'd been slapped in the face.

Kate gave her mother a scorching look.

Celia took Kate's wrist and they left the kitchen. Richard followed close behind.

I felt bad for Liv. She didn't have a mother or father to take care of her. Only her grandfather. But when I looked at Nathan and Ingrid, I realized she'd be okay.

After I went up to check on Elle, I retrieved my boots and hearing aids from the Jeep. Elle's pickup was still loaded with things to go in Rebecca Crandle's cottage. I got inside and headed for Hither Hills—only a five-minute drive from Sandringham.

When I pulled into the Hither Hills neighborhood, I checked the rearview mirror to make sure I wasn't being followed, then realized my stalker hopefully thought I only drove a Jeep, not a turquoise pickup truck.

This time, I parked next to Rebecca Crandle's kitchen door. I got out and grabbed a box from the back of the pickup. I remembered which stone held the cottage's key. Duke and Duke Junior were the only other people who knew about the key besides Rebecca, and she was on a book tour promoting her mother's and her latest mystery. The mother/daughter writing team took turns traveling so the other could write.

There was a note taped to the door. I grabbed it and went inside.

Duke and Duke Junior had done their magic. The walls were down, molding added and painted. The area under the stairs had an open storage area on one side and a wine rack on the other and looked better than I had imagined.

I went to work unloading the pickup. Each item had a Post-it taped to it, telling me where it belonged. Later, when everything was in place, I'd arrange items based on the plans I'd drawn to scale on a new user-friendly computer program I'd purchased.

As soon as I finished unloading, I went to the kitchen and grabbed my handbag. The note that had been taped

to the door was on the counter. It was from Sylvie Crandle. She wanted me to stop by her cottage.

This time when I climbed the steps to Sylvie's porch, there was no dog to greet me.

Sylvie ushered me in. I smelled baked goods, but was disappointed when I saw a lit maple syrup candle on the living room coffee table. I'd skipped lunch: fish and beet salad to be exact.

Sylvie looked less put together than the last time I saw her. She sat on the sofa and I sat next to her.

She said, "I know it's Sunday and you designers only work Monday through Thursday."

Say what? "I've been known to work seven days a week and all hours."

Her face remained calm, but she clenched her fist. "Ms. Gayle told me that's the way it works in the Hamptons."

It dawned on me that perhaps Tara had another gig at Mickey's Chowder Shack on the weekends. "I don't think that's a Hamptons rule. Maybe Tara's personal rule?"

"I thought you two were friends. She said you coordinate your designs and help each other out."

"No. I've never worked with Tara Gayle."

Sylvie looked flustered. "Well, that's what I wanted to talk to you about. I've been to Becca's cottage and I see things are coming around. So far there hasn't been one visit from Ms. Gayle, and I was hoping you could fill me in on where she was. I need to know when this cottage is going to be worked on so I can set up my writing schedule between

here and the city. I prefer to write here. Plus, I need to know if I can bring Trixie when I come to Montauk, or if she'll be in the way of the design team."

Team? That explained why the dog hadn't greeted me.

I looked out the front bay window, where I hoped Tara planned to put a window seat, and saw the ocean view. A great muse if there ever was one. "I'm sorry, but I'm not in contact with Tara."

"If I show you the pictures of what Ms. Gayle plans to do, do you think you could give me an estimate on how long it will take?"

She passed me a cheap-looking scrapbook. One you'd buy on sale at a craft store. I opened to the first page and recognized the photo right away. It was of Elle's White Room at her shop in Sag Harbor. And so was the next page, and so was the next. There were also photos of rooms from last year's Hamptons Showcase house that Tara claimed to be her own. Tara had nothing to do with the showcase because I'd perused every room for inspiration and talked to every designer. Tara would've gotten along well with Pierce—not an original thought between the two of them.

"Wow. I don't know what to say. Did Tara tell you she was going to do any construction or painting? Or just place similar items like in the pictures?"

"She only came by once after I hired her when she dropped this off." Sylvie pointed to the scrapbook. "She said she couldn't duplicate everything exactly because her former clients would be upset, but promised not to stray from the gist of what I'd told her I wanted."

Gist?

She unclenched her fist and bit at her lower lip. "I had to

give her fifty percent of her proposed fee so she could purchase items similar to those in the photos. Ms. Gayle finally
returned one of my calls last Thursday. She said she'd have
to up her fee. A container of antiques she'd ordered from
England had taken on water damage when it arrived at a
New York City pier during the nor'easter."

Oh, it just kept getting better. "Well, I can't advise you
on that, but I'm sure if she had antiques sent from Europe,
they should be insured." Cargo ship. Right. Just like me,
Tara only went to garage and estate sales. "And I wouldn't
give her any more money until you see some work being
done." I handed her my Cottages by the Sea business card.
"I wish I could help, but if you decide not to go forward
with Ms. Gayle, give me a call."

"Becca says you talk to her and text often."

"Yes. It's important for a good relationship."

I chuckled to myself on the way out when I thought of
the items I'd taken from Elle's White Room that were going
into Sylvie's daughter Rebecca's cottage; some of the same
pieces were in Tara's faux portfolio. How would Tara
explain that one?

After I left Sylvie's, I decided I needed comfort. The
only place I could think of was The Old Man and the Sea
Books.

When I walked in, Georgia was in one of the wing
chairs, her feet up on an ottoman. Mr. Whiskers was curled
up in the other chair, snoring. He was about one-third the
size of Jo. It was chilly enough for a fire, and one was
crackling in the hearth.

Georgia took off her reading glasses and placed them
on the table. She'd been reading Patrick Seaton's book,

Tales from a Dead Shore—A Biography of Tortured Poets, only she was much further along than I was.

"Have a seat. You look awful."

"Thanks a lot."

"Sit." She picked up Mr. Whiskers and placed him inside the cat bed behind the counter. Then she poured me a cup of tea.

The tea reminded me of Ingrid's homegrown tea leaves, which reminded me of Sandringham. There were so many things going on around me. A murder that happened twenty years ago and the stalker who caused me to look over my shoulder at every turn, not to mention the forgone conclusion that Little Grey would never be my Little Grey. It would belong to Sgt. Gordon Miles.

Georgia's strong hand rested on my shoulder. "Drink. You don't have to tell me a thing."

After I drank half the cup, she said, "Okay. Close your eyes and picture the following. The Kittinger cottage after you completed it last spring and how good it made you feel. Next. One of your father's meals. And finally, a walk on an empty beach during an Indian summer. The sand between your toes as you breathe in the scent of the ocean."

I opened my eyes. "How'd you do that?"

"You attract what you think about. So, when you find yourself going down a dark path, distract yourself with something that feels good. It doesn't make your problems disappear, it just clears your head of what-ifs and worry. And replaces stress with light and calmness. Distract from your demons. Distract. Distract."

She sat in the other armchair, and we talked about the latest things going on at Sandringham and the extraordi-

nary time I had at the Barkers' film festival party. Georgia confirmed she knew Patrick Seaton's book publicist, Ashley Drake, had been invited to the Barkers', so it could've been her and Patrick at the party.

She said, "Hey. What's up with the photo you sent me of those awful paintings?"

"I wanted to know if you recognized the artist."

"Not from my phone, but I'll transfer it to the computer screen and see what I can figure out."

"I also wanted to ask if you knew anything about Brandy, Harrison's assistant and nurse?"

"Brandy Port? Easy name to remember, both after-dinner drinks. Don't know much about her except she has worked for Harrison Falks and lived at Sandringham for years."

"I think she truly cares for Harrison."

"She had a wackadoodle mother. I know that."

"Ingrid told me."

"How is Ingrid? Tell her I said hi. We used to volunteer together on the seal walks at the lighthouse. Before she took the job at Sandringham."

Talking about Ingrid reminded me of the photo of her as a toga-draped artist's model. "I have something to show you." I took out my cell phone, found the photo, and passed it over.

Georgia reached for her reading glasses and put them on. "Oh my. I'd forgotten about this. Actually, this is how I first met Ingrid. She worked in a gallery in Bridgehampton, then modeled to make some extra cash to pay for culinary school."

"That's nice, but look who else is there."

"Celia. That's not a surprise."

"For me, the surprise was Richard and Ingrid. I didn't know they knew each other. And I didn't know Richard had been in the picture back then." I recalled his midwestern accent.

"Who's Richard?"

"He's Celia's chauffeur and houseboy at Sandringham."

"Hmmm, the plot coagulates."

"It sure does. What about Pierce's wife and Liv's mother? Wasn't she a local Montaukian?"

"Sonya Falks. I was friends with Sonya's mother in high school. Sonya was a sweet girl. Too sweet for the likes of Pierce Falks. She was beautiful, like her mother, but she was small-town and Pierce was a spoiled rich boy. Harrison forced Pierce to marry Sonya when he found out she was pregnant."

"Did you know Uncle Harry's second wife, Tansy?"

Mr. Whiskers came over to Georgia and jumped on her lap. "Did anyone know Tansy is a better question. Not much intellect, but she sure knew how to have fun. She was from Springs. Didn't care about money. Just wanted to be where the action was. I never had two words with her, and she was always surrounded by men. Gay and straight alike. Harrison didn't know what to do with her, so he gave her anything she wanted, including her freedom from monogamy."

I picked up *Tales from a Dead Shore* to see which poet Georgia was up to. Coleridge.

"Don't ask," Georgia said. "I know Patrick Seaton lived

through his own tragedy, but this book can be a little much. I bet he never guessed it would hit the bestseller list."

"Maybe he'll write a sequel: *Tales from a Vibrant Shore*, about poets who led happy lives. If they existed? It seems most prolific artists, especially the Romantics, had their crosses to bear."

After I left The Old Man and the Sea Books, I grabbed a pint of chili from Bobby's Drive-in, Montauk's only fast-food burger joint. When I got home, I would add fresh cilantro, sour cream, extra hot sauce, and shredded locally made cheddar cheese. I thought about visiting Little Grey but didn't think I could take any more drama. Tomorrow I'd be back in my Jeep, a bull's-eye for my stalker's arrow.

My neighbor was in Florida, so I parked in her driveway just in case my stalker came cruising by. When I walked into the rental, Jo was waiting on the banquette.

"Sorry, ma'am, it's too early for dinner."

She acted like she understood and took the prone position and closed her eye. I felt guilty about eating in front of her, even though I was starving, so I left the chili on the counter and went to the answering machine and read the phone messages on the screen.

Byron had called and didn't sound happy. "Thought you were going to call. Did Kate and Liv show up? You owe me a rain check for lunch. And I know you were upset I ordered for you, but I knew you loved striped bass from the fishing yarn you told me on the way to Chez Noelle. Take care."

Oh boy. He was sensitive and hot.

I got his number from caller ID and dialed.

A woman answered.
I hung up.

Later that night, I tried to sleep, but couldn't. I flipped to
Samuel Taylor Coleridge in Patrick's book and read a
stanza from "The Rime of the Ancient Mariner."

> *I woke, and we were sailing on*
> *As in a gentle weather:*
> *'Twas night, calm night, the moon was high;*
> *The dead men stood together.*

I snapped the book shut. Now I really wouldn't be able
to sleep.

When I arrived in Sag Harbor to pick up Maurice, my hands and knees were shaking. This morning, after I came up from the beach, there was a message on my machine telling me today at three P.M. Sgt. Gordon Miles was scheduled to make an appearance at the East Hampton courthouse.

I let Maurice drive to Sandringham. The plan was for him to pick up Elle, drop me at my Jeep, and bring Elle back to Sag Harbor.

Maurice looked comical driving Elle's big ole pickup. He was slender and well groomed, reminding me of an elegant bird, not exactly truck-driving material. He lived in Sag Harbor, a block away from Elle, in a tiny Victorian he and his partner renovated and filled with items from Elle's shop. Elle said Maurice had a good eye for picking out the "cream of the crap." But last year, when I attended

Maurice's New Year Eve's party, I didn't see one piece of crap, it was all cream.

We talked about the Barkers' party. I didn't have to paint it more glamorous than it was. It was something I'd remember forever, but I had a hard time recalling what all the celebs wore. I could tell Maurice was disappointed.

Maurice said, "The truck came yesterday with the furniture from the bungalow. Everything's in the carriage house. Looks like you two did well."

"Elle's going to want to check it out. Don't let her overdo."

"Like I could stop her."

Maurice pulled through the gates at Sandringham. Thankfully, everything looked copacetic. He parked and we went to the kitchen door, where Elle had texted that she was waiting.

When we walked inside, Maurice oohed and aahed at the kitchen décor. Then nearly fell off his chair after eating one of Ingrid's pumpkin scones. When he'd finished his second one, he licked his fingertips in a very ungentlemanly, non–Professor Higgins way.

Elle was sad to leave, and I didn't blame her. She still looked pale and fragile, so I didn't tell her about my three o'clock court appointment.

I accompanied Elle and Maurice to the pickup, telling Elle to call if she needed anything. As they pulled away, Liv opened Sandringham's front door. She called out my name, and came down the steps to meet me on the circular drive.

Her hair was pulled back in a ponytail and she wore a Brown University sweatshirt and sweatpants. "I'm so sad to see Elle go. She's such a great person."

"Yes, she is."

"I have a favor to ask. I want to give you these and see if you can find out anything. I know my father is trying to tell me something, and I can't quite figure it out." She handed me her father's journal and the four children's books he had printed for her when she was a child.

I didn't feel worthy. I knew how much they meant to her, and I also knew how Celia's snub about Pierce's artwork yesterday had wounded her. I was happy to take them. Now I knew how I'd pass the time before my court date. But first I was going to Little Grey. Possibly for the last time.

When I reached the side of the garage where my Jeep was parked, I didn't see any sign of Richard. I still had the keys, so I wrote him a note and taped it to the now-locked side door, got in the Jeep, and left the estate.

A few minutes later, I pulled the Jeep into the old Eberhardt property. I might as well get used to its new/old name. But I refused to call it the Miles property. Doc had canceled our standing Monday morning date at Paddy's Pancake House because he and Georgia had a surfing lesson. He'd offered to buy me my own board and invited me to join them. But with this afternoon's court date, I didn't feel up to it.

The cottage looked as forlorn as I felt. Sun reflected off the corners of the upstairs windows, reminding me of eyes with tears ready to spill. I knew mine were. The attic! All the items were still in the attic from the day I signed the papers. I'd left them untouched, planning on renovating the first and second floors, then bringing out each item one at a time from the packed attic and incorporating them into the cottage.

Back where they belonged.

Would Sgt. Miles keep the cottage or tear it down and build something new?

I got out of the Jeep and grabbed the tube that held the landscape plans.

Once inside the folly, I spread out Byron's landscape plans, using clay flower pots to hold down the corners. The plans were wonderful. There was a gray walled-in space just like at Grey Gardens in East Hampton, but smaller, with circular openings cut out of the southern wall for glimpses of the Atlantic. Byron included a plethora of hedges and trees and a revamp of the outdoor stone fireplace, now in ruin. He'd even drawn two lanterns on the mantel.

In front of the fireplace was a slate patio with thick-cushioned teak outdoor furniture. There were loads of perennials, flowering bushes, and trees. I'd told Byron no annuals, except for the herb beds and, of course, Anna Gilman Hill's delphiniums, considered biannuals because they usually only lasted a couple of years. There was a cutting garden and arches and trellises. Each proposed species of flower was numbered with a key in the bottom right-hand corner: phlox, wisteria, lavender, wild lupines, and heirloom roses. And, of course, he'd included steps leading down to the ocean.

I'd also told Byron no vegetables. I'd leave their growing to the local farmers. Tending a vegetable garden and planting annuals were a little beyond my patience level. Plus, if I grew my own vegetables, there'd be no reason to visit farm stands in the area. One of my guilty pleasures— no gourmet cooking degree required—just steam and herbed butter.

Clouds moved in and lowered the temperature in the folly about ten degrees. No sense in buying a generator. Soon I'd be thrown to the curb.

I rolled up the plans and headed back to my rental—a rental whose lease ran out in two months. I planned for an hour of looking over Pierce's journal and books, then on to the slaughter/courthouse.

Before I turned onto the street of my rental, a white van caught my attention in the rearview mirror. I swore it was there. But when I looked again, it was gone.

I walked into the cottage and for the first time, Jo greeted me. Even allowing me a rare scratch behind the ear. After filling her bottomless dry cat food container, which always seemed to have a bottom, I made a peanut butter and banana sandwich. I bundled up, took Pierce's journal and my sandwich to the wooden swing that hung under the eaves. I sat on the cushioned seat. It was funny how you only appreciated things once they were threatened to be ripped away— like the view of the ocean I now enjoyed.

There was definitely a common thread in each page of Pierce's journal—secret hiding places. Like Liv, I also suspected there must have been a hidden door in the wine cellar. I looked again at the sketch of the beach below Morrison Manor with its rock wall and, more importantly, the fire pit. What if Sandringham had underground tunnels built from the old Montauk bootlegging era? Or even further back to the days of pirates, like Captain Kidd— possibly a tunnel that connected Sandringham to Morrison Manor with access to the ocean?

I was in a bit of a time crunch so I got out my cell phone and took photos of the pages in Pierce's journal

for future reference. Then I went inside and opened my laptop. I looked at the photos I'd sent from my cell phone of Sandringham and Morrison Manor's landscape plans. They were charming and well thought out, but I didn't see anything that would suggest secret tunnels leading to the ocean.

It was two thirty. I needed to get going. Before I left the cottage, I took out the slim leather volume on Montauk I'd taken from the bungalow and put it on the coffee table as a reminder to look through it when I returned.

Thunder sounded when I got out of the Jeep, announcing my arrival at the East Hampton courthouse. I'd given myself a good talking-to on the way over. I needed to stand up for what was mine. I just hoped I'd be given a chance.

There was a black unmarked car at the curb with a driver waiting inside. I knew it belonged to Sgt. Gordon Miles.

After my handbag and I passed through security without incident, I was told to go to Conference Room 2, not the courtroom. The pulse in my neck thumped and the Barrett Curse reared its ugly head: I felt red welts bloom over my face and neck, my constant companions in times of bereavement, anger, excitement, and public speaking. What was waiting for me at the end of the hallway seemed to encompass all four.

I walked into the room. At the head of the conference table was a man dressed in a military uniform. Sgt. Gordon Miles. He smiled when I walked in, all white teeth and white hair. He had crinkly wrinkles around his hazel eyes,

like laughing was his favorite pastime. Then I noticed he wasn't sitting in a chair. He was in a wheelchair. He'd served his country, and now it was time for his country to serve him.

It felt like a boulder had been lifted from my back. He wasn't my stalker, and whatever happened with Little Grey, I'd be okay. It was just a building and some land. I knew I could make a home anywhere as long as I lived in Montauk and had the ocean nearby.

I could tell Sgt. Miles was a glass-half-full kind of guy when he held out his hand. "Meg Barrett, I've been looking forward to meeting you. I'm so sorry I couldn't get here sooner, and I'm sorry for the heartache all this must have caused you." He patted the top of the table next to him. "I've saved you a seat." The heartache he'd caused me? How about what he endured after being held captive?

All parties were present, except for Judge Ferry. Unbeknownst to me, my attorney and Justin Marguilles had agreed to mediation. The mediation attorney started the proceedings.

When we finished, I had no idea where I stood. Sgt. Miles had a letter from his great-aunt Amelia, which proved they'd been in touch before her death. The letter was of a friendly nature. Also, the church hadn't spent any of the money from the sale, so that wouldn't be an issue. The only light I could see at the end of my booby-trapped tunnel was that Sgt. Miles lived in California with his wife and daughter. Little Grey would be a vacation home, not a primary. Sgt. Gordon Miles wasn't poor, and he wasn't homeless. It was something.

Wasn't it?

When I got back to the cottage, I spent the late afternoon ordering window treatments for Rebecca Crandle's cottage, along with a chair cover for my *New York Times* reading chair. Dinner for two at the banquette consisted of sardine-delight for Jo, tuna mac 'n' cheese for me—dump a can of tuna into microwaved macaroni and cheese, top with crushed garlic salad croutons, and add fresh-snipped chives.

After we finished eating, I sat on the sofa and looked through the book on Montauk I'd found in the bungalow. Jo kept busy rolling her head back and forth over the catnip tiger until her eye glazed over in ecstasy.

The book, titled *On Montauk*, was published in 1930 and reiterated the story Nathan told Elle about Morrison Manor. Bootlegging and rum-running were standard operation during the Volstead Act, which lasted from 1919 to 1933. Many locals participated in transporting booze via fishing boats to the shores off Montauk Point then sent them due west to New York City. However, I wasn't able to find any connection between bootlegging and Sandringham, so I returned to Pierce's journal and got out a magnifying glass to analyze the drawing that caused Liv and Kate to spend the night in the wine cellar. There was a row of old wood barrels, and above them Pierce had drawn where an arched door might be—possibly what had led Liv to the cellar in the first place. Then I turned the picture in the cellar sideways and I saw it. The scribbling of lines representing knotholes in the barrels weren't scribbles at all. I brought the journal to the mirror and the word "enter" appeared.

Later that night when I went down to Patrick Seaton's

beach, the sand was bereft of sandscript. Everything that helped me feel safe and secure about my new life was deserting me. If I called Byron, I was afraid a woman might answer.

Lightning zipped across the ocean sky, followed by thunder. For the first time in my life, I didn't revel in it. My nerves were stripped bare.

When I walked into the cottage, I said, "It looks like it's just you and me, Jo."

She got down from her chair and walked upstairs.

Wrong again.

CHAPTER

❧⁓❧

TWENTY-SIX

The bad weather continued. It was a wet, miserable Tuesday, and I was out the door by six A.M., having been unable to sleep and needing to keep busy.

I planned to investigate the wine cellar at Sandringham. I'd already texted Liv and she was at the kitchen door waiting for me. Ingrid wasn't awake and when I looked in the dark kitchen, it seemed cold and uninviting without her presence.

Liv looked like a teen. Her hair was in pigtails and she wore pj's and a robe. "Shush. This way."

The door to the stairs leading to the wine cellar was in the mudroom. Liv unlocked it with a skeleton key from her robe pocket. We went down a twisting set of concrete steps. At the bottom was another door. The key to the wine cellar door was in the keyhole on the outside.

She opened the door and handed me the key. "Just in case, so I can't lose it."

I flipped the light switch, and we both went to the wall with the barrels. I was disappointed. There wasn't a curved outline above the barrels to indicate a door, like in Pierce's sketch. "Let's move those barrels."

Liv said, "Been there. Done that. But I'm game to have you see for yourself."

She was right. Behind the barrels was only the stone cellar wall. The room was windowless and the walls and cellar door thick and impenetrable, making it impossible to be heard. Just like the recording studio where we'd found Pierce's skeleton.

There was a rough wood table and four chairs in the center of the room and rows of stacked wine bottles on eight wooden floor-to-ceiling racks. On the wall opposite the wood barrels, I saw a large electrical fuse box.

I walked over and opened the metal door. The fuses were labeled with a *G* followed by a number. At the top of the list it read, *Gallery*.

Liv stood behind me. "Are you thinking what I'm thinking?"

I was. When the fuse box went in, someone must have moved the barrels to the other side of the cellar. Pierce's drawing must have represented the cellar before the move.

We went to the last wine rack to the right of the fuse box and managed to shimmy it forward.

Liv took a flashlight out of her robe pocket and shone it on the wall. She must have been a Girl Scout to have come so prepared. Then I remembered how long she'd

been exploring Sandringham—a flashlight was status quo.

Sure enough, there was an outline of a small door. Next to the door, attached to the wall, was a gas lantern.

It was too easy. I let Liv do the honors.

She bent the lantern forward, like she'd done with the head bust that opened the secret staircase. I stuck the fingertips from both my hands into the small crevice at the top of the door and it opened.

The doorway was only big enough for a hobbit to walk through. Liv got on her hands and knees and crawled forward. I followed. When the ceiling got higher, we both stood.

I felt like I was inside a trendy Manhattan underground bar. The space was more likely a Prohibition speakeasy.

"What a hoot," Liv said. "This is the interior drawing we thought was Morrison Manor. Does that mean there's also a tunnel leading to the shore like the old-time Montauk rumrunners used?"

I used my phone as a flashlight and reached over the bar to see what was behind it. When Liv gasped, I turned around. Her flashlight illuminated something against the far wall.

On a bar stool, wearing a creepy grin, was a skull.

Liv made a whimpering sound.

I stifled the gag reflex and turned her around, coaxing her out of the room.

When she finally made it back out, I left her sitting on the cement floor in a fugue state—motionless and unblinking.

I went back inside the hidden room. Beneath the bar stool was a whisky crate and inside was a pile of bones.

TWENTY-SEVEN

Elle and I shared a glass of wine in her carriage house. I was taking Elle with me for the final walk-through of Rebecca Crandle's cottage. During the past week all had been quiet on the eastern front. We were waiting for confirmation that Liv and I had indeed discovered the bones of Helen, Nathan's wife, a.k.a. Pierce's lover, in the speakeasy. I and everyone else had no doubt it was Helen.

Things were also quiet on two other fronts: the status of Little Grey and Byron Hughes.

Morgana had left a message on my machine with the names of the owner of the boat *Wrestling with the Wind*, Bill Bates, and the owner's two part-time workers, Kurt Pinkus and Fred Slocum. I felt confident my stalker had nothing to do with Sandringham or Sgt. Miles, but I had to be sure. I'd called my father with the names Morgana left, along with the name Richard Challis.

Someone had killed Helen. The obvious suspect was Nathan Morrison, but I wasn't sure. Why would he leave Pierce in the bungalow and his wife, Helen, in Sandringham's wine cellar? As a neighbor with open access to Sandringham, Nathan could've found numerous other places to get rid of their bodies. Plus, Nathan had twenty years to do it. Once again, the big question remained: where was the Warhol?

Elle took a sip of wine. "I'm so happy I missed finding Helen Morrison's skeleton. One advantage to having a sprained ankle—no more dead bodies."

"Have you talked to anyone at Sandringham?"

"Yes. Ingrid. She wants us to come over tomorrow. It's Kate's birthday. She said it might be Kate's last at Sandringham because Justin Marguilles served Celia with divorce papers. I wonder if we should pass. Tomorrow's Devil's Night, October thirtieth. Not a good omen."

I gave her "the look."

"Hey. You're always telling me I should inform you of my premonitions beforehand. Well, I just did."

"Okay, I'll bring my amethyst."

I loaded the back of Elle's pickup with some of the furniture stored in her carriage house that we'd taken from the bungalow, and set off for Hither Hills.

Elle claimed she was good enough to drive, but her limp said otherwise. Also in the bed of the truck was the flattop locked trunk from the bungalow attic. I wanted to use it on my rental's screened porch. I also wanted to unlock it without ruining the fabulous brass lock, which Elle and Maurice had threatened to do.

*   *   *

Elle was the first one inside Rebecca Crandle's cottage. "Wowza! It's so bright and airy. Can't believe the difference."

The first level of the cottage had the loft-like feel I wanted, yet there were cozy surprises around each corner. With the exception of a small office with pocket doors and a guest bathroom, the great room/open kitchen took up the entire first floor.

The kitchen and great room were painted white, including the bead-board walls and trim. There were pendulum lights over the unvarnished salvaged wood center island with cement countertop. The island had a cooktop on one side and seating on the other.

Inspired by Sandringham's kitchen, the far wall was faced in bricks by Duke and Duke Junior, then whitewashed. I'd added a large farm table and an assortment of mismatched vintage chairs painted white.

I couldn't bring in live herbs because there was no telling when Rebecca would be in Montauk. I did buy some seed packets and coordinating porcelain name stakes and stuck them in vintage flower pots on the windowsill over the farm sink. The stakes were made by a local potter known for her fantastic glazes.

Elle was prone on the cushioned window seat, looking out at Hither Hills beach. I handed her one of the Crandles' mysteries to keep her busy while I carted in the furniture from the back of the pickup with my trusty hand truck.

I started to unpack a collection of vintage spyglasses

I planned to put on the fireplace mantel, when there was a knock at the kitchen door. My first thought was, *stalker calling*. But would he knock? Plus, I had Elle's pickup, not my Jeep.

When I boldly walked to the door, I saw Sylvie Crandle's face pressed against the glass.

I let her inside and introduced her to Elle.

She walked from the kitchen to the open living area and saw the pieces I'd taken from Elle's White Room. "I don't understand. Thought these items were from Tara Gayle's clients' homes?"

Elle looked at me and I nodded my head.

She said, "Ms. Crandle, please have a seat. There's something you should know."

"Please, call me Sylvie."

I left them for "the talk" and ran upstairs to make sure I hadn't forgotten something.

I'd stuck to a soft palette in all of Rebecca's rooms and let my carefully chosen garage and estate sale smalls mesh with Montauk's raw beauty peeking through the cottage's windows. Furniture that needed to be painted, was. Items that needed to be left as is, were. Freshly updated and new fit together with worn and well used.

I loved imagining what rooms and humans my vintage and antique pieces belonged to before incorporating them into a client's cottage. At estate sales, the items I found in attics and basements were usually hand-me-downs from a past generation, not the current generations. My mother's antique shop in Michigan had been named Past Perfect. The shop sowed the seeds of my love for all things old. I think she would've been proud of me if she saw the life I'd carved

out for myself. Scratch that. I believed she *was* proud. She stood next to me on every purchase, every decision.

One of my favorite spaces upstairs was the writing nook in the hallway I'd converted from a walk-in linen closet. I'd painted the entire space a palest-of-pale robin's-egg blue and removed all the shelving with the exception of two upper shelves on the back wall. They would house Rebecca's writing reference books, including true crime and police procedurals. I made a desk surface by adding a salvaged white Formica countertop cut to size that was bolted to the wall under the bookshelves. A white leather bucket chair with Lucite arms and base, which I'd taken from the bungalow, fit perfectly. On the wall between the desk and the shelves, I'd added a thick corkboard with clear pushpins.

The antique inkwell I'd purchased from Grimes House Antiques went on the desk in the downstairs office. The linen closet turned writing nook had room for only a laptop, a lamp with a Lucite base, and a pad of paper.

When I came downstairs, Sylvie Crandle was gone. Elle knew my unspoken rule. Rebecca, my client, would get the first official tour. If she wanted to bring her mother, Sylvie, that was fine. I believed personal taste was just that. I never got upset when certain items didn't resonate with a client. So far I'd been pretty lucky on that score, but I still felt the elevator free-fall in my gut as I waited for a client's feedback at the end of a job.

After Hither Hills, Elle and I had an early dinner at Pondfare, the hot in-season restaurant on Fort Pond Bay and yummy off-season stop for us year-rounders.

Pondfare specialized in small plates—tapas-style. My favorite way to dine. I'd rather share six appetizers with Elle than a main dish any night. Another perk to visiting Hamptons restaurants off-peak were their prices: discounted menus for early birds and special prix fixe dinners that cost one-third the summer price.

I halved the Spanish sausage in squid ink risotto, put it on a plate, then passed it to Elle. She took a bite and her eyes glazed over. She handed me Sylvie Crandle's card. "You're hired," she mumbled between bites. "Sylvie stopped payment on Tara's check."

We talked about what Liv told Elle before Ingrid, Nathan, and I walked into the kitchen after the girls had been locked in the cellar. One thing seemed slightly strange; Liv told Elle that she hadn't had her inhaler with her but that Kate had brought an extra. If the girls got locked in accidentally, why would Kate have Liv's inhaler? Also, how had Richard gotten a photo on his laptop from Pierce's sketch journal? From Kate?

Maybe Kate didn't fall asleep from drinking too much wine but made sure Liv did. Richard and Kate had a connection. Was it Richard who killed Pierce and Helen?

Back at my rental, I left Elle playing with Jo while I moved the trunk to the screened porch. I fed Jo at the table, and Elle couldn't stop laughing. Over the past four days, I'd been gradually making Jo's suppertime fifteen minutes later. She hadn't seemed to notice. But just to make sure, I set the clock backward one hour. Any cat that could drag my top to her litter box could probably tell time.

Elle insisted we take Jo in the car with us when I dropped her home. It took only seconds and a single treat to get Jo in the carrier. When we turned onto Route 114, Elle's cell phone rang. It was Detective Shoner. The skull and bones had been positively identified as Helen Morrison's. Nathan Morrison was already at the station for questioning.

Jo howled and I felt like joining her.

When Jo and I returned home, I was exhausted, but I couldn't let the trunk from the bungalow's attic remain locked. I got out the huge key ring I'd found at Little Grey, the one with the magic key that had opened the door to Little Grey's attic, and went out to the screened porch. Jo followed.

She jumped on the trunk, gave it a few sniffs, then settled down on a wicker chaise.

The trunk would be perfect for storing cushions from my porch furniture. And it also performed double duty as a coffee table.

A dozen vintage oil lanterns hung from the porch ceiling, all in different sizes and colors. I'd purchased the lot at a house sale in Montauk. Their former owner was an elderly gentleman who'd spent his entire life working for the Long Island Railroad.

Jo's gaze followed me as I lit each lantern with a butane torch.

It took me thirteen tries with the key ring before I opened the trunk. Lucky thirteen. Good thing I didn't have triskaidekaphobia.

There weren't any historical documents or signed constitutions worthy of bringing to an antique appraisal television show. There were items I was sure Liv would cherish till the end of days.

Under a stack of *Rolling Stone* magazines were three journals, and a scrapbook filled with magazine ads featuring Tansy holding cans of Aqua Net hairspray. At the bottom of the trunk was a box from Tiffany's. I opened it. Inside was a sterling silver rattle. Also in the box was a dated receipt. The space on the rattle where there should've been an engraving was left blank. Someone meant to have it engraved, hence the receipt.

I emptied the trunk and brought its contents to the table at the banquette, then went down to the beach to look for sandscript.

Nothing.

Feeling bereft about Pierce and Helen Morrison's demise and the thought of a rattle-less baby, I left a quote in front of Patrick Seaton's cottage from Emily Dickinson, someone who knew about a solitary life:

> *It might be lonelier*
> *Without the Loneliness*
> *I'm so accustomed to my Fate.*

After I came back up to the cottage and fed Jo, I made her scoot over, then sat on the banquette to look over Pierce's journals. It appeared Pierce had been much younger when he'd drawn them. Younger and less schooled. The amazing thing was, he had actual living things in his sketches: horses, dogs, and humans. What had turned him

away from living, breathing things and caused him to draw mostly interiors? Interiors hiding secrets?

I closed the books, even though I was curious. My brain was too fried to look for secret codes hidden in Pierce's drawings. I'd go over them with Liv after Kate's birthday party. When I thought about it, what were we looking for? We had Pierce and Helen's bodies. The murderer most likely had the Warhol, and I didn't think Pierce would have sketched "killer" into the folds of someone's jacket before his demise.

Pierce and Helen's murderer would probably be caught by high-tech DNA testing and cutting-edge CSI work.

CHAPTER

❧❧❧

TWENTY-EIGHT

Everyone was in Sandringham's dining room for Kate's party, except Ingrid and Brandy. Maurice had dropped Elle off, and she'd saved me a seat. I was surprised to see Nathan Morrison was there, not in jail. He hadn't shaved and his eyes were downcast.

Sandringham's formal dining room brought to mind all the PBS miniseries I'd watched over the years, ones set in English manor houses or castles; eighteenth- and nineteenth-century breakfast buffets: kippers and eggs in sterling hot water-warmed chafing dishes and buttered toast in silver filigree toast servers. Today, the table was set casually—more in line with Kate's style. I added my gift to the others on the glossy polished sideboard that smelled of beeswax. It made me wonder about the crew that came in daily to keep the mammoth house clean. I

knew from my Realtor and friend Barb, many of the housecleaners who worked in the Hamptons had to commute from towns more than thirty miles away. Not a bad ride off-season, but in-season, it could take an extra hour or two.

I'd had a hard time picking Kate's gift. What did you get someone whom you suspected was up to no good? In my case, I bought her a Grateful Dead T-shirt from Montauk's Rockin' Retro because I remembered Kate had worn one the day we had chowder.

Ingrid had outdone herself, which I didn't think was possible. I even heard Celia thank her for going the extra mile for Kate. Celia seemed as low as Nathan, validating the news she'd been served with divorce papers. Brandy arrived in time for the main dish or should I say dishes: six huge pizzas all with different crusts and ingredients, ranging from a classy pie of lobster, shrimp, and clam in a garlic-butter sauce on thin crust; to a campy White Castle pie with thin square burger patties with onion-filled holes, topped with pickles and ketchup on flatbread. The White Castle pie looked pretty bad, but it tasted more than pretty good. Brandy had taken the only seat left, which was next to Nathan. She kept inching her chair away, perhaps afraid she'd catch his killer cooties.

Uncle Harry was the biggest surprise. He was clearheaded and told jokes in which he remembered the punch lines. Everyone laughed with him, not at him. I believed he had a fondness for Kate and might have felt guilty about kicking her and Celia out of the house.

Ingrid brought in the cake with its twenty-three lit

candles. After the last "you" in the birthday song, a banging came from the direction of the front door.

Ingrid said, "Ignore it, Kate. Blow out your candles."

Richard left the room.

Kate hesitated for a second, then blew. It took two tries, but she finally got them all out.

Detective Shoner entered the dining room, followed by Chief Pell and two Suffolk County officers. Chief Pell was top brass in the Hamptons' law enforcement hierarchy. We'd met last spring under similar circumstances.

Detective Shoner walked up to Nathan. "Nathan Morrison, you're under arrest for the murders of Pierce Falks and Helen Morrison."

The two officers went to Nathan's chair. He stood and one of the officers put him in handcuffs, while the other read him his rights.

Nathan turned his head toward Ingrid.

Ingrid said, "I'll call you a lawyer. They've made a mistake."

He nodded and Liv ran to his side. "Uncle Nathan. Tell me you didn't do it?"

"I didn't do it."

Then the officers prodded him out of the dining room and into the hallway.

Chief Pell, who could have been a professional wrestler in another life, lumbered over to my chair. "How are you, Ms. Barrett?" Like it wasn't strange for me to be at the site of another murder in the mostly crime-free Hamptons.

"I'm well. Thank you."

Chief Pell went over to Detective Shoner, mumbled a

few words, tugged on the detective's pocket square, and left the room, his head barely clearing the doorway.

Elle hobbled over to Detective Shoner and he whispered something in her ear. I read his lips, "We found Helen's handbag and Pierce's wallet in the Morrison gatehouse."

CHAPTER

✌︎⁓✌︎

TWENTY-NINE

The birthday party disbanded. Maurice came and retrieved Elle. Before she left, she told me Helen Morrison's purse and Pierce's wallet were found in the bottom of a humpback trunk in Nathan's bedroom.

It seemed too obvious a spot to keep evidence from a murder committed twenty years ago. On the day we hoofed it over to the gatehouse, Liv had opened the door with a key that was hidden outside. Who else knew about the key? The missing Warhol could have been another motive for their murders.

I'd woken with my own theory about the Warhol. As soon as I left Sandringham, I planned to go to East Hampton and visit Detective Shoner.

I'd told Liv earlier about her father's journals that I'd found in the trunk from the bungalow. As soon as the police

left and Uncle Harry was taken to his suite, we went up to her room.

When I gave her the first journal, a smile spread from ear to ear. Her hands trembled as she placed it on the desk in front of her.

Maybe this wasn't the best time, especially after Nathan Morrison's arrest. "If you want to do this another day, that's fine."

"I'd rather do this than go down and see Mrs. Anderson. Did you know her and Uncle Nathan are in love? Even if they won't admit it to themselves. I don't know what to think anymore."

I thought I heard a slight hesitation before the word "Uncle."

She opened the first journal, her eyes bright as she turned the pages.

After a few minutes, Liv said, "I've been looking at these drawings of these two girls, and I think I've figured out who one of them is. But I'm stumped on the other."

She slid the journal closer and I scanned the sketch. "Celia, right?"

"Yes. Hard to picture her and my father dating in high school, and then to think she married Granddad." She pointed to the page. "See how my father drew that hardness in her eyes. She still has it. Let me show you something."

She took a chain from around her neck; hanging on the chain was a small key. She turned the key in a locked bottom desk drawer and pulled out a scrapbook. Below the scrapbook were her father's sketch journal and the children's books I'd returned to her after we'd found Helen's bones.

Liv opened the scrapbook to the first page. There was
a newspaper article with the headline:

Falks Sells Fake

and an UPI photo of Harrison and Pierce on the steps of
the East Hampton courthouse. Pierce was quite an attractive guy, probably homecoming king to Celia's queen. I
shivered when I thought of my first meeting with him in
the bungalow.

The article was about the Jackson Pollock scandal,
recounting that Pierce had brokered the sale of a bogus
Pollock to a museum in Czechoslovakia.

Liv pointed to a young girl in the crowd.

"Celia?"

"Yep. I always suspected she had something to do with
the Pollock. It sounds like something she'd orchestrate,
especially after knowing she wanted Granddad's power
of attorney."

"It's possible."

"Celia went right from high school to an art gallery in
Bridgehampton. Four galleries later and a gig at the
MoMA, she marries Granddad."

Liv put the scrapbook away and we looked at the
sketch of the other young girl in Pierce's journal.

I pulled the journal closer. "If I had to guess, I'd say
it's Brandy. Look at her bosoms and sweater."

Liv giggled. "Bosoms? You could be right."

Pierce hadn't been too kind to the features on her face.
He'd drawn Brandy's nose bigger and her eyes smaller,
like two little slits. But in the chest area, he'd been on
target. Brandy looked to be in her teens. She sat Indian-
style on the floor, with a blanket on her lap. There was

no mistaking which room Pierce had drawn her in. It was the attic in the bungalow. The bungalow where his skeleton was found. Pierce's go-to hideout. I knew I was right because in the background was the easel holding the portrait he'd made of his mother, Tansy. Also pictured was the trunk that was now on my porch and on top of it, a *Rolling Stone* magazine.

Liv looked closely at the page. "Brandy practically grew up here. Her mother was sick and her father was Granddad's financial assistant. Granddad took her under his wing after her father passed away. It turned out to be a good thing because she's the one who stopped all the prescriptions Granddad was on. I don't know what he would do without her."

I couldn't agree more.

The other pages in the journal had numerous drawings of Tansy. Maybe they'd been practice for Pierce's portrait of Tansy.

I'd saved the last sketch journal for last. It was smaller than the rest and had only two pages of drawings. The surprise was the handwriting at the bottom of each sketch.

Liv opened to the first page. "Oh. This is wonderful! This might be the first time my father got his idea to do my children's books."

The drawing was of a baby's nursery with a crib. And there was the figure of an infant inside the crib. Tiny penguins dangled from the strings of a mobile. At the bottom of the page Pierce had written: *It was a cold and snowy night and the penguins wanted to come out and play. But baby wanted to sleep*. Liv turned the page. Pierce had reverted to one of his non-human sketches. It looked like

the interior of Liv's bedroom, with the huge fireplace, mantel, and the mahogany four-poster bed. There was a fire burning in the fireplace and a blanket on the floor. And on the blanket was a baby rattle. The rattle was similar to the one I found in the trunk from the bungalow. The caption read: *Where have you gone? Are you hiding with Grandma?*

"Is that your father's room in the drawing?" I didn't want her to know I'd been snooping in her room on the day she and Kate got locked in the cellar.

"It was. Now it's mine. We're sitting in it. I took it over after college. Do you think the reason for my father's drawing is that I'm meant to look for clues in the picture and find out where the baby is hiding, so I can find more treasure?"

"Maybe."

I left Liv in her bedroom, holding the drawing from the journal up to a mirror to see if there was any reverse writing, like she'd found before. I thought about saying good-bye to Uncle Harry and Ingrid but wanted to get to East Hampton to talk to Detective Shoner about the Warhol.

When I was almost at my Jeep, something hit me. The date on the Tiffany's receipt for the sterling baby rattle I'd found in Pierce's trunk had been dated years before Liv was born. Then I thought about Pierce's drawing with Brandy and the blanket in the bungalow attic. He had drawn little squares in the blanket. Granny squares. Thirdly, I thought about the small white suitcase in Brandy's armoire.

I needed to see what was in that suitcase.

Heading to the side of the mansion, I approached the

kitchen door, knowing it wasn't usually locked in the day-
time. The door opened before I reached it. Ingrid stepped
out wearing her coat and carrying a handbag. "I'm going
to the courthouse to see if anyone has set bail." Her eyes
were red and swollen.

"I forgot something in Liv's room."

She held the door open. "He didn't do it. I know he
didn't."

As I passed by, I put my hand on her shoulder. "Keep
the faith." Then I stepped inside.

I took the secret stairway up to the second floor, then
crept down the hallway toward Uncle Harry's and Brandy's rooms. The door to Brandy's sitting room was open
and so was Uncle Harry's. Brandy was reading aloud to
him in his room. After Nathan's arrest, Uncle Harry had
been so distraught, she had to bring him to his suite in a
wheelchair. Sad, because he'd been doing so well with
the walker after the competency hearing.

I tip-toed into Brandy's sitting room, unlocked the
armoire, and took out the suitcase. I could still hear Brandy
reading, but her words were getting fainter and fainter. I
cupped my hand to my right ear. No feedback. My right
hearing aid battery was dead. I looked around for something
to use to pick the suitcase's lock. Time was of the essence,
so I grabbed a letter opener and pried open the latch.

Inside the small suitcase were photos of Brandy pregnant and ready to pop. In the background of the photo, she
was standing in a room with two single beds, almost like
a dorm room. She wasn't smiling. On the bed was the same
granny square afghan from Pierce's sketch. I turned and
looked through the doorway to Brandy's bedroom. The

same crocheted blanket from the photo lay on the rocking chair. There were also photos of Pierce as a young man. Candid shots. Under the photos were crocheted baby clothes: a pink hat with satin ties and a pair of matching booties. Below the clothing was a newborn's plastic bracelet, which read: *Millard Fillmore Hospital, F and Port.* The bracelet had been cut, but before someone taped the ends back together again, they'd threaded the bracelet through a man's wedding ring.

Through my left hearing aid I heard, "Well. Well. Aren't you the nosy one?"

Then I felt pain like I'd never felt before.

CHAPTER

THIRTY

I woke up in the living room of the bungalow in Uncle Harry's wheelchair. Brandy stood in front of me. "What are you doing?"

"Don't talk. Things will go easier if you don't talk."

"What kind of things?" My tongue felt coated with peanut butter.

I tried to stand. No good. I touched the back of my head and felt a huge gash. My hand came away slicked with blood and I had a hard time moving my arms and legs.

"Time to top you off." Brandy reached in her coat pocket and took out a syringe and glass vial. She stuck the needle into the top of the vial and pulled the stopper. The syringe filled with clear liquid. She tapped the syringe until a few drops beaded on the needle's point.

"I don't understand. What's that for?" Unfortunately, a similar experience taught me to keep the killer talking.

Maybe when I survived this one I'd do a seminar: things to say when you're confronted with a murderer.

"Stop talking."

Or in my case, things not to say. "I think you misunderstood."

"Ha. I misunderstood? I misunderstood you rifling through my private things? Her things? Did you see his ring?"

"No. What ring? I, uh, I wanted to return something that belonged to you."

"What are you saying?" She came closer. And so did the needle.

"The rattle."

"What rattle?"

"The one Pierce bought for your baby."

"How do you know?"

"I found it inside a trunk that had been stored upstairs in the attic." I tried to point above me to the attic, but my arm felt so numb, I could barely raise a finger.

Her eyes filled with tears. She wiped them away with the sleeve of her sweater. "Show it to me."

"I don't have it. Must've dropped it back at Sandringham."

"There's no rattle. Pierce didn't care about the baby. Not even when Harrison told him she died. And he certainly didn't care about me. Sixteen, scared, and alone. He used me. At school he was with Celia. At home he was with me. After the baby died and I came back to Montauk he barely talked to me. Then when he married Sonya, I almost forgave him. I wasn't even mad that Pierce had married Sonya when she was pregnant with Liv. Harrison forced him to

do the right thing. Sonya was real. She wasn't one of the stuck-ups. She was my friend. I even told her about the baby. But I was mad when I found him cheating on Sonya with Helen Morrison."

She moved closer.

I tried to stand but only managed to fall back into the wheelchair. "Then I must have been wrong. The rattle must have been for Liv."

"Oh no, you don't. A rattle doesn't explain why you broke open the case. Plus, you saw Pierce's wedding ring. I am sorry, but you won't feel a thing. You'll fall asleep before the smoke enters your lungs." She jabbed the needle in my arm.

I twisted away but she had the advantage. Every last milliliter entered my right arm. "They know," I said. "Liv knows you killed Helen and her father."

She tucked the syringe in her pocket. "You're bluffing."

"Why did you do it?"

"I caught Helen and Pierce here. In the recording studio. Their little love nest. This used to be our place. But that didn't matter. When I found out they were meeting here, I had to do something. Not only for myself, but for Sonya and Liv. Pierce was married, and had a three-year-old. Cheating snake. So I bolted and locked the door to the recording studio on the outside and pushed the bookcase against the door, then filled it with heavy books. I packed some of Pierce's clothing, wallet, passport, and toiletries, snuck into the gatehouse, and did the same with Helen's things.

She took a box of matches from her other pocket.

"So you let Pierce and Helen die and let Sonya think Pierce ran off with Helen?"

"It was all for the best. And don't forget the Warhol. Pierce had moved it to his suite. I took it and hid it in the speakeasy room in the cellar so it would look like Pierce and Helen had stolen it before they left Montauk. Everyone believed Pierce took off with the painting, especially after he was blacklisted in the art world for the Pollock scandal. We were all better off without Pierce in our lives. Even Harrison. Poor Harrison. I started doubling and tripling his meds so he'd become confused and out of it. Then right before the competency hearing, I weaned him off so he'd be lucid. I knew Celia would be blamed. He doesn't need that bitch in his life. I'll always take care of him. I made it look like Celia was a gold digger, which she is. Where do you think Celia got the names of Harrison's shrinks? From me."

Whatever Brandy had injected, kicked in.

She continued her diatribe. "No one knew about the recording studio but me. I was privy to most of Pierce's secret places that he sketched in his journals. We played in some of them as children." She looked over at the door to the recording studio. "Twenty-seven years ago, when I told Pierce I was pregnant, he told me to get an abortion. My father sent me away to 'boarding school' to have the baby. After my drunk of a mother, Father couldn't stand any more scandals in our family. Harrison told my father he'd take care of the baby if Pierce wouldn't. But my father insisted I give her up. It really didn't matter anyway. She only lived an hour."

"So killing them was an act of kindness?" I slurred.

"I never thought of it that way. But yes, I suppose it was. If you knew Pierce, you'd understand. When I found out

Harrison planned to move the bungalows, I needed to relocate Pierce and Helen—or what was left of them—to the hidden speakeasy room in Sandringham's wine cellar, the same place I'd hidden the Warhol. I didn't know Harrison told you and Elle to clean out the bungalow, so I'd only had a chance to move Helen, before the two of you showed up."

"Where is the Warhol now?" It hadn't been in the cellar with Helen.

"I have no idea."

My jaw felt heavy and I couldn't keep my eyes open.

"So you planted Helen's purse and Pierce's wallet before you came to Kate's party to frame Nathan. What about him? He's innocent."

"I suppose. But I don't have a choice."

She went out of the bungalow's front door and came back with an armful of wood from the porch. She put the wood against the back wall of the living room. "It'll take time to reach you. It won't be painful. The smoke and carbon monoxide will kill you first. I'm sorry to do this, but Harrison needs me. He's been like a father to me, and I can't desert him."

At this point I could barely move my lips. Whatever she'd given me felt good. It was like I'd taken a dozen muscle relaxers, then chased them down with a bottle of vodka.

Brandy gave me a wistful look before she scratched the match against the box. She lit the logs and then the bottom of the curtains at each window. Elle had wanted to take them. I should have let her.

The sun had gone down and the room turned orange. Heat reached my back.

Even if Brandy did get away with killing me, how did she plan to explain Uncle Harry's wheelchair?

I got my answer when she tipped the wheelchair forward and I slid to the floor. No need for duct tape or rope. I couldn't move a muscle—not even my tongue.

She took one last glance at the bungalow and rolled the wheelchair out the front door.

The room got brighter and brighter. I was drenched in sweat.

Then, through the smoke, I saw him.

The man in the neon orange cap.

My stalker.

CHAPTER

∾⟫⟨∾

THIRTY-ONE

"Kurt Pinkus saved your life," Elle said.

"Who?" The name sounded familiar but I couldn't place it.

I was in a bed in a private room at Southampton Hospital.

Elle handed me a glass of water. I tried to get up on my elbows to take it but fell back against the pillow. She held the glass with a straw to my mouth. I drank and immediately started coughing.

"You're lucky. Nurse Freeman said you suffered very little smoke inhalation."

My shoulders relaxed. Nurse Freeman was looking out for me. We'd met last March after the Seacliff incident. "Brandy?"

"In jail."

"How?"

"Kurt Pinkus cracked her hard in the jaw. Knocked her flat on the sand."

The room was spinning. I closed my eyes. I knew the name sounded familiar. "Who is Kurt Pinkus?"

I could barely hear her through my left hearing aid. How long had it been since Brandy bashed me on the head in her sitting room?

"You should rest. Your father took a plane and should be here any minute. Are you sure you're up to talking?"

I opened my eyes and gave Elle a dirty look. Did she know me at all?

"Okay. Okay. Kurt Pinkus was your stalker."

That's why the name sounded familiar. Kurt Pinkus was one of the part-time deckhands on *Wrestling with the Wind*. The boat with the orange bucket. One of the names Morgana had left on my voice mail.

Elle said, "Doc's waiting in the hall. Can I tell him to come in?"

"Of course."

It was good to see Doc's face.

I held out my hand and he took it. "I leave you on your own and look what happens."

"Tell me about Kurt Pinkus."

He said, "You should rest. You have a nasty bump on your head."

My throat felt scratchy and I coughed again.

Elle handed me the glass of water. "Doc, you know she won't do anything until we tell her what we know."

"Okay. Okay. Your father learned Pinkus had a relationship with Sergeant Gordon Miles. He served with him in the Middle East. It was a case of misguided loyalty. He

wanted to scare you away from fighting for the ownership of the cottage in order to help his hero, Sergeant Miles, win the case. Apparently, Sergeant Miles saved Kurt's life when they were on tour. Pinkus thought he was doing Sergeant Miles a favor, but Sergeant Miles had no hand in his pranks. Today, Kurt Pinkus followed you to Sandringham. He planned to fill the back of your Jeep with another bucketful of fish guts, but on his way to your car, he saw Brandy carting you out of Sandringham unconscious in a wheelchair. So he followed you and Brandy to the bungalow."

"Wow. Who would have thought having a stalker would be a good thing?"

"Which reminds me," he said. "Why didn't you tell me about these stalking incidents?"

"I told Dad. I thought they were just pranks." Not completely true, but he had known about the bucket of fish guts.

Elle glanced up from her cell phone. "Detective Shoner's downstairs. He wants to know what happened with Brandy. Are you up to talking about it?"

"Yes. And you can call him Arthur."

She blushed.

A few minutes later, I explained to everyone how Brandy was sent away to have Pierce's baby when she was only sixteen. After the baby died, Pierce wouldn't have anything to do with her. Seven years later when Brandy found out Pierce was cheating on Sonya with Helen, she lost it. She entombed Pierce and Helen in the bungalow's recording studio. Then she moved Helen to the cellar where she'd hidden the Warhol. She was just about to move Pierce when Elle and I showed up. Brandy planted Helen's purse

and Pierce's wallet in the trunk at the gatehouse before Kate's party, because she knew that Helen could no longer be blamed for Pierce's murder.

Detective Shoner said, "Quite the game of musical bones. However, if Brandy put the Warhol in the speakeasy, where the heck is it?"

I said, "Brandy didn't know. When she had moved Helen to the secret cellar room, the Warhol had been there. Brandy never cared about the Warhol, she just wanted retribution."

I thought I understood why Pierce stopped drawing living beings in his journals. After his and Brandy's baby died, he'd found his own way to grieve.

Elle said, "Pinkus also overheard Brandy's confession and promises to testify in court."

My stalker was my savior.

CHAPTER

THIRTY-TWO

Applause broke out when Elle and I walked into the kitchen at Sandringham. Everyone was there. Except Brandy.

Ingrid came over and gave me a huge hug. "We're so happy you're okay."

It had been two weeks since my near-death experience in the bungalow. I'd only stayed in the hospital two nights and that was because Nurse Freeman had been overprotective.

When my father arrived in New York, he not only filled me in on what he'd found out about Kurt Pinkus but also what he learned about someone else.

He'd stayed a week, and the kicker was, he got along famously with Jo. She even stood on his lap at the banquette while she ate her supper. I tried the same routine after he'd left, but Jo pooh-poohed my advances. What else was new? Although it might have had more to do with her

being spoiled by the cooked-to-order grilled seafood plate my father prepared each night in lieu of her Purrfectly Organic canned food.

Last week I'd sent Elle on some recon work, and today I was going to solve the mystery of the missing Warhol. It was my Hercule Poirot/Jane Marple moment.

When everyone was seated at the farm table—Elle, Ingrid, Nathan, Kate, Liv, Celia, Richard, and Uncle Harry—I began. "Brandy had no idea what happened to the Warhol. She told me the last time she saw it, the painting was in the secret cellar room with Helen's skeleton."

Ingrid took Nathan's hand.

"Kate, when you were *supposedly* locked in the wine cellar with Liv, why did you take photos of Pierce's journal with the cell phone you supposedly didn't have, then send them to Richard?"

Celia jumped up. "What is this? What are you talking about?"

Kate said, "Sit down, Celia. Let Meg talk."

"Richard, why did you keep it a secret that you are the son of Tansy and the artist Frederic Challis? And Pierce's half brother?"

"What?" Celia seemed totally surprised, and here I'd thought she'd known Richard was Tansy's son the whole time.

My father had found Richard's birth records in Milwaukee. The two huge paintings in Richard's apartment signed F. C. were done by Richard's father, the artist Frederic Challis. The same man Tansy had followed from the South of France to Milwaukee. Richard's father must have taught

him the double-double French air-kiss, and his Wisconsin childhood explained his midwestern accent.

Elle had taken Tansy's hairbrush from the glove compartment of her Shelby convertible. Detective Shoner compared Richard's DNA with the DNA from Tansy's hair. Voila! Mother and son.

I nodded to Elle. "Go ahead."

She typed a word on her cell phone.

Seconds later the kitchen door opened. Detective Shoner and another officer carried in the Andy Warhol painting of Aqua Net hairspray.

Richard jumped up. "It's mine. Warhol made it for my mother!"

Celia said, "Richard, you idiot. What have you done?"

Richard ignored her and tried to grab the huge canvas, but Kate stopped him. "For once, Celia is right. I'm ready to confess everything." Kate turned to Liv. "I'm so sorry, Livvy. I never meant to hurt you. I just put one sleeping pill in your wine and I brought your extra inhaler in case you had an asthma attack. When I told Richard about the journal and the drawing of the wine cellar, he came to the cellar that night and we found the speakeasy room. Richard took out his precious painting. I didn't go inside."

I said, "But why would you help Richard?"

Kate sighed. "We had a deal. If I helped him find the Warhol, he would help me find more treasures from clues found in Liv's father's journals. These people are multimillionaires. I only meant to sock away a few goodies for when Stepdaddy kicked us out and divorced Mommie Dearest."

Tears slid down both Liv's and Ingrid's faces. They'd both trusted Kate and felt betrayed.

I walked over to Liv and handed her the box with the diamond heart I'd found under Kate's bed. Liv looked at Kate, and Kate ran out of the room in tears. Celia followed. On the way out the door, she kicked Richard in the shin. I could have thought of a better place, but that was me.

It was obvious Richard wanted what his half brother had: the Warhol and Celia. He wasn't a murderer, but he hadn't disclosed he'd found Helen's skeleton in the speak-easy for fear someone might suspect he'd taken the painting. When I learned Richard was Tansy's son, I looked back at the photos I'd taken of Pierce's first journal—the same journal Kate had taken pictures of when she was in the cellar while Liv was passed out. She had sent them to Richard, which explained the photo I'd seen on his computer. Another photo in Pierce's drawings was of the apartment over the old stable/garage. An upside-down horse's head had been sketched in the mahogany paneling behind Richard's desk. It was the perfect spot to hide the Warhol, as Richard also figured out.

Detective Shoner went over to Uncle Harry. "Do you want to press charges?"

"Not at the moment." Then Uncle Harry clapped his hands. "Well done, Meg Barrett. Well done."

THIRTY-THREE

Elle and I had stopped for lunch at Sandringham a week after the Aqua Net unveiling, and Ingrid informed us she and Nathan were engaged. I was happy for her and I was glad she didn't turn out to be a murderess, not just because she looked like my mother but because she had a similar heart to my mother's.

Ingrid told us Harry gave the Aqua Net painting inspired by Tansy to his granddaughter, Liv. Liv put it in the gallery with her father's drawings. I wondered what other things she'd find hidden at Sandringham. When I thought about it, we'd never checked for revolving bookcases.

Now that Uncle Harry's head was clear, he promised to work with Liv to try to remember other secret spots around the mansion. I envied them the hunt.

When Richard had the gall to ask for Tansy's Shelby

convertible, Uncle Harry said that was a no-go. He sold it to a local collector. He did, however, let Richard keep Tansy's can of Aqua Net hairspray from the car's glove compartment, then he sent him on his way.

Uncle Harry also went easy on Celia because I'd told him Brandy was the one screwing around with his medication, not Celia. Celia wouldn't admit she had anything to do with the Pollock scandal. Uncle Harry and Celia were still slated for divorce because Liv had told him about what we'd witnessed between Richard and Celia on the beach.

Ingrid put in a good word for Kate after she returned all the jewelry she and Richard had found from the drawings in Pierce's journal. Uncle Harry wouldn't be pressing charges.

Apparently, Richard came to Montauk when he was twenty-one, after his father died. He wanted to find out more about his mother's other life and his half brother. His father had told him stories about Tansy and the Warhol painting inspired by his mother. Richard hooked up with Celia when she was working in an art gallery in Bridgehampton.

Twenty years ago, when Pierce and Helen disappeared with the Warhol, Richard went crazy trying to track it down. Then after we found Pierce's skeleton, he obsessed even further. Richard enlisted Kate's help in finding the Warhol after he heard from Kate that Liv found jewelry from clues in Pierce's sketch journal.

I had no idea on the status of Liv and Kate's relationship. I doubted it would ever be repaired, even though Kate had remembered Liv's inhaler when they were in the cellar.

On our way out the door, Ingrid gave Elle and me a huge container of chowder and our own loaves of bread. We each picked a cheek and kissed it.

I had a feeling our lunch date might turn into a weekly event.

CHAPTER

THIRTY-FOUR

The fickle finger of good fortune pointed itself in my direction.

I was at 221*B* Surfside Drive.

After hearing what I'd gone through at the hands of Kurt Pinkus, the good and the bad, the court, under recommendation from Sgt. Miles, granted me half ownership of the land at Little Grey. I received a refund of more than half my down payment because Sgt. Miles got the side of the property with Little Grey and I got the folly side with the garden.

Sgt. Miles said he'd hire Cottages by the Sea to do the interior design in Little Grey, using whatever I wanted from Little Grey's packed attic. Anything left over was mine to use in my own future cottage.

A small glitch was that I only had through December until my lease ran out, which would bring me to January.

I didn't think Jo and I would make it in the glass folly during a Montauk winter. The space heaters that ran on my new generator in the folly were adequate for forty-degree weather, but I didn't think they'd do much good in a deep freeze. And who wanted to visit The Watercloset in the middle of a frigid winter's night? I didn't.

Duke and Duke Junior had helped me find a contractor to build a small cottage on my half of the property. However, we wouldn't be breaking ground until the spring.

I waited in the folly for Byron Hughes's text.

Byron had shown up at my rental after he'd read in the papers about Brandy's arrest. I never asked him about the woman who answered the phone. I had a tendency to put those kinds of questions on the back burner. Today he was bringing new landscape plans he'd drawn up free of charge. I'd given Sgt. Miles the other plans.

My phone vibrated. I read the message from Byron.

Meet me by the cottage. Now!

Okay. A little terse. But I'd give him the benefit of the doubt.

I threw on my jacket and followed the bluestone path Duke and Duke Junior had just laid down.

Byron was sitting on Little Grey's porch. A bottle of champagne in one hand and two cut crystal glasses in the other. "Hey, stranger."

"Hey, yourself. What have you got there?"

"Time to celebrate."

I sat next to him. "Well? Pop her open."

"You have to wait."

"For what?"

"You'll see."

The sound of gears grinding made me look in the direction of the drive that led from Route 27. I stepped off the porch and put my hand over my eyes to block the sun. Byron joined me. A huge tractor trailer approached, flattening bushes and shrubs as it inched forward.

"What's going on? Is this your doing?"

"No. But I am a part of the plan." He smiled that smile.

The truck kept coming. Smoke billowed from a pipe next to the cab. The front of the truck had a banner stretched across the front grill, which read, OVERSIZED LOAD.

Then all was quiet.

Byron put the champagne glasses on the porch step, grabbed my hand, and pulled me toward the truck. He still held the bottle of champagne in his other hand.

We stopped. My mouth opened wide. "Holy smokes!"

On the back of a flatbed truck was a bungalow. Not Pierce's bungalow, because that had burnt to the ground. But it was one of its sextuplet siblings.

Byron said, "Courtesy of Mr. Harrison Falks. May I present you with your own Cottage Sweet Cottage."

I was floored.

"Time to christen it." He handed me the champagne bottle. When I hesitated, he laughed. "I have another one on ice in the car."

I took my left-handed batting stance and swung. The bottle broke, the champagne fizzed down the porch railing of the bungalow, and just when I thought things couldn't

get any more intense, a three-legged dog bounded in my direction.

Tripod!

And right behind him, Cole, Tripod's master, blue eyes stormy as hell on his handsome face.

I looked from Cole to Byron.

Hang on, Meg Barrett. I think you're in for a bumpy ride.

Meg and Elle's
Think-Outside-the-Box Guide
to Repurposing Vintage Finds

Meg: Rub scented essential oils, such as lavender, orange, or sandalwood on the underside of wood furniture: the oil is good for the wood, and at the same time, scents the room.

Elle: Place a vintage ironstone or graniteware pitcher by the kitchen sink to store your bottle brushes, dishwashing soap, and other dishwashing odds and ends.

Meg: Create a piece of art by gluing a map to the back of an old salvaged window. Look for old folded travel maps at garage sales or vintage shops. It's even more fun if the map represents places you've traveled or hope to travel. If you want, you can reinforce the paper maps with a few coats of matte decoupage glue. When dry, glue the map to the back side of the window frame and hang on the wall. This works for windows with or without their panes of glass.

Elle: Search thrift shops and estate sales for inexpensive vintage or antique china dinnerware in assorted transferware patterns; try to stick to the same color family—it makes for a festive, eclectic table setting.

Meg: Put outdoor iron wall planters in your bathroom. Spray-paint the planters to match your room's color palette. As long as your bathroom has a window, potted houseplants flourish in the steamy environment. Or, put vintage American pottery flower pots in the planter's iron rings and instead of inserting plants, use the pots to store your toothbrushes, makeup brushes, etc.

Elle: Buy vintage or antique oil lamps with clear glass chimneys. Insert a photo in the brass slot where the wick comes out. A grouping of three or more oil lamps on a mantel, dresser, or piano creates an interesting photo gallery. Odd numbers are best for displaying similar collectibles in a group.

Meg: You can also fill the bottom of vintage Ball jars with buttons in one color, or a mixture of colors. Stick a photo or other ephemera at the bottom of the jar, using the weight of the buttons to keep the photo upright, then replace the lid. Or, place a flower frog lid found at craft stores on top on your Ball jar. Use the jar as a vase for your fresh flowers, leaving the buttons inside to hide the bottoms of the stems.

Elle: Spiky iron flower frogs perform double duty as a way to display photos, business cards, or vintage postcards.

When it's cold outside, treat yourself and buy a single stem of freesia or a single scented lily stem, cut the stem straight across the bottom, and put in the center of the spiky flower frog. Display the flower on its frog in the center of a footed Depression glass dish with a lip, or in the center of your favorite piece of vintage pottery. Only use enough water to cover the top of the flower frog. Flowers last longer on spiky flower frogs because the water travels up the flower stem.

Meg: Set up an indoor herb garden by hanging vintage tiered vegetable baskets from the ceiling near a kitchen window. Fill the baskets with herbs in clay pots or herbs planted in vintage tea or coffee cups. This way your cat won't eat your cilantro. Grow edible cat grass in an accessible pot for your wayward kitty. Tiered vegetable baskets also work as an outdoor herb garden; just add moss, hanging basket liners, dirt, and your herbs. Hang the baskets under the eaves, near your outdoor grill.

Elle: Vintage or antique tablecloths make great coverlets for your bed, or use vintage tablecloths to upholster chair seats. Instead of buying a matching set of kitchen or dining room chairs, buy different chairs in a similar style, then spray-paint them one color for cohesiveness.

Meg: Find a vintage suitcase and remove the top, insert a bed pillow or cushion on the bottom, cover with a soft blanket or vintage piece of fabric—voila! You have a cozy kitty or doggie bed. A rubber-edged window squeegee removes pet hair from cushions and upholstered furniture—especially

handy if you have a fur-ball like my Maine Coon, Jo. I can't think of a suitcase large enough for Tripod.

And remember, a modern home can meld perfectly with that little touch of vintage or antique.

Wishing you great finds!!

Recipes

❧

JEFF BARRETT'S
CAJUN BBQ SHRIMP

It's called Barbecue Shrimp, but these shrimp don't go anywhere near the grill, which has a couple of very important advantages. Shrimp are difficult to grill properly because they cook so fast, and when overcooked tend to dry out and get rubbery. These shrimp are cooked in a pan, where you can control the heat and moisture content much more readily. Moreover, you cook them within a very tasty and robust sauce you create. That allows the shrimp to actually absorb the sauce, which improves the flavor even more. In fact, this is one of those dishes that really does taste better the second day, so don't be afraid if you have leftovers–feel free to make a large batch.

WHAT YOU'LL NEED:

2 pounds jumbo shrimp (about 25)
1 cup shrimp stock, or chicken broth

FOR THE SHRIMP STOCK:

2 bay leaves
1 teaspoon Old Bay Seasoning

FOR THE SPICE MIXTURE:

1 tablespoon dried thyme

*1 tablespoon dried rosemary, crushed (you'll need to
    crush it; it doesn't come that way)*

1 tablespoon oregano

1 tablespoon hot paprika

1 tablespoon chili powder

*1 teaspoon crushed hot pepper flakes (more or less
    depending upon your tolerance for heat!)*

2 sticks unsalted butter

3 cloves fresh garlic, chopped or crushed

2 tablespoons Worcestershire sauce

1 12 oz. bottle of beer (not light beer)

2 tablespoons or 1 oz. of your favorite barbecue sauce

Clean the shrimp, leaving the tails on. Save the shells for stock. Place shrimp in a bowl of cold water and set aside.

If you're feeling ambitious, and you have time (at least an hour; the longer the better) cover just the shells with water, add two bay leaves and one teaspoon of Old Bay Seasoning, and bring to boil, then simmer for at least 1 hour. You should have no more than 1 cup stock. If you do not have the time, you can substitute the shrimp stock with chicken stock.

Assemble your spice mix in a large sauté pan.

With the spices in the pan, heat pan on medium high heat. The heat will bring out the natural oils in the herbs and accelerate the release of flavors. After 1 or 2 minutes, add 1 stick of butter (you'll be adding a second stick a bit later in the process). After the butter has melted, add 3 cloves of chopped garlic. Then add 2 tablespoons Worcestershire sauce.

Then add 1 bottle of beer, the more flavorful the better. (Light beer is to be avoided if possible.) Let the sauce cook down until syrupy. Add the stock and cook down again. Add 1 or 2 tablespoons of your favorite barbecue sauce and stir it in.

Now add the peeled shrimp to the pan. Try to get the shrimp in a single layer. If the pan's not quite big enough for that, just be careful not to let the bottom shrimp overcook. Shake the pan while cooking the shrimp. Turn them with tongs. The shrimp will be done when the tails are orange in color and the bodies are white and curled. You want them to just be cooked through. Be careful not to overcook the shrimp or else they will be tough. When they have all cooked through, usually about 3 to 4 minutes, remove them to a clean bowl, leaving the sauce in the pan. The shrimp will have added to the liquid in the pan so it needs to cook down a bit more. Add the second stick of butter and shake the sauce as it melts. The sauce will thicken. When the butter begins to separate from the sauce, it is done. Remove from heat. Place shrimp and sauce together in your serving dish, pouring sauce over the shrimp. Garnish with fresh parsley.

You can serve two ways. As an appetizer, serve with crusty French bread for dipping. For a main course, prepare the Roasted Carrots, Sweet Potatoes & Onion Recipe.

JEFF BARRETT'S ROASTED CARROTS, SWEET POTATOES & ONIONS

Coated in spices and orange juice, these oven-roasted vegetables make for a great side dish.

WHAT YOU'LL NEED:

2 large sweet potatoes (about 1 ½ pounds), peeled and
    cut into ¼-inch by 3-inch strips
8 medium carrots (about 1 pound), peeled and cut into
    3-inch pieces
1 large onion, cut into ½-inch thick slices
2 large garlic cloves, minced
1 orange for its juice (about ½ cup juice)
3 tablespoons butter, melted
2 tablespoons olive oil
1 teaspoon kosher salt
1 teaspoon high-quality paprika
¼ teaspoon ground cinnamon
½ teaspoon ground ginger
¼ teaspoon freshly ground black pepper
⅛ teaspoon cayenne pepper
20 fresh mint leaves for garnish

Preheat oven to 400°F.

In a large bowl add sweet potatoes, carrots, onion, and garlic.

In a small bowl, whisk together orange juice, melted butter, oil, salt, and dried spices. Pour over vegetables in the large bowl and toss until coated.

Transfer to a roasting pan and roast 35 to 45 minutes, then switch oven temp to broil and cook until crisp, 3 to 5 minutes.

Top with fresh mint leaves for garnish.

MEG BARRETT'S INSTANT
PUMPKIN ICE CREAM

WHAT YOU'LL NEED:

*1 quart high-quality French vanilla ice cream, softened
    slightly in the refrigerator*
*1 cup canned pumpkin pie mix (includes sugars and
    spices)*

Empty the ice cream into a large bowl. Fold in pumpkin pie
mix until blended. Refreeze in airtight containers.
   Could it be any easier?
   Enjoy!

Also from
National Bestselling Author

KATHLEEN BRIDGE

Better Homes and Corpses

A Hamptons Home & Garden Mystery

In between scouring estate sales for her new interior
design business, Cottages by the Sea, Meg visits
the swanky East Hampton home of her old college
roommate, Jillian Spenser. But instead of seeing
how the other half lives—she learns how the other
half dies. Jillian's mother, known as the Queen Mother
of the Hamptons, has been murdered. Someone
has staged a coup.

When she helps a friend inventory the Spensers' estate
for the insurance company, Meg finds herself right in
the thick of things. Cataloging valuable antiques and art
loses its charm when Meg discovers that the Spenser
family has been hiding dangerous secrets, which may
have furnished a murderer with a motive. As Meg gets
closer to the truth, the killer will do anything to paint
her out of the picture…

"A delightful sneak peek into life in the Hamptons, with
intricate plotting and a likeable, down-to-earth protagonist.
A promising start to a promising series."
—Suspense Magazine

kathleenbridge.com
facebook.com/authorkathleenbridge
penguin.com